RRAC

D1711220

Trust No Bitch

JUL - - 2022

Ca$h & NeNe Capri

**Lock Down Publications
Presents
Trust No Bitch 3
A Novel by *Ca$h & NeNe Capri***

Ca$h & NeNe Capri

Lock Down Publications
P.O. Box 1482
Pine Lake, Ga 30072-1482

Copyright 2013 by CA$H & NeNe Capri
All rights reserved. No part of this book may be reproduced in any form or by electronic or mechanical means, including information storage and retrieval systems without permission in writing from the publisher, except by a reviewer who may quote brief passages in review.
First Edition 2014
Printed in the United States of America
This is a work of fiction. Names, characters, places, and incidents either are products of the author's imagination or are used fictitiously. Any similarity to actual events or locales or persons, living or dead, is entirely coincidental.

Lock Down Publications
Ca$h
Email: ldp.cash@gmail.com
Facebook: Cassius Alexander
Like our page on Facebook: Lock Down Publications @
www.facebook.com/lockdownpublications.ldp
Amazon: http://www.amazon.com/Ca$h
NeNeCapri
Facebook: NeNeCapri
Twitter: @NeNeCapri
Instagram: @NeneCapri
Cover design and layout by: **Marion Designs**
Book interior design by: **Shawn Walker**
Edited by: **Shawn Walker**

Acknowledgements

We would first like to acknowledge our fans nationwide. Thank you for supporting our individual careers and this collaboration Trust No Bitch. To our loyal supporters on the social websites, in the book groups, and the distributors, you fuel our drive. To the readers, you make us what we are authors. Thank you Shawn Walker for your boss editing. Keith, we thank you for the cover and look forward to more of your work. Friends, family, associates, and fellow authors we thank you all.

Dedications

CA$H: To the one who prefers to remain anonymous, they can't destroy what they can't see.

Nene Capri: To My beloved daughter Princess Khairah everything I do is for you. Mommy loves you.

Prologue

As Wa'leek drove back home with the bag of money on the seat next to him he thought of all the ways he would torture Treebie before killing her. " 'Til death do us part," he said as he reached the house.

Treebie's other whip wasn't in the driveway so he knew that she wasn't home yet. It didn't matter, he was going to patiently wait on that ass to return then he would show her no mercy. Deception and deceit were unpardonable.

He hit the remote and pulled back into the garage. He waited for the garage door to come down then he grabbed the money off of the seat and went inside the house. As he stepped through the door headed for the bedroom. Treebie crept up behind him and put a gun to the back of his head. "You should've left well enough alone," she muttered.

Even through the distorter that she wore over her throat, Wa'leek recognized his wife's voice. He stopped in his tracks trying to steady his breathing as he let the bag slip from his grip and fall to the floor as he contemplated his next move. "Stop playing, baby," he chuckled, trying to throw her off but Treebie wasn't fooled.

"Nah, you stop playing, nigga. I know you found the shit in the basement. You left the door to the cabinet wide open and the lock on the floor. Seek and you shall find, you ever heard that?" she asked ominously.

"I ain't ever heard shit," he spat.

"Well you heard it now. Take it to the grave with you," she replied coldly.

"Would you really kill me, ma?" he asked as his chest began to heave up and down.

"Try me and get your shit blown the fuck out your head," said Treebie. She gripped the banger with both hands and widened her stance. "Kiss the carpet nigga or kiss this life goodbye."

Wa'leek remained standing but nothing moved but his mouth. "This Wah, baby—your muhfuckin' husband—not some random ass nigga you're about to jack." He slightly raised his voice with his eyes settled on a picture of them that probably captured the last of the bond they had left.

"I know who you are but ask me if I give a fuck. The question is 'do you know who I am'?" spat Treebie.

Wa'leek's mouth tightened and his response came out bitter and hard. "I thought you was my baby but I guess I was wrong because the Treebie I knew would never put a gun to my head. So nah, I don't know who the fuck you are, why don't you tell me?" His anger was now replaced by hurt that resonated from his tone. No matter their differences he had thought that she loved him.

"You can miss me with all that bullshit and lay the fuck on the floor before I put your brains up on the ceiling," she commanded.

"Nah, ma. You know I'm not going out like no bitch. Fuck lying face down, if it's really like that you're gonna have to look me in my eyes and take my life," he said. "Can you really do that to your nigga?" Wa'leek tried his hand at reason.

"You know how it goes, I'm 'bout that Blood Money. I'll kill you and sit down and smoke a blunt, have a drink and pour some out for the niggas who ain't here. I'm that bitch," she reinforced.

"Blood Money, huh?" he said, recalling how vicious they had been when they ran up in Riz's spot. The memory of that night was forever ingrained in his mind so there was no mistaking it, Treebie was indeed a killah. But would her trigger finger be as quick and merciless towards him as it had been towards others? "Blood Money," he repeated, shaking his head in disbelief.

"You wanted to know," she gritted. "Now you have your answer but it's going to cost you your life."

Wa'leek couldn't help but chuckle. Treebie had been a herb from the burbs when he first cuffed her and introduced her to the game years ago. Now she was turnt all the way up, willing to spill his

8

blood to protect Blood Money's identity. Hell no, he couldn't believe that she would really pull the trigger. She had to be bluffing.

"So you're gonna choose Big Zo and some bitches over me, is that how you get down?" He challenged her loyalty.

"Shut the fuck up with the sermon and put your dick in the carpet!" Her voice barked on the back of his neck.

"You put it there." Wa'leek called her bluff. "You that bitch. Bust that muthafucka then." Wa'leek's chest filled with fury and hate. In that moment he decided that if she didn't make a move quickly he was going to put her on her ass.

Treebie was a split-second away from spraying Wa'leek's noodles all over the living room. As she gnashed her teeth and stared at the back of his head, memories of them together in blissful times flashed through her mind and pain struck her heart. Her knees wobbled under the weight of the decision that lie at the tip of her finger. Just a bit more pressure on the trigger and his head would explode, and her complicity with Blood Money would go to the grave with him

The room fell silent as Wa'leek waited for her to do what she had threatened to do. He closed his eyes and accepted his fate. When he didn't hear her gun clap or feel something hot blast through the back of his head he slowly spun around and faced her.

Treebie now held the gun pointed between his eyes but her hesitation gave Wa'leek the upper hand. In the dim light that illuminated the living room, he looked into those blood red eyes and shook his head. "You're pitiful, ma. For real, look at you. Is this what you let Big Zo turn you into?" His gray eyes were admonishing.

"Big Zo didn't turn me into nothing, you did this shit," she yelled.

"Don't blame this on me. That nigga got a hold on you. What the fuck did he do to you?" Wa'leek asked choosing his words wisely.

"What he didn't do was fuck my friend," she hurled.

The unexpected accusation bounced off of the walls and settled in Wa'leek's ear hard. "What the fuck is you talking about?" he replied with a creased brow and a set jaw.

"You know exactly what I'm talking about!" Tears began to form against her blood red shields.

"I don't know shit," he maintained.

"Nigga, I know all about you and Donella." Treebie felt sick as the words slid out of her mouth. The tears she had held in for years were now running down her face.

"Who told you that stupid shit, Lissha? You letting her fill your head up with lies against me? Fuck is wrong with you? You can't trust that scandalous ho."

"Lissha, didn't tell me shit, I got it straight from the horse's mouth." She stared coldly into his eyes.

Wa'leek's brow dropped and the anger in his face softened.

"Yeah, look shocked nigga. She came to me while you was locked up and confessed everything." Treebie's lied to get him to confess. "Why do you think I haven't moved back home with you? You betrayed me, nigga. I gave you all of me and you traded it for pieces of the next bitch. 'You love me'? Fuck you, your love don't mean shit." Her voice shook with fury.

Wa'leek knew in that moment that she was not bluffing, the secret he had tried hard to protect her from had been exposed. Now that the truth was laid out in all if its ugly nakedness there was nothing left for him to do but confront it head on. He looked at Treebie and the red in her eyes behind the contacts was as hot as the flames of hell. Wa'leek's heart pounded in his chest as fear and regret coursed through his body.

Treebie looked in his gray eyes and clacked one in the chamber. With her other hand she removed the distorter from over her throat; her breathing quickened and her lips tightened as her mind replayed the images she formed of Donella riding and sucking Wa'leek's dick. When she spoke again it was in her natural voice and its tone *was as lethal as the ratchet in her hand. "My girl, Wah? Really? That's how you do me?" She lowered the gun below his waist. "Nasty ass muthafucka! I was faithful to your dirty ass." Treebie sneered.*

Wa'leek sneered back at her. "Fuck that bitch," he spat. "You gonna kill me cause a nigga busted a nut? That bitch didn't mean shit to me. As soon as I took the condom off and flushed it down the toilet I flushed that bitch with it. It was nothing but a nut. You're the only woman I ever cared for, you know that. That shit was business."

"Yeah? Well this is about to be personal," she said harshly.

"Personal? Fuck you think it was when you was running around taking orders from Big Zo over me. How do I know you didn't fuck that nigga?"

"You know what, Wah? Fuck you. You out here sticking your dick in the dirt and you questioning my fidelity? This pussy always confirms my loyalty. Don't insult me. I'm a loyal bitch." She lifted the gun to his chest aiming it at his black heart.

Wa'leek braced himself for the blast but he didn't turn pussy. "Do what you do. But like I said, that bitch ain't mean shit to me."

"Neither did I, obviously," Treebie snapped. Her feelings were collapsing and the wall she had built between them was crumbling at her feet.

She was talking that murder shit but her gun hadn't popped off so Wa'leek knew that she was wavering. She might've been that bitch but he was her weakness. He held out his hand and softened his voice. "Hand me the gun, ma, before you fuck around and do something you'll regret."

"Back the fuck up." Treebie raised the Glock back up to his head. Her palms filled with sweat as she tightened her grip around the handle. A lump formed in her throat and her heart raced with uncertainty.

Wa'leek let his arm fall down to his waist while continuing to hold her stare. Treebie watched him intensely, if he reached for his

*banger she was going to put a whole clip in his dome and go have
that stiff drink that was summoning her.*

*Wa'leek wasn't about to test her gun but he damn sure was about
to play on her love. He flashed her a puppy dog look and appealed
to her heart. "Baby, we're bigger than that one mistake. You don't
wanna kill me over that punk ass shit. We can move past that and
the Blood Money stuff. You're my wife fuck everything and everybody else. We can team up against all those muthafuckaz. Fuck 'em
all with a fat ass dick, it's you and me against the world. Ya boy,
Spank, is dead, I did that nigga and his bitch a little while ago. And
I'll do the same to Kiam and any other nigga. You don't follow but
one nigga's lead and that's mine."*

"I can't trust you, Wah."

"Since when?"

"Since you played me with my own girl."

*"I didn't play you, baby. Yeah, I fucked up but charge that shit
to the game not my heart. You know I don't give a fuck about nobody
but you. Don't you know that?"*

*"I thought I did," she replied a little over a whisper. She lowered
the gun and wiped at the tears that streamed from her eyes with the
back of her hands.*

*Wa'leek made his move. He stepped towards her and gently took
the gun out of her hand and brought it down to his side. "C'mere,
ma," he whispered lovingly, pulling her into his arms.*

*"No, Wah, your shit ain't working this time." She squirmed to
be free.*

*"Let me make this right, ma," he spoke softly, tossing the gun
on the couch and holding her tightly in his arms.*

*Treebie stiffened momentarily then surrendered to her heart's
call and melted into his familiar embrace. "Baby, why you do me
like that?" she cried against his chest.*

*"I'm sorry, ma," he said, holding her closely and kissing away
her tears. His touch felt like a thousand apologies. As tough as her*

exterior was his whispered 'I love you's' seemed to melt away that shell that protected her emotions. He could still reach that softness inside of her that made her a woman. "I'll make it up to you, ma, that's my word," he promised as his mouth covered hers and she gave into the desire that she still felt for him in spite of his transgression.

Treebie wrapped her arms around the only man that she had ever given her heart to and accepted his tongue in her mouth hungrily. Her body pressed against the rock in his pants and his hands set her on fire as they slid up and down her back with passion that made them both pant.

As each layer of her clothes came off and littered the floor of the living room a piece of her rage fell with them. Entering her bedroom their passion erupted into a heated flame that begged to stay kindled. Their bodies hit the cold sheets as apologetic hands caressed and gratified places that heightened their desires. Wa'leek lifted his body off of hers, removed his heat off his waist and sat it on the nightstand. Treebie who was already naked and throbbing to feel him inside of her reached up and helped him remove his shirt and jeans. When they hit the floor she stood next to the bed and encircled his girth with her hand, stroking it up and down. "Let me taste you baby," she panted.

"This your dick, do what you do, ma."

Treebie licked around the bulbous head and savored the taste of the pre-cum that seeped out. "Ummm," she moaned then took him into the warmth of her mouth inch by glorious fat inch. She looked up at him as she slurped the lollipop noisily.

Wa'leek looked down at her and what he saw almost made his engorged dick go limp. "Take them shits out of your eyes," he said in a gruff tone.

Treebie pulled back and removed the red contacts, then she stepped back to her business. From her knees she had Wa'leek standing up on his tippy toes and moaning like they had switched genitals. She licked his balls and gobbled the dick until he rewarded her skills with a mouthful of cream. "Give me all of that shit," she urged, pumping his pole firm within her grip.

"Get it, ma," he moaned, taking his pipe and slapping it on her tongue.

Treebie didn't waste a drop, she made it disappear then smacked her lips and looked up at him delightfully. Wa'leek slowly opened his eyes and smiled down at her. "Til death do us apart," he proclaimed.

"Yes, daddy," she agreed.

He lifted her to her feet then guided her down on the bed and parted her thighs. When he knelt before the alter it was with the desire to bring her all the way back into the fold. After today she would move as he commanded, fuck Big Zo and Lissha. This was his pussy and it was time to re-stamp that muthafucka.

Wa'leek's tongue had Treebie's clit screaming and in no time at all her juices flowed like a river. She gripped the back of his head and cried out his name while she coated his mouth with her sweetness. He made her come back to back and it felt like her head was spinning. Treebie laid back breathing heavily from the intense orgasm.

Wa'leek took charge, stroking himself to another full erection. "I want your face down and that ass in the air."

Treebie was as weak as a wet paper towel but the sight of all that meat instantly re-energized her. She rolled over and got on all fours, head down; ass up. Her pussy was sopping wet and Wa'leek slid in easily, pushing deep. "This my pussy," he boasted as he began rough riding that shit.

"Yes, daddy, this is your pussy."

"Chant that shit."

"It's your pussy. It's your pussy. It's your pussy," she moaned over and over again as he plowed in and out of her with powerful strokes that were meant to fuck her mind along with her body. This was the type of raw make-up fucking that nothing else could compare to. Wa'leek had that pussy talking to him.

Treebie was trying to run from the dick but he held her by her hips and made her take it. Pain mixed with pleasure as she begged him to stop. Looking to the side, her eyes settled on the nightstand and her mind wondered back and forth between the hard heat between her thighs and grabbing his heat and ending the command he had on her body and her mind. There was a battle between her thoughts until he began fucking that spot that took over her soul.

"Baby, baby, baby, do that shit, daddy," she moaned, throwing her ass back hard making him connect with every thrust.

"Come on this muthafucka, ma. Make me nut with you," groaned Wa'leek. "I wanna bust all up in this pussy."

Treebie couldn't hold back another second, she cried out in ecstasy as he hit that spot that took her over the edge. "I'm coming, Wah. Oh, my god!"

Wa'leek went deeper. "Arghhhh," he growled like a wild animal as his nuts exploded. He rested up against the softness of her ass cheeks watching her back heave up and down as she tried to capture her breath. Wa'leek pulled out slowly and fell next to her trying to slow his breathing as well.

"You a fucking beast," Treebie confessed, crawling into his arms as she looked into his eyes.

"You already know," he said, kissing her lips.

Afterwards they laid in each other's arms sharing a blunt. No words were spoken as they each retreated into their own thoughts. Treebie's head rested on Wa'leek's chest and she played with the coarse hair that covered his pecs. He stroked her hair tenderly and kissed her forehead.

Awhile later Wa'leek's cellphone lit up with a call from Riz. He reached over and grabbed it off of the nightstand. "What's up?"

"That's what I'm calling to ask you," said Riz. "What have you found out about Blood Money?"

Wa'leek looked down at Treebie and put a finger to his lips. "I'm all over that," he reassured Riz.

Treebie slid out of bed. "I'm going to fix a drink. You want something?" she mouthed.

"Ciroc," Wa'leek mouthed back returning his attention to the call.

"Do I need to send Bones down there to help you shake the city up and smoke out Blood Money?" Riz was saying.

"Nah, I already know who they are and where they're at and I'm about to get at them," Wa'leek whispered. "And you'll never believe who the fuck they are."

"Humor me."

"I'm going to do better than that, I'm bringing you their bodies one by one, starting with the most treacherous," Wa'leek promised as he kept his voice low and his eyes on the door.

Riz loved the sound of that. "A'ight, I'm giving you a month then I'm sending my goons," he declared.

"Trust me, you'll have the bodies long before that."

When Wa'leek hung up the phone his mind was set, Treebie was a dead bitch and her girls were next. He reached over the side of the bed and grabbed his banger off of the floor beside his pants. With a firm mind on what had to be done, he slid the Nine under the pillow beneath his head and laid back and waited. He was about to give the saying "getting some brains" a brand new meaning.

Wa'leek folded his hands behind his head and half-closed his eyes as he formulated Lissha's death next. When he looked up Treebie stood at the foot of the bed in full Blood Money gear with a pump shotgun leveled at his chest.

"Did you think some good pipe was going to spare your life, nigga?" she gritted. "I just wanted the dick one last time before I sent you where all disloyal niggas belong."

Wa'leek knew that this time there would be no reprieve. Treebie was one cold-hearted bitch. He just looked at her and tried to disarm her with his cool demeanor and piercing stare.

"Finally," he said, "Loyalty is us over them."

"Nah, you wanted Donella now I'm about to reunite you with her," she rasped.

"Like I told you, I fucked the bitch, I didn't want her. You're the only woman I've ever wanted."

"Nigga, please!" Treebie threw her head back and laughed mockingly. This was the slip up that Wa'leek had been waiting for and he was about to make it her last one.

Wa'leek moved swiftly. His hands came from behind his head gripping heat and spitting lead. Boc! Boc!

The first two shots missed wildly but the semi-automatic fired in rapid, deadly succession. Boc! Boc! Boc! The bullets slammed into Treebie's chest sending her stumbling back against the wall, but she remained on her feet.

"Punk ass bitch!" spat Wa'leek, sending the next shot at her head, but his aim was high and the bullet lodged into the wall. He lowered his aim and squeezed the trigger again and again.

Click. Click. Click. Click.

Wa'leek looked down at the gun, it had jammed at the wrong gotdamn time.

Treebie was wobbled but the heavyweight Kevlar vest had done its job and she was quickly getting her orientation back. She used the wall behind her to brace herself as air returned to her lungs and her stance became firm.

She brought the shotgun back up and stepped towards Wa'leek as she slid her finger back inside the trigger guard. "I guess it wasn't my time," she taunted and leveled the shotgun at his chest.

Wa'leek lunged at her as the pump sounded off like a cannon. Boom! His body flew backwards and he crashed back down on the bed with a hole the size of a baseball in his gut. Treebie pumped another slug in the chamber, stepped closer and leveled the shotgun down at his chest. "Til death do us apart muthafucka," she spat. Boom!

Wa'leek's chest opened up like a busted can of tomatoes and he stared at her disbelieving as his vital organs quickly began to stop functioning. "Donella didn't tell me shit, stupid ass nigga," she admitted. "I always suspected it though. Grimy ass niggas ain't good for shit but stiff dick and good tongue. Still think I love you? Punk muthafucka."

Treebie looked down at her husband unmercifully as his eyes slowly began to glaze over from death's call. He gurgled on the blood that had quickly filled his mouth but Treebie felt no pity. She let the pump slip from her grasp and fall to the floor. She reached in her pocket and pulled out a crisp bill, then crawled up on the bed and grabbed Wa'leek by the head. "Blood Money, bitch ass nigga," she snarled as she forced the bill inside his mouth and watched him slowly succumb to death.

As Treebie stepped out of the shower, her phone began to sound off with a familiar ringtone. She wrapped a towel around herself and hurried to answer it before Big Zo hung up. "Hello," she answered, ignoring Wa'leek's body on the bed.

"Hey, baby girl. I need you to handle something for me ASAP. Are you still down?" Big Zo's voice conveyed urgency.

"You don't even have to ask me that, just tell me what you need done and I'm on it," she assured him.

"Good. I always knew you were the one I could count on most. Here's what I need you to do…"

Treebie listened without interruption. When Big Zo was done she didn't even question his request. "Consider it done," she said.

Treebie hung up the phone, dressed quickly, and grabbed her gun. She covered Wa'leek's body with the bed spread before leaving out. She would deal with it when she returned, he damn sure wasn't going anywhere.

Chapter 1
A Pained Cry

Kiam's mind was so preoccupied with Lissha's disappearance he drove straight through the red light as he neared the twins' complex. "Shit!" he exclaimed glancing over to his right and spotting a police cruiser parked in the lot of a strip mall. Adrenaline rushed through Kiam's veins like a live current of electricity.

When the car pulled out and got behind him he saw that they were two hillbilly looking cops in the vehicle. He knew that if they pulled him over they weren't going to just write him a ticket and keep it moving, Jakes like them always wanted to search your shit. What they would find in his vehicle would open up a floodgate of trouble for Kiam, trouble that would bring his rise to the top to an unceremonious halt. His hand went to the Nine that he had sat on the counsel between the seats; the gun had mad bodies on it and he was about add two more to it if they flashed their lights.

Going back to prison wasn't even an option. *Court gets held in the muhfuckin' streets,* he instantly decided. That was the code of every real nigga that had ever done a bid. Fake niggas talked it, trill niggas walked it. In a minute the Jakes were going to have the misfortune of pulling over the wrong muthafucka at the wrong time.

Kiam scanned the area for the quickest escape route after he opened up on po po. Within minutes the helicopter would fly in and every available patrol car would flood the area where he had left two of their brethren leaking in the snow. He would have to abandon the truck, snatch a bitch up and make them drive him away from there. To think that after all the blood he had spilled since coming home, his downfall would be something as trivial as running a red light!

Kiam felt a pang in his heart as the realization of how this would drastically change the lives of Faydrah and their unborn. A picture of her flashed in his mind intensifying the ache in his heart. He had promised her before walking out of the door that everything would be alright. Guilt leaped up in his chest but his gangsta forced it back down.

"It is what the fuck it is," Kiam said aloud as he slid the Nine over onto his lap and stared in the rearview mirror waiting for the flashing lights.

Nothing but head shots. He clicked off the safety latch and slid his finger inside the trigger guard. "Eyez, I love you baby," he whispered as if she was in the seat next to him. "Take care of my seed."

As the words left his mouth the police cruiser turned off and went about their business. Kiam relaxed his grip on his gun but the anxiety he felt remained strong. Where in the fuck was Lissha? Shit like this threw a nigga off his square.

JuJu and Isaiah was standing outside with their whistles tucked underneath heavy winter jackets when Kiam pulled up to the condo. As soon as he brought the truck to a complete stop JuJu hopped in front and his cousin climbed in the back.

"What's up, Boss? Let's go make the city tremble," said JuJu.

"Muhfuckin' right," intoned Isaiah bringing out his fo-fo and checking the clip.

"Where's Isaac?" asked Kiam.

"I sent him to stand guard at your house," JuJu informed him.

Kiam nodded his head and pulled out his cellphone to try Lissha again but her phone just rang until he was sent to voicemail. Kiam sighed. "Yo shorty, call me as soon as you get this message and let me know you're good," he said with a heavy undertone of trepidation.

Next Kiam called Treebie but got the same results. *Fuck everybody at? Muthafuckaz need to be on call 24/7.* The crease in his forehead spread across both brows. He hung up without leaving a message. With a look of frustration written across his face he turned to JuJu. "Youngin we gotta tighten up the ship. We're becoming too lax and I don't like that shit. I wanna know where everybody is at all times, no exceptions," he spewed.

JuJu nodded his understanding.

Kiam put both hands on the steering wheel and stared out of the window at the snowfall wondering where in the fuck Lissha could be. If she was lying somewhere dead he would never forgive himself for letting Big Zo down. If she was somewhere all in her feelings and ignoring his calls he was going to fuck her up for real this time!

His cellphone rung in his hand. Expecting a call back from either Lissha or Treebie, Kiam hurriedly answered without paying attention to the caller ID. "Yeah?" His tone was hard and admonishing.

"Have you heard from my daughter yet?" Big Zo's strained voice boomed in his ear.

Kiam softened his tone. "Not yet, Pop. But I promise you I'ma find her," he uttered.

"I expect you to and I expect her to be in perfect health when you do."

"Yes, sir," he respectfully replied.

A long silence followed Kiam's response before Big Zo muttered, "Son, Lissha is all that I have left in this world and if something has happened to her..."

Big Zo couldn't even complete the thought. Kiam thought he heard Big Zo's voice crack, and the sound of his mentor's pain heightened the concern that had washed over him. "Pop, I'ma find her," he promised. *Or I'm killing everything in my path.*

"Turn that whole city upside down until you do. Don't underestimate Wolfman, he has survived in the game a long time and he's a ruthless muthafucka," Big Zo advised. The sincerity inflected in his words hid his well-orchestrated deceit.

By the time Kiam got off the phone he was convinced that nobody that he loved would be safe until he had demolished Wolfman and his entire squad. He looked over in the passenger seat at JuJu and said, "Call Isaac and check on Eyez."

As soon as Isaac turned onto the block, he noticed the pizza delivery boy's car parked in front of the house, but he thought nothing of it. He pulled into the driveway, parked, and hurried towards the porch. He stopped in his tracks when he saw what looked like a man's body sprawled out across the threshold of the front door.

"What the fuck!" he uttered.

The first thought that came to mind was that the driver guy had slipped and injured himself, but when he stepped up on the porch he immediately became alarmed. Blood circled the man's head and the front door stood wide open. A black cloud of death seemed to darken the sky.

Isaac's hand went inside his coat and he brought out his ratchet as he cautiously stepped inside the house, eyes on alert, and trigger finger poised to squeeze a few off. He slipped and almost lost his balance as his Timbs stepped into a small puddle of slowly congealing blood that was on the hardwood floor just inside the door.

Regaining his balance, Isaac tightened his grip on his Desert Eagle and quickly scanned the living room. His eyes followed a trail of blood and his feet followed his eyes. What he saw when he got closer rocked his world because he knew that if she was dead it would devastate Kiam's. Blood was all over her face, chest, and stomach.

Isaac swallowed hard as he knelt down and lifted her blood stained hand off of her stomach and checked her wrist for a pulse. Feeling nothing, he put his face to her mouth and felt faint breath on his skin. Her hazel green eyes fluttered open but that were glassy and unfocused.

Faydrah mumbled something that Isaac couldn't quite understand.

"Don't try to talk," he urged her. But she repeated it.

Again her voice was faint. It sounded to Isaac like she was saying "ba...by".

Judging from all of the blood on her stomach he didn't think there was a chance that her baby would have survived this. Isaac was just praying she didn't die. "Just hold on Faydrah I'm going to get you to the hospital," he pleaded.

"I—can't," she gurgled.

A gush of blood spilled from the corner of her mouth and her head fell slack. Her beautiful eyes went lifeless. "Noooooo," Isaac cried.

His phone rung in his pocket causing him to jump and squeeze off two shots that shattered a mirror on the wall. "Damn," he uttered when he realized what had happened.

He fished his phone out of his pocket and answered dourly. "Yeah, fam."

"Where you at, cuz?" asked JuJu.

"I'm at Kiam's and, cuz, this shit is fucked up! Blood is everywhere and she's not breathing."

"What the fuck is you saying, Bleed?" snapped JuJu. "Who's not breathing?"

Kiam's head jerked to the side. He snatched the phone out of JuJu's hand and put it to his ear. "What are you saying, man?" he demanded to know.

"Man, oh man, it's bad, fam. Somebody shot your girl up. They did her so dirty." His tone relayed the grave reality, but Kiam didn't want to believe it.

"What the fuck are saying?" he belted.

"Boss, the door was wide open when I got here. I came inside and found her on the floor. She's been shot up. Blood is all over her face and stomach," Isaac repeated as he knelt over Faydrah's body.

"Is she still alive?"

Isaac knew the answer to Kiam's question but he could not force himself to give it.

"Hello! Hello!" Kiam took the phone away from his ear and looked at the screen to see if the call had dropped.

"I'm still here," said Isaac in a low tone.

"Just tell me the truth, man. Is she still alive?" Kiam demanded to know.

Isaac didn't respond.

"I asked you a question," Kiam boomed.

Isaac took a deep breath and slowly forced the truth out of his mouth. "Nah, fam, she's dead."

Kiam let out a loud cry that echoed throughout the truck. JuJu and Isaiah bowed their heads as Kiam's pain resonated deep in their souls. Their eyes clouded up with the closest thing to tears that thugs could shed.

Silently they communicated to each other that they were going to put the city under siege. For this, Cleveland, Ohio was about to become the new murder capitol.

Chapter 2
Wounded

Kiam stood motionless at the foot of the cold slab that held her body; he was afraid to see what was under the white blood stained sheet. His chest felt like an empty cavity that contained no heart. The blood that used to pump through his veins with the love of Faydrah Combs now felt like thick clots that threatened to clog his arteries and stop his heart from pumping. He was there to identify her body but his mind had yet to accept that she was dead.

No, that's not my Eyez. It can't be.

He had just left her at home an hour or so ago; had just kissed her lips and looked into those beautiful eyes of hers and told her not to worry. Now they were telling him that it was her on this steel gurney. Fuck no! He had to have firm confirmation. His shorty wasn't dead!

Kiam's gaze eased slowly down her covered body and settled on her belly. *My baby* rang loud in his mind and for the first time in years tears clouded his eyes and forced themselves down his face. He let out a deep breath fighting back more tears as he thought of the excitement that he and Faydrah had shared over her pregnancy.

I'm going to give you a son who's strong and handsome just like his daddy, she had gushed exuberantly.

Kiam could hear her voice as clearly as if she was whispering it in his ear. He closed his eyes but the tears continued trickling down. He sniffled them back and stilled the ache in his heart that was contracting with the intensity of unbearable pain. Again he blew out a deep breath and tried to stiffen his legs. Slowly he reached out and uncovered her face.

What Kiam saw wobbled his knees and crushed whatever kindness resided in his heart. Some muthafucka had done the ugliest thing to the most beautiful person in his life and for that the world was going to pay.

"I fucked up, baby. I let you down," he said as a lump formed in his throat. He stood there in virtual shock, wanting to hear her voice; needing to have her reach out to him, but that was not going to happen. What the enemy had done to his girl was irreversible and ruthlessly final.

He dropped his head under the guilt of knowing that he had left her alone and open to the revenge of his enemies. It was a mistake that he was powerless to undo and the reality of that was like a pair of strong hands wrapped around his throat strangling him. But Kiam was not one to wilt.

He lifted his head, straightened his shoulders, and stiffened his back. Then he placed a hand on her arm and whispered, "I'm sorry, baby. Just know that I will love you forever and no other woman will ever take your place. You will never die in mind, heart or soul." His voice cracked. "I love you so much, Eyez."

Kiam took a deep breath and swallowed the huge sob that was right at the front of his throat. The enemy had hit him where he was most vulnerable but he refused to bow. The love of his life was lying before him cold and lifeless; the gravity of that would forever rob him of the happiness that he sought but there was no way it would go unavenged.

"With everything that I am, I will make them muthafuckaz bleed from the inside out," he vowed as he stroked her leg.

A sharp intense pain hit Kiam's chest and weakness settled at the back of his knees. He steadied his legs and brought his hands to his face and wept silently as thoughts of Faydrah and their unborn ripped the lining of his heart. A sharp scream came from the hallway, jolting him out of his painful remembrance.

"No! No! No!" Ms. Combs cries were as loud as thunder.

Kiam turned and walked to the door and took a deep breath before opening it to face the music. Once he saw Ms. Combs on the floor being comforted by two nurses the heat left his body.

"Oh, God, please. Not my baby. Not my baby," she yelled. Her cries chilled Kiam to the bone.

He looked over at the twins who were booted and suited; they had the look of evil and the smell of death and carnage oozing from their pores. JuJu stood next to Bayonna who was standing there in an oversized sweater hugging herself with tears in her eyes.

Kiam moved over to Ms. Combs and tried to help her from the floor. When she looked up and saw Kiam's face she snapped. "Don't you touch me!" She swung her arms trying to be free and in seconds she was on her feet and grabbing at Kiam's clothes. "This is your fault. Her blood is on your hands!" She raged as she pummeled him with both fists.

Kiam absorbed her blows as he wrapped his arms around her and allowed her to release her pain. "Why my baby?" she cried against his chest.

Three security guards came from different directions posting up around the waiting room. "Mind y'all muthafuckin' business," Isaac barked, pulling his hood back. He was itching for a reason to act up.

JuJu gave him a stern eye. "Chill my nigga," he cautioned. Then he turned to the toy cops with his hand held up and projected his voice in their direction. "Y'all muthafuckaz can stand down we got it under control."

The rent-a-cops were in uniform to earn a paycheck not a burial plot. They sensed that the young niggas across from them didn't give a fuck either way so they piped down and relaxed their postures.

Bayonna covered her mouth and stomach at the same time. The pain in Ms. Combs' cry was making her nauseous. She had killed many and danced to the pleas of mercy from the mouths of her victims, but this was different. Kiam's despair was shared by everyone in the room and for the first time she knew exactly what death did to the survivors.

"Kiam, what are we going to do without her?" Ms. Combs incoherently sobbed, clinching his hoodie tightly in her fist.

"I don't know, Ma," he replied, but his thoughts contradicted those words.

I'm turning this city into a killing field.

Ms. Combs lifted her head from his chest and locked eyes with him. "I want to see my baby," she said.

"No, Ma, you don't want to see her like that," he pleaded.

"Take me to see my baby!" she demanded tearfully.

Kiam conceded reluctantly. He took her hand in his and led her inside the room that held Faydrah's body. Both of their steps were heavily weighed down by a grief that no amount of time would ever lessen.

When Ms. Combs saw what they had done to her only child she fell into Kiam's arms weeping. "Why would they do my baby like this? What kind of animal would do this to a pregnant woman, Kiam? My baby had never harmed anyone," she wept uncontrollably.

"Let's go, Ma," he whispered consolingly.

"No! Wait." Her sobs were heart-wrenching.

Kiam allowed her cries to subside as he held her tightly. Ms. Combs wiped her face then stepped back to the head of the gurney and placed a kiss on Faydrah's lips. Her tears splashed onto her daughter's blood encrusted face. "Momma loves you, baby," Ms. Combs cried.

Kiam watched on with grief stronger than any emotion he had ever known. Ms. Combs raised up and turned to him with a coldness in her eyes as frigid as the subzero winds that blew in off Lake Erie. "You kill everything they love. Make them hurt more than we hurt." Her shaky voice pleaded in a hushed but stern tone.

Kiam saw the seriousness in her eyes; it was as irreversible as her daughter's tragic demise. "I promise we won't be the only ones mourning, Ma. I vow that on my soul and on the soul of my son," Kiam uttered.

Ms. Combs grabbed his collar with both hands and shook him. "When you find the one that did this to my baby and my grandchild you make them suffer in the worst way. You hear me, Kiam?"

"Yes ma'am."

When they emerged from the room Kiam stepped over to JuJu and the twins and issued a firm directive. "From now on ain't nobody safe. If you think a muthafucka is a problem—kill 'em, and when they get to heaven Jesus can explain it," he ordered.

Beside JuJu, Bayonna swallowed her spit hard. She knew that Blood Money was a number one target and if she could not hide it from JuJu she would be on their list. Kiam was going to murder muthafuckaz and ask question later. It was time to disband Blood Money.

Kiam's eyes met hers and as if he could see her thoughts floating above her head, he gritted, "Where in the fuck is Lissha and Treebie?"

Bayonna couldn't answer because she was wondering the same gotdamn thing.

Ca$h & NeNe Capri

Chapter 3
The Alibi

Kiam turned and headed for the door and the others silently filed out behind as grief and unspoken suspicions choked off any words that were on anyone's lips.

Bayonna walked a few steps behind JuJu running the whole night's events through her mind. She knew one thing for sure and two things for certain, Kiam suspected that Lissha's and Treebie's unexplained whereabouts had something to do with Faydrah's murder. In his present state of mind he was unpredictable and even more dangerous than usual.

She looked at the twins who were on Kiam's heels itching to cause a bloodbath in revenge of Kiam's loss. JuJu was hard to read, even though his heart was hers, she knew that he was fiercely loyal to Kiam. The one thing she could not let happen was the murder of her bitches. There was a tacit agreement amongst the Blood Money crew—kill a nigga before they killed you.

JuJu was her boo but she would turn his insides out and his mans could get it too, for that matter, if they came for her bitches. Slowly she pulled her hand back from his and slowed her pace. JuJu turned slightly recognizing her hesitation to continue to the car. "What's up?" he asked with a wrinkled brow and tight jaw.

"I'ma ride alone, if anybody can find them it's me," she said softly, trying to ease his suspicion.

JuJu paused for a minute, looking over her face trying to capture her angle. "Yeah, a'ight. But as soon as you connect with them bitches you hit me first." He issued firm instructions.

"I got you." She moved forward and placed a kiss on his lips.

JuJu kept a hard stance, he was on his murder shit and being loving was far from his mind.

"It's going to be okay, baby," she assured him. The love in her voice calmed that beast in him momentarily.

"Be careful," he warned as she hit the alarm to her car. He saw her inside then flipped back into beast mode.

Turning to the twins he ordered, "Isaac follow Kiam. Isaiah come with me." Each man stepped to their position with murder at the front of their mental.

Kiam made sure that Ms. Combs could drive herself home in her present condition. "I'm okay. You go out and find the person that did that to my baby," she replied stoically.

He hugged her and stood watching as she drove off. With the sleeve of his coat he wiped a lone tear that trickled from his eye. When Ms. Combs exited the lot Kiam walked to his whip with a single purpose that leaked from his pores.

Bayonna pulled out the parking lot, grabbed her cell and begin hitting numbers. Again no answer. She combed her mind trying to replay the puzzle of events that had just brought hell to all their door steps. As she disconnected from Treebie's voicemail a call came in from Lissha.

"Hello," she answered in a rush.

"Yeah bitch, why you blowing up my shit, don't that little boy keep you busy?" Lissha said.

"LiLi, we got trouble."

"Maybe *you* have trouble but I'm good. I'm about to smoke some loud, drink some Ciroc, and get fucked up."

"You better change those plans. Faydrah got killed and you're a suspect in Kiam's eyes. I hope you have a good alibi."

"What?" Lissha's voice was full of surprise. "When did that happen?" she asked.

"A couple of hours ago."

"Shit! That nigga about to go ham." Lissha sat the Ciroc down on the table heavily as she conjured up a lie that would explain her absence at the time of Faydrah's murder.

As Treebie pulled up to her house, she noticed Bayonna's car parked only feet away from her driveway. She slowed down and darted her eyes around the area. Seeing that Bayonna was alone Treebie pulled past her and parked. She grabbed her gun from the console, took off the safety and slipped it in her jacket pocket. When she exited the vehicle Bayonna hopped out and began moving quickly in her direction.

They met up at the edge of Treebie's front lawn. Bayonna pulled up the collar of her coat to combat the freezing cold; huge flakes of snow cascaded down from the sky. Treebie was only rocking a jacket, she seemed oblivious to the low temperatures and gusting wind. "What's with the serious face? And why are you parked out in front of my damn house like I'm in trouble or something?" asked Treebie, looking at Bayonna curiously.

"Because you might be if you can't explain where you've been?" *How could she know already?* Treebie wondered.

"Excuse you?" She looked at Bayonna like she had grown another head. "Since when do I report to a muthafucka? I'm not that bitch. That dick that young boy giving you must have you confused." She headed up the walkway with Bayonna closely behind her.

Inside the house, Treebie stepped out of her shoes and hung her jacket up in the front closet. Bayonna rubbed her hands together and blew into them. "Damn. Bitch, turn the heat up in here it's freezing cold," she complained.

"You can do a U-turn. You always trying to run what goes on in the next person's shit." Treebie was so not in the mood for the bullshit. She had put in work today and still had tracks to cover.

"What's your problem?" Bayonna asked, walking across the room to the thermostat on the wall to crank the heat up.

"See that's why you need to keep your ass at home in your own shit," said Treebie, taking a seat on the couch. Her mind was elsewhere.

Bayonna ignored her snide remark as she headed back across the room wearing a gloomy expression on her face. She sat down across from Treebie and spoke in a harried but hushed tone.

Treebie sat staring at Bayonna as the last words left her lips she had said a mouth full but all Treebie heard was "Faydrah is dead."

"Hold the fuck up. What did you just say?" she asked.

"I said everything you think I said?" Bayonna replied. She had an accusatory expression on her face.

Treebie picked up on it immediately, "Bitch, you better lower your brow. If I would have killed Faydrah you would be mourning Kiam too. I would never leave that nigga alive to come for us." She stood up and began pacing back and forth.

"Well that nigga coming and if we don't have a sound story our ass gonna be lying right next to her," Bayonna said, rubbing her hands together still trying to warm them.

"Did you get in contact with Lissha?" Treebie asked.

Before Bayonna could respond the doorbell rang.

Treebie froze in place looking over at Bayonna. Bayonna looked at the door as if it had blood seeping from the frame. Treebie moved to the closet and grabbed her piece from her coat just as Bayonna retrieved hers from the small of her back. Treebie moved to the door and Bayonna moved to the window. Silently, they both checked to see who was at the door uninvited; this was the wrong time to be dropping in on them. Treebie cautiously looked out the peep hole while Bayonna settled her eye through a small opening in the curtain.

"It's Lissha," Bayonna mouthed.

"She alone?" Treebie mouthed back.

Bayonna nodded then Treebie stepped back and slowly opened the door.

"Why y'all bitches acting all scary open the fucking door." Lissha pushed through the small crack Treebie had provided. Lissha looked over at Bayonna who was standing firm with her gun at her side. "Bitch, why the fuck you standing over there looking like a damn Charlie's Angel?" she said, moving to the couch.

"Lissha don't play. This shit is serious," Bayonna said, checking the window one more time then went back to her seat.

Treebie also looked out the peep hole then stood next to the couch staring down at Lissha and Bayonna. "She told you what happened to Faydrah?" Treebie asked while watching Lissha's body language closely.

"Why you looking at me like that?" Lissha instantly caught feelings.

"Bitch, don't play. Did you kill that girl?"

"Tree, you know me better than that. I didn't like the bitch but I don't roll like that. Shit, you didn't like the ho either. Where was yo ass?" She turned the heat back to Treebie's corner.

"Don't worry about where I was. Kiam is going to come for yo ass first." Treebie gave her a swift wakeup call.

"He is fucked up right now. Neither one of you are safe." Bayonna looked up from her seated position as she replayed the pain she saw on Kiam's face. "We gotta cover y'all tracks right. I am not trying to bury another one of us." Bayonna's eyes rotated back and forth between Treebie and Lissha.

"Look, I was with Spank," Lissha said, throwing her hands up in the air. "I just left him."

Treebie's brow creased as she heard the lie leave Lissha's lips. She started to blow her shit up but she needed more information before she pulled her card.

"Well, I was with JuJu so I'm good." Bayonna also tossed an alibi on the table.

At the same time Bayonna and Lissha looked up at Treebie who was in deep thought. Treebie felt the heat coming from their direction and snapped out of her trance. "Bay, I already told you but I will repeat it for the bitch that was not here. I'm not sloppy. I would never take the body and leave the head," Treebie spat, glaring down at them.

"This shit is fucked up," Bayonna said. "We got this Blood Money trail and now we got Kiam and them on our ass tight."

"I took care of the Blood Money thing." Treebie's voice cracked as she thought about Wa'leek's dead body laying only thirty feet away.

"What is that supposed to mean?" Lissha questioned with her brow raised.

Treebie stood there for a minute; she took a deep breath, shook her head, and then said. "Come with me."

Bayonna and Lissha rose to their feet and followed her to the bedroom. When Treebie opened the door and Lissha's eyes rested on Wa'leek's dead body she gasped and covered her mouth with her hand. "Tree, what did you do?" She looked at her with teary eyes.

"Who is that?" Bayonna asked, gape-mouthed.

"Tree. What the fuck?" Lissha continued to grill her girl.

"I had to, Lissha."

"Why? Wah was one hundred."

"He found everything, LiLi." Treebie's heart started to pound in her chest as Lissha's reaction made her actions real.

"But Tree," she looked bewildered, "that's Wah."

"Lissha I know," she said as a little pain hit the back of her throat.

Lissha moved closer to the bed to get a better look. She shook her head in utter disbelief. *If Treebie could murk her own husband nobody was untouchable to her.*

"Who is that Treebie," Bayonna repeated her unanswered question.

Treebie swallowed her spit. "It's my husband, Bay."

"Oh, shit. What happened?" Bayonna also moved in closer. Wa'leek's whole chest was opened up.

"I came home and he had found everything in the basement's cabinet: guns, masks and voice distorters. He knew everything," Treebie said, looking over at Lissha.

"What we gonna do?" Lissha put the ball in Treebie's court.

"We gotta do like Bayonna said tighten our shit up and get rid of the only thing that connects us to Blood Money." She pointed at Wa'leek. "We gotta stay strong. We all we got," Treebie said as they looked in her direction.

Lissha nodded her head up and down and Bayonna was stuck shaking hers from side to side.

"This shit is fucked up," Bayonna said again as she realized that things were going to only get worse. Kiam was no fool and her girls apparently had more than she could imagine hiding behind their pretty smiles. "This is too fucking much. I need some fresh air." She sighed heavily as she left out of the room.

Lissha and Treebie stood there silently. Finally Lissha threw her hands up and headed for the door too. Treebie reached out and snatched her by the arm, turning her around.

"Bitch, what is your problem?" asked Lissha. She looked down at Treebie's hand on her arm.

Treebie didn't flinch. When she removed her hand off of Lissha it was only to close the door. Then she stepped up in her girl's grill. "Bitch, come clean or I'ma get in that ass."

Lissha put her hand up and tried to move Treebie back a step but she was planted in that spot. "Talk or fight, bitch," spat Treebie.

"I don't have shit to say because I haven't did anything. And I'm not doing anymore fighting." Lissha's hand went inside of her coat. "We can let these tools pop off if it's that serious."

"Say that." Treebie's hand went to the small of her back.

Over Treebie's shoulder Lissha caught a glimpse of Wa'leek's body on the bed with his chest turned inside out. That was one hundred percent proof that Treebie's gun didn't hesitate or discriminate.

Lissha was the one to blink. "What are you asking?" she asked, letting her hand fall to her side.

Treebie kept hers where it was, wrapped around the butt of her hammer. "So, you was with Spank, huh?" she set the trap.

Lissha unsuspectingly stepped right into it. "Yeah. I told you that already. If you don't believe me call him and ask him. Not that I owe you an explanation of my whereabouts."

"You don't but you're lying."

"Bitch, please. I don't have to lie about nothing I do. Miss me with the accusation." She brushed past Treebie and snatched the door open.

"Lissha," Treebie called out. "Wa'leek killed Spank and his girl last night before he came here so you might want to come up with a stronger lie."

That stopped Lissha in her tracks. She turned around and looked at Treebie, trying to read her. Was she bluffing? Nah, she knew what she claimed to know. Lissha saw that in her face. But she still wasn't confessing her whereabouts.

"Just play your position. This is still Daddy's shit, he's the only one I answer to. Don't get it twisted," Lissha spat, looking down her nose at Treebie.

"Maybe so, but I'm your sistah. I'll bust this gun for you 'til the grave but don't leave me in the blind about the way you're moving. Did you kill that girl, yes or muthafuckin' no?" Treebie again stepped towards her aggressively.

"Bitch, is you *slow* or something? What part of no don't you understand— the N or the O? And back the fuck up out of my face." Lissha's hand shot up and she mushed Treebie in the mug.

That's all it took to get it cracking. Treebie drew back and popped her dead in the mouth. But Lissha didn't fold, she had to let her know that in order to get some ass she had to bring some. They tore into each other like alley cats. Treebie was throwing knockout blows; Lissha's arms were flailing.

The fight quickly spilled out into the living room where they fell over an end table with Treebie ending up on top.

"Stop it!" Bayonna screamed. She rushed over and used all of her might to pull Treebie off of Lissha before she inflicted serious damage.

Lissha got up huffing and puffing, and the look on her face was one of a die-hard fighter.

"She saved your ass," smirked Treebie, looking at her victoriously.

"No bitch, she saved *your* ass, I'm just getting crunk." Lissha kicked off her heels and pulled her hair back in a ponytail.

"Oh, you want some more? Are you serious?" Treebie's eyes hardened. She pulled her shirt over her head and tossed it on the couch. Her stomach was well-toned below her sports bra. She crooked a finger a Lissha. "Come get some, bitch."

Lissha was about that life. Even if she didn't win, she never ran from fight. She threw up her fists and came flying at Treebie. Bayonna jumped between them, catching the brunt of their blows.

"Y'all stop this shit!" she wailed, as she managed to wrap her arms around Lissha's waist and pull her back.

"Bitch, you was about to get knocked the fuck out," Treebie hurled.

"Yeah, yeah, yeah," Lissha smirked. "You wish."

After a minute or two of fierce stares and tearful pleading from Bayonna, they both calmed the fuck down.

"We can't be fighting each other!" Bayonna cried. "Kiam is going to be problem enough. I don't know which one of you killed his girl and I don't want to know, but y'all need to get your stories together or we might as well kill him too because that nigga is about to go ham."

Lissha looked from Bayonna to Treebie. "I told y'all I didn't do it," she uttered unconvincingly.

"The mere fact that Kiam is still breathing is proof that I didn't kill his bitch," Treebie reaffirmed.

"It doesn't even matter. Let's get a concrete story together and get ready to face this fool," said Bayonna.

She had witnessed the anger in Kiam's heart so she knew that regardless to how concrete of a story they concocted, there was no way to guarantee that Kiam wouldn't execute them on sight. She desperately tried to convey that to them.

"Hmph! I ain't no punk. Me and that nigga will kill each other," snorted Treebie as she rechecked her clip then slid the gun back in the small of her back.

Bayonna and Lissha checked their weapons as well.

Treebie headed back into the bedroom to fix her hair and freshen up. Entering the room she stopped and stared at her husband's dead body. A moment of regret threatened to crack her hard exterior but Treebie fought it off. As she stood in the mirror pulling her hair back into a ponytail. Lissha's voice came from the doorway.

"Tree, we gotta do something with Wah's body. You can't just leave him there like that."

"Why not? He's definitely not going anywhere," she quipped morbidly.

Lissha's mouth fell open. She was just as much of a killah as Treebie, but damn, she thought. There was no way she could've murked Big Zo and remained sane afterwards. *This bitch is the truth,* she silently paid homage to Treebie's gangsta.

Treebie glossed her lips then reached in the top drawer of her dresser and pulled out a chrome .380 and an ankle holster. She walked over to the bed and moved Wah's leg out of the way. Taking a seat on the edge of the bed she strapped up.

She stood up, and walked over to Lissha and hugged her. "We're still in this together. We'll talk when things cool down, okay?"

"Fine," Lissha replied.

They joined Bayonna in the living room where she was whispering into her cell phone. When she saw them she disconnected the call.

"That was JuJu," she volunteered. "I was letting them know that we're on our way."

They took a few minutes to rehearse their story. Lissha and Treebie eyed each other suspiciously as they concocted a strong lie to cover the truth about where they had been when Eyez was killed.

Satisfied that their story would withstand the harshest interrogation, the women were all set to go. It was time to face the music but they were prepared for a death dance if it came to that. But nobody said it had to be *their* blood that was about to be spilled.

"If this shit doesn't hold up I'm pulling out and killing everything with a dick between its legs," warned Treebie. Turning to Bayonna, she added, "If you're too in love with that young boy to heat up his cabbage you can get it too."

"I'm boss with my shit. You don't have to question my loyalty," Bayonna declared.

They looked at Lissha.

"Can you kill Kiam if it comes down to that?" Treebie issued the challenge

Lissha didn't bat one of her long, pretty eyelashes. "Fuck I care about dick I ain't never had." Standing in a semi-circle, they put their fist on top of each other's. "Blood Money," they said in unison.

Ca$h & NeNe Capri

Chapter 4
Deader Than Dead

Kiam and his most trusted men sat around his living room in silence. JuJu was flipping a coin in his hand, over and over again mindlessly. Isaiah was staring at a wall, not seeing anything but red. He was ready to murk some muthafuckaz and it didn't matter who. Next to him Isaac rose up off of the couch and paced the living room with his tool down at his side. The memory of finding Faydrah covered in so much blood ran through his mind and heated up his head. She had literally died in his arms.

Nobody knew what to say. Kiam's anger and grief was too intense to gauge. Last night he had gone out and made the firsts of many feel his pain. The victims of his heat were random niggas whose mouths had uttered the wrong thing in the streets about Kiam's come up.

Kiam had walked up on the first one coming out of a bar on Lee Road and hit him in the face with two shots. JuJu had left an unlucky witness slumped beside the big mouth nigga.

Just an hour later Kiam had stepped out from the side of a house and filled the second victim's chest with .40 caliber death. Then he stood over him and crushed his melon in the snow with the heel of his boot. The man had made the small mistake of wishing Kiam bad to the wrong person.

"Death to all haters," Kiam had spat as he stared down at his carnage.

The next day Kiam wore an identical look on his face as he sat silently on the couch with Trapstar on his lap whining for Faydrah. Normally Kiam didn't fuck with Trapstar, but holding him now was like holding onto a part of Faydrah. He unconsciously stroked the dog's head as he recalled how Eyez' whole face had lit up when he surprised her with the puppy.

Trapstar licked his hand as if he somehow understood their connection.

Kiam's eyes roamed around the living room and came to rest on the closed casket that sat near the far wall. He stared at it for a full minute, thinking. *Fuck it! It is what it is now.*

His heart was now colder than the bleakest winter.

His hardened gaze moved from the coffin to the spot on the living room floor where his woman and their unborn son had perished. JuJu had tried to clean the carpet but the blood stain was still evident.

"My beautiful Eyez," mumbled Kiam.

Isaac had told him what Faydrah's last words were. "Ba...by."

"Our baby," Kiam uttered.

Bitch made muthafuckaz had forever robbed him of that joy. There would be no cutting of the umbilical cord or holding his little man in his arms as Eyez looked on proudly.

The streets were about to feel his wrath. And to his enemies, real or imagined, he was going to deliver hell on Earth.

Kiam stroked Trapstar's white coat and bit down on his bottom lip to contain the fury inside that was bubbling like boiling water. JuJu turned his head away and wiped at his eyes.

He stood up, walked over to Kiam and placed a hand on his shoulder. He opened his mouth but nothing came out.

The sound of a car pulling up in the driveway put them all on alert. JuJu whipped out his Desert Eagle and moved to the window. The twins posted up on both sides of the door, whistles ready to sound off.

Kiam sat Trapstar down and grabbed his fo-fo off of the table.

"Relax, Boss," said JuJu, peeking out of the blinds. "It's Lissha and 'em."

Bayonna pulled into the driveway first. Lissha parked her BMW behind her and turned off her headlights as they waited for Treebie to arrive before going inside.

Treebie turned onto the block a short while later and parked her truck at the curb.

She stepped down from the SUV and met her girls in the driveway. In a hushed tone she issued a hurried reminder. "Remember, we're going up in here as three and we're coming out as three. If one of us dies all of us go tonight, and we take somebody to hell with us. Is that understood?"

"You're damn right," Lissha agreed without hesitation as the strong winter wind blew through her hair.

"All for one and one for all," added Bayonna, ducking her head against the chill.

Treebie looked at her *'bout it bitches* and felt reassured that they were prepared for whatever mood Kiam was in. If she could smash her own husband, Kiam could certainly get it.

"Let's go see what's on this nigga's mind," she said.

When they stepped it was in unison, one behind the other. Femme Fatales ready for whatever a nigga had on his mind. Their heels clicked with each step and their hearts beat a cacophony of fearlessness.

The door swung open almost as soon as Lissha pressed the bell. She stepped into the house followed closely by Treebie with Bayonna bringing up the rear.

The twins greeted them with a stiff hello but neither of the girls took offense. Bayonna stepped around them and hugged JuJu. "You okay, bae?"

The softness in her voice and in her eyes disguised the truth. If any gunplay popped off she would ride with her bitches not him.

"I'm a'ight," JuJu replied. It was no secret that he stood firmly on Kiam's side.

Behind them Treebie's face was stone but her eyes and instincts were alert. She felt an immediate tenseness in the room that rushed up on her like a whoosh of stale, hot air.

Lissha made a beeline straight for Kiam who was seated on the couch with his fo-fo in hand and a bottle of Jack on the table in front of him. She leaned over and hugged him. "I'm so sorry," she said, sounding genuine.

Kiam saw the tears well up in her eyes but he wasn't sold on their authenticity. Crocodiles always appeared to be crying.

"What happened?" she asked.

Kiam ignored her question.

"Y'all sit the fuck down and start explaining where y'all been all day."

Lissha sat next to him on the couch. Bayonna squeezed into an overstuffed chair across from them with JuJu. The twins remained standing, posted up around the room.

Treebie remained standing too. She placed her back against the wall and watched everyone closely.

Kiam noted her paranoia but he said nothing. If her guilt became obvious he would address it with three up top.

Lissha took his hand in hers and spoke first. "Kiam," she said, looking him squarely in the eyes. "Faydrah and I might have had our differences but I knew how much you loved her. I would never touch you like that, baby."

Kiam knocked her hand off of him. "Don't touch me," he gritted. "I hear all that sweet shit but what I wanna know is where the fuck were you at."

"I was with Treebie. We went to meet with a lawyer for Daddy out in Akron. He's supposed to be the best appeal lawyer in the state, but he said that he doesn't think he can help Daddy."

"We were depressed after that so we went back to my house and got fucked up," Treebie cut in.

"Did Big Zo know that y'all were meeting with the attorney?"

The wrong answer was going to get their wigs pushed back.

Lissha replied, "No, I don't tell Daddy things like that because I don't like to get his hopes up."

Bayonna had prepped them well.

Kiam fired one question after another at them, trying to trip them up, but they had their story down pat. Kiam let out a heavy sigh and relented—for now. He turned his head towards the casket that sat across the room and everyone's eyes followed his gaze.

Like her girls, Lissha had noticed the black coffin as soon as they entered the house. Now she asked the question that was on her mind. *Why had he chosen black to bury Faydrah in?*

"I would think a softer color would be more appropriate," she opined.

Kiam chuckled.

"What was the rush to pick out the casket?" Bayonna chimed in.

Treebie remained quiet, she had a feeling that the casket wasn't for Faydrah at all. She eased her hand behind her back and wrapped it around her Nine. If that nigga thought he was putting her in that muthafucka, he should've bought two because his ass was going to need one, fucking with her.

Isaac stepped towards Treebie with his strap already out. "Let me get that," he said.

Treebie was tempted to test his gangsta but looked in his eyes and thought better of it. She recognized a killah when he was in her presence. She slid the burner out and gave it up without protest.

Isaac grinned.

Treebie did too, but inwardly, as she felt the weight of her spare gun on her ankle. *Sleep on a bitch if you want to.*

Lissha and Bayonna looked at each other nervously.

"If I wanted y'all muthafuckaz dead it would be done already," said Kiam, rising up from the couch. "Follow me," he commanded.

The twins held their posts while JuJu remained seated, they already knew what Kiam was about to disclose.

Lissha and Bayonna followed Kiam across the room wondering how he had managed to get Faydrah's body from the morgue so soon. Out of mere curiosity Treebie joined them in front of the casket.

Kiam's expression was hard as granite but they could still hear the grief in his voice as soon as he began to speak. "A lot of people are going to pay for what happened," he said.

He took a deep breath and let it out slowly as the loss that he had suffered tugged at his heart and strained his voice. He placed his palms on top of the coffin.

"Beginning tonight I'm murdering any and everybody that I have beef with. The nigga inside this casket is supposed to be like a brother to me. We grew up under the same roof but I don't trust his bitch ass so he has to die. Let what I'm about to do to him be a lesson to any muthafucka in this room that might think about betraying me."

Kiam opened the lid of the casket and looked down at DeMarcus. He was bound and gagged, his face was hideously swollen, and one eye hung out of its socket in a grotesque manner, resembling an egg yolk. But he was still alive.

When Lissha peered inside the casket she almost fainted, and it was not because of the blood and gore. She steadied her legs but her mouth remained open.

DeMarcus looked up out of the one eye that wasn't gauged out, hoping that she was his reprieve, but that wasn't happening. Lissha had a vested interest in his immediate death.

She looked from DeMarcus to Kiam. "If this nigga called himself your brother and violated you, this is what I think of him." She leaned inside the casket and spat in DeMarcus' face. Take that to hell with you.

DeMarcus squirmed around and muttered out pleading sounds as he saw her whip out her ratchet. Kiam reached to remove the gag out of his mouth; he wasn't too cold to not allow the nigga a few last words. But the bitch beside him could not chance what DeMarcus might know.

Lissha aimed the whistle inside the casket, and blasted him in the head and chest.

Boc! Boc!

For insurance, she put another shot in his thinker. Blood and bits of skull splashed up in her face. She turned to Kiam and proclaimed, "Fuck whatever that nigga had to say. Your enemies are my enemies, baby."

She took a final look at DeMarcus and let her gun bark again.

Boc! Boc! Boc!

Now DeMarcus was deader than dead and Lissha was determined not to let Kiam find out why she hadn't wanted to chance letting him speak.

Chapter 5
Saying Goodbye

Kiam stood looking down inside the casket, but this time it was with a heavy heart. The church was packed with Faydrah's extended family, friends from her professional life, and with a horde of street types that came out of respect for Kiam. Silent tears ran down his handsome but weary brown face and dripped onto the soft blue dress that Faydrah was being sent home in.

The organist strummed a song that was likened to a chorus of angels crying. Ms. Combs wails could be heard over all other sounds. "My baby," she cried. "Lord Jesus, why did you take my only child? You said that if I served You faithfully, I would receive Your blessings. Is this how You treat Your child?" she challenged.

Ms. Combs raw grief had become stronger than her faith. It was times like this that made mothers temporarily forsake God.

If you're omnipotent, bring her back dammit! Bring her baaaccckkkk!

She looked down into the face of her baby and realized that there was no prayer she could utter that would ever give Faydrah life. The reality of that was more than Ms. Combs could bear; she collapsed into Kiam's arms, sobbing from the turmoil of a mother's tortured soul.

Ms. Combs' grief intensified Kiam's. He held her in his arms and let her weep against his chest. His face was as wet as hers but there was no sound coming from his mouth. He helped her back to her seat in the front row and left her in the care of a church member.

With leaden feet he returned to the stage to say goodbye to the only love that he had known.

In spite of the brutal manner in which she had been murdered, Faydrah looked beautiful. Kiam had hired one the best morticians in the state to make his baby as pretty in death as she had been in life. "But no amount of money can bring you back, my love," he said.

He fought hard not to choke up as he reached down and gently stroked her face.

"Eyez, you were the only soft thing in my life; the one person that loved me for *me*. What we had transcended any love that anyone has ever known. Your love kept me human and sane, it was my only comfort in this cold, cold world and now you're gone." Kiam's head fell down on his chest. Grief was such a heavy burden to bear.

JuJu walked over and put a hand on Kiam's shoulder but didn't trust his voice to communicate his condolences. Kiam's pain was his pain and it was immense.

"Eyez, I don't know what I'ma do without you," Kiam continued. "I just know that I'll never smile again. Every bit of my happiness died with you and my seed. Every bit."

He leaned in the casket and kissed her lips as his tears wet both of their faces. "Sleep in peace, baby."

When he rose up, the anger inside of him bolted high in his chest and ricocheted to his mind before settling on his darkened soul. So many muthafuckaz were gonna suffer for this! They had cut out his heart so now they were going to feel the wrath of a heartless man.

Kiam looked over at the tiny white casket that sat next to Faydrah's. It was in memory of his unborn son that had died inside Faydrah's womb.

Died?

Hell no! My li'l dude ain't die, they murdered him. They took his life before it had a chance to begin.

The organist played *Eye on the Sparrow* as Kiam stepped over to the small closed coffin and laid his hand atop it. He closed his eyes and pictured a little hard head just like himself; a fearless li'l dude with crazy swag. The little girls would've loved him and other hard heads would've feared him.

Kiam's chest threatened to collapse. The game had served him the cruelest loss imaginable. His mouth was like a slash across his face.

52

"Daddy gon' make 'em pay, that's on our blood," he vowed.

With the weight of vengeance on his shoulders, Kiam turned and walked back to the front of the pews where Ms. Combs sat stone-faced. Her tears had dried, leaving streaks down her face that might as well have been blood. Her overwhelming misery had been replaced by bitter anger that she whispered into Kiam's ear.

"Every day I open the newspaper I better read about somebody else's mother crying. Do you understand me?"

Kiam slowly nodded his head up and down.

In the back row of the church a tall, thin but shapely woman watched from under the black veil that covered her face. There were no tears falling from her eyes and she would have gone unnoticed had she not been texting on her cell phone.

When she looked up, Isaac was staring at her with a strong interest.

In the blistering cold, the funeral procession traveled to The Highland Cemetery on Chagrin Boulevard to lay Faydrah and baby Kiam Jr.'s coffins in the ground.

Kiam proceeded up the path to where his family would be laid to rest with his arm around Ms. Combs. His team flanked him in heavy numbers and with even heavier artillery underneath their coats.

JuJu and the twins were on alert for anything suspicious. *I wish a muthafucka would,* JuJu thought. His head was on a swivel and his hand inside his coat. Other soldiers were equally ready for whatever.

Lissha, Treebie and Bayonna walked together in silence and blended in with the other mourners.

The graveside service was respectfully brief, to spare everyone from more tears. Gina, a close friend of Faydrah's from work, sang *I'm Going Home to Jesus,* acappella. Her voice was angelic and it tugged a few more tears from eyes that were already red-rimmed.

Kiam bit down on his bottom lip as he watched both caskets lower into the earth into the same allotted space.

The preacher announced, "Ashes to ashes and dust to dust," then he tossed a handful of dirt on top of the caskets.

Kiam put two fingers to his lips and blew a kiss to his girl and his son. Lissha came up behind him and wrapped her arms around him. "I'm here for you if you need me," she whispered.

"Don't you touch him!" Ms. Combs hissed, recognizing her from the description Faydrah gave of her nemesis.

Lissha drew her arms back and stared at her with restrained heat. Slowly, she backed away and rejoined her girls.

Ms. Combs looked at Kiam and said, "My daughter didn't like that bitch and I don't either. Whatever you do, don't you trust that tramp. I can see deceit in her eyes."

Kiam was a bit taken aback by her quick assessment of Lissha, but he didn't discount it. Since Faydrah's death Lissha had shown him a softer side of herself. Whether it was genuine or simply the guile of a treacherous ass bitch, Kiam didn't know. But he planned to adhere to the old adage "Keep your friends close and your enemies closer" until the truth came to the surface.

Faydrah's death had rocked his foundation but his mind remained sharp, and his thirst for vengeance was absolute. He would take a few days to rearrange his operations and shore up any holes in his team, then there would be hell to pay.

God have mercy on the souls of the muthafuckaz that had darkened his.

Chapter 6
Uninvited

Xyna removed the veil from over here face as she walked into the bedroom. She placed her purse on the nightstand, eased her hammer out, and looked down at her lover with a glint of mischievousness in her dark eyes. Quietly, she slipped the gun under the pillow and sat down on the bed and began undressing. The black dress that slid easily off of her slender body matched perfectly with the color of her heart.

Wolfman watched her out of one eye. When she had undressed down to nothing but her birthday suit she slid under the covers and spooned her little soft ass against him.

At the feel of her nakedness Wolfman came fully awake from a long night of business, during which he had handled a one hundred kilo drug deal. When he had come in that morning Xyna was already gone to the funeral.

He wrapped his hairy arms around her and pulled her closer to him, allowing that morning hard-on to slide in the crack of her butt cheeks. Wolfman nuzzled his nose in her hair and inhaled its fragrance. Then his thoughts went to the funeral.

"So, how did it go?" he asked in his normally gruff voice.

"A lot of slow singing and flower bringing and tears of course. But, yeah, that bitch is definitely dead. Her and the baby," she replied cold-heartedly.

"Damn, that's some wild shit. I'm still tryna figure out who the bitch is that killed her."

"I don't know, baby. I told you what happened that day."

Xyna was parked a half a block away watching the house from behind dark shades and an open newspaper. She perked up but slid further down in the seat when she saw Kiam leave in his truck.

Over the top of her shades she saw him turn the corner. She sat the morning edition of the Plain Dealer down on the seat, grabbed her gun, and slipped it inside her handbag.

She would've made her move right away — walked up to the door and when the bitch answered shot her right in that pretty face. Bang! Bang! Bang! But a neighbor came outside to clear the snow off of their front steps.

Not wanting the man to notice her car parked at the curb in such a quiet, affluent neighborhood, Xyna decided to bend a few corners. When she returned, driving slowly, fresh snow flakes descended from the sky and the neighbor had retreated inside. But now a car with a freaking Dominoes' sign on the hood pulled into Faydrah's driveway.

This bitch must carry a rabbit's foot! Xyna huffed.

She watched as the pizza delivery boy climbed out of the car and strolled up on the porch. Xyna eyes narrowed when she saw a woman step from around the side of the house and creep up behind the delivery boy. The door swung open and Xyna caught a quick glimpse of Faydrah just before the sounds of muffled gunshots echoed lightly then got sucked up in the wind. The boy's body dropped just like what it was, dead weight, and the woman stepped over him, forcing herself inside.

Xyna sat up in her seat as if she was at the drive-in watching a movie. There was no way she was going up in that house now, but neither would she leave until she knew the identity of the murderess.

She strained her ears and listened for confirmation that Faydrah had met the same fate as Dominoes' boy. Moments later faint claps of gunshots reached her ears and a curious smile enveloped her face.

The chick came out of the house moving casually, as if murder wasn't anything new to her. She wore a long wig and dark shades, a thick coat, black gloves and boots. As she strolled through the snow she kept her head down as she moved quickly to a car that was parked directly in front of the house.

Xyna started to follow her but decided against it. As long as Kiam's bitch was deceased it didn't matter who had turned her lights out. She left there and drove straight home to deliver the news to Wolfman.

"I've been wrecking my brain tryna figure out what bitch is bad enough to go up in there and do that gangsta shit. Lissha and her crew is about that murder shit but why would one of them touch Kiam's people?" Wolfman was puzzled.

"It doesn't matter though, he'll think I did it and he'll come for me but I'll be ready," he added. "This is the major leagues over this way."

"And those three little Barbie doll hos he has on his team can't fuck with your one bad bitch."

Wolfman smiled. "Talk that shit, Slim," he said proudly and pulled her on top of him.

"You better know," replied Xyna confidently even though she hadn't murked nothing.

She leaned down and ran her tongue inside Wolfman's ear. "After seeing all that death today, a bitch needs to be reminded that she's alive. Put something long, hard and fat in my life," she purred as she reached down and stroked him.

Wolfman's dick rocked up. He closed his eyes as Xyna lifted up and inserted the head inside her moistness. He gripped her small ass and pushed deep inside of her, feeling her tight wet walls. If there was a bitch on Earth with wetter pussy than Xyna's, Wolfman was yet to hit it and he had fucked hundreds of women.

He hadn't been inside that wetness a full minute yet and already his nuts felt like they were about to explode. Xyna put her hands against his chest. "Just lay back and let me ride," she said.

Wolfman surrendered control. He laid back and allowed Xyna to do her thing. She lifted her hips until only the tip of his dick remained inside of her opening. When she slid back down on it her grip caressed his girth and her bottom opened up to accommodate his length. "You like this good pussy, baby?" she asked in a sultry tone that heightened his desire.

"I love it. Bitch, you're the best." He couldn't help grinding up in that shit.

Xyna looked down at him. "Be still, nigga, I got this," she said.

Wolfman smiled at her spunk.

She moved up and down, working her hips and muscles in a slippery harmony. Her pussy was gushy wet and hot, causing Wolfman's dick to swell up inside of her to a new thickness. He filled her completely but she rode it like a champ.

Wolfman reached up and pinched her erect nipples as he bit down on his lip almost drawing blood. "Ride this muthafucka," he grunted.

Xyna's speed increased and her pussy started talking to his wood. The squishy sounds mixed with her moans as she tried to swallow all that pipe with her pussy made him moan like a bitch.

"Turn around," he said. "I wanna watch it go in and out."

"You know you can get this pussy any way you want it," she said.

Xyna's tight grip held the dick inside as she rotated into the reverse cowgirl position and spread her thighs wider so that he could get a good view.

"Fuck yeah," Wolfman said. That pussy was wide open as she began sliding up and down.

The dick was hitting the bottom causing Xyna to close her eyes as she enjoyed the combination of pleasure and pain. Wolfman gripped her hips and pulled her back and forth. Xyna was moaning and he was grunting. Both of them were caught up in the moment, oblivious to everything but the hot friction of pussy and dick.

The bedroom door eased open and in stepped Dontae flanked by two goons. Wolfman looked up into the barrel of a .357.

"Go ahead and get your nut nigga. But when you get through somebody has to answer for Two Gunz," said Dontae.

Wolfman sat on the edge of the bed pulling on his boxers. Beside him Xyna had wrapped a blanket around herself. Dontae and his armed goons watched them closely, ready to turn the room into a bloody crime scene at the first false move.

Wolfman put an arm around Xyna and looked into Dontae's face without a trace of fear on his own. "What are you doing up in my house uninvited?" he asked.

Dontae shook his head. "You don't get to ask the questions, I do. And one wrong answer will get two people killed."

Wolfman wasn't no bitch so his lips didn't quiver when he replied, "Ask your question and get the fuck out of my house."

Dontae couldn't help but to respect that nigga's courage, he was staring death in the face and not humbling to it. It didn't matter though, courageous muthafuckaz got their tops blown the fuck off too.

"Blood Money hit one of my spots last week. They killed my right-hand man and some other people. As usual they left one alive to tell the story—and the story that's being told is that *you* sent them after me. What do you have to say about that?" asked Dontae.

"You can't be serious." Wolfman grinned.

"You don't think so?" said Dontae. He raised his aim from Wolfman's chest to his head.

"If you kill me you still won't know who sent those niggas at you, because it damn sure wasn't me. Fuck I need to rob you for? Do I look like I'm hurting for anything?"

"Some people are just greedy." He cocked one in the chamber and re-leveled the barrel.

He repeated to Wolfman everything that was told to him by the girl that Blood Money had left alive, concluding with the mentioning of Wolfman's name.

Wolfman shook his head at the utter foolishness of what he was hearing. He said, "From everything that you know about me, what would make you believe that I'm stupid enough to send a message with my name attached to it? I don't send messages, I send pall bearers. And my people would've killed everybody up in there."

"I damn sure would have," co-signed a voice that came from behind Dontae and his mans. The click-clack of his street sweeper exclamated his point.

Dontae's head snapped around and his eyes met with the fearless eyes of a ponytailed killah.

"Did y'all muthafuckaz think y'all was gonna have a party without inviting me," smirked Chino, Wolfman's top lieutenant and number one gunman.

He stood with the semi-automatic shotgun braced against his hip and primed for bloodshed.

Xyna's hand came from under the blanket, gripping heat. "Now this shit is even," she exclaimed rising to her feet butt ass naked. "Who wants to be the first to die?" Her Glock .40 moved from Dontae to his goons and back.

Five muthafuckaz stood braced for death and murder, and nobody's palms sweated or eyes blinked. Every nigga in the room was a certified killah with huge nuts, and the only pussy amongst them belonged to a bitch that was real anxious to prove her gangsta.

"Let's get it popping," she said.

"Let's do it," chimed one of Dontae's henchmen.

Time froze as a black cloud of death moved over the room like a blanket of foreboding smog. Hearts pumped hard and trigger fingers held steady; jaws tightened and eyes darkened.

"Everybody just calm the fuck down and we'll get to the bottom of this," Wolfman said, composed.

Dontae was the first to lower his gun and Xyna was the last.

Wolfman looked at Dontae. "Take your people out in the front room so I can get that nut you interrupted. I'll be out after that."

As soon as the bedroom door closed Xyna made sure that those niggas wouldn't have to wait too long.

Ca$h & NeNe Capri

Chapter 7
Calm Before The Storm

JuJu and Bayonna entered his apartment with heavy hearts and shattered spirits. Bayonna walked to the kitchen to grab something to drink as JuJu sat heavily on the couch with his head down.

Bayonna watched her beloved take a few deep breaths, holding his hands together. Faydrah's life had been cut short and not having the killer's identity was weighing on the whole crew. She took a few swigs of her Pepsi then headed back to where JuJu sat.

"You want something to eat or drink, babe?" Bayonna asked in a low tone as she rubbed her hand gently up and down his arm then sat the bottle on the table.

"Nah, I'm good," JuJu responded as the memories of Kiam and Faydrah's family played in his head. He had sat by many caskets but today would be marked as one of the saddest of his young life.

Juju tried to erase the piercing sound of Faydrah's mom's cries but every time he tried they would rush back to the front of his mind and send chills up his spine.

"Kiam is going to need you now more than ever." Bayonna spoke softly as she laid her head on his shoulder.

"I know. I can't even imagine how my nigga sleeps at night."

Bayonna took a deep breath as she thought about the alibi they had concocted and the reality that Kiam probably wouldn't completely trust them ever again until the truth was found out. The thought that one of them may be at the head of all the pain that had seeped into the very core of the organization had to scorch his soul.

And what hurts Kiam definitely hurts JuJu.

No sooner than the thought ran through her mind JuJu confirmed it.

"I need you to keep it gully with me no matter what. The one thing I can't deal with is a crooked tongue and dirty hands." JuJu paused and looked over at her.

Bayonna lifted her head from his shoulder and connected with his gaze. "I got you, no matter what. I promise to have your back." She gave him a stern look.

"Who holds your loyalty, me or your girls?" He put her on the spot.

"Baby, it doesn't ever have to come down to that, they're my girls and you're my man. One relationship doesn't prohibit the other. I'm loyal to this thing of ours and if a bitch or a bitch nigga on our team violates I'll make them pay with their life. It doesn't matter who that is, disloyalty will be met with death."

JuJu nodded his understanding then looked down at the floor as he began processing all the blood that would be shed over Kiam's losses. Killing for personal reasons was usually not his get down but Faydrah was more than Kiam's woman she was family and the way they touched her was definitely unforgivable.

A nagging thought resurfaced in his mind. He looked deeper into Bayonna's eyes and asked a question that would test her sincerity because the one thing he couldn't afford to do was sleep with the enemy. "Can you swear to me that Lissha or Treebie didn't kill Faydrah?" he asked.

Bayonna considered her answer before speaking. Finally, she said. "Baby, I wasn't with them that day so I can't swear to you that neither of them did it. But I can tell you that nothing will ever convince me that they did."

JuJu had to respect that.

He leaned further back on the couch and sighed. What he wanted more than anything right now was to serve Kiam the culprit's head on a platter, literally.

Bayonna saw the determination in his eyes. She also could see the stress on his baby face and his loyalty to Kiam was a big turn on.

"I want to make you feel better, baby," Bayonna cooed while sliding her hand down his leg and reaching for his zipper. "Let me relieve some of your stress."

JuJu didn't refuse the offer; he knew that once the bloodshed began they would be going hard. Right now he needed something soft.

As soon as Bayonna touched him, he felt himself stiffen. Bayonna positioned herself at his feet and pulled his dick from its encloser. She looked up at him with a low gaze. "Lay back."

JuJu sat back and rested his arm on a pillow next to him. He looked on as Bayonna's petite hands stroked along his length.

Bayonna slowly ran the tip of her tongue over the head of his dick. JuJu took in a little air as she placed his steel between her wet lips and tightened her jaws.

Bayonna reached up and placed her hands on his waist and brought his pulsating rod in and out her mouth sloppy wet with every motion. When she rotated her head and tightened her grip around his thickness a slight hiss left JuJu's lips.

"Ssss. Suck that dick, baby," he mumbled, placing his hand on the back of her head.

Bayonna complied, taking him to the back of her throat allowing her saliva to slide down his shaft onto his nuts. She gripped firmly around the base, released him from her jaws and ran her tongue over his balls then sucked along his thickness, taking him back into her mouth. Fast quick motions caused JuJu to grip the collar of her shirt as the feeling to release rose in his gut.

"Damn, ma," he moaned on heavy breath.

Knowing he was right on the edge, Bayonna stopped and stood up, lifting her skirt over her butt. "I want you to come in your pussy, baby," she panted then turned and bent over, grabbing the edge of the coffee table.

Barely able to stand JuJu rose to his feet and dropped his pants and boxers to his ankles.

Bayonna licked her fingers and rubbed her throbbing clit in anticipation of feeling him deep inside of her.

JuJu spread her cheeks and slid all the way in.

"Ahhh," she moaned as he gripped her hips and pulled her into his forceful push.

Bayonna was on fire. The more he stroked the hotter and wetter her pussy became.

"Touch them toes for daddy." JuJu pushed her back down as he stroked from side to side watching his dick get wetter with every stroke.

"I feel it coming, baby," she cried out.

"You feel it?"

"Yes. Yes baby I feel it." She closed her eyes tightly holding her ankles.

"Make me cum Bay," he commanded pulling her back and forth into his thrust.

Bayonna tightened her pussy muscles and rotated her hips. JuJu had her on the brink. "Come in your pussy baby. I need to feel you," she panted.

"You want me to come in my pussy?" he mumbled.

"Yes. Come deep in your pussy, baby," she moaned as she began to release hot sticky juices all over his dick.

JuJu's knees buckled when her pussy began to contract sending heat through his whole body. He pushed deep inside of her and let it rain.

Bayonna held the edge of the table and pushed all the way back into him and slowly rotated her waist calling for him to give her every drop.

JuJu stood still enjoying the softness of her ass up against his legs. He slid his hand down between her legs then brought his fingers to his mouth. "Just like I thought, sweet as hell."

Bayonna turned and looked at him over her shoulder and licked her lips. Even though round one was finished she was nowhere near done.

"You act like you want me to put my pussy out of commission."

"I want you to make your pussy feel good, let me have your pain baby," she moaned.

JuJu looked into her hungry eyes and instantly his dick rocked back up. He pulled his dick out to the tip then slid back into her warm and wet kitty.

Bayonna moaned loudly as he searched then tickled her spot. She knew that she needed to do whatever it took to make sure all his aching turned into pleasure. And it was her hope that the shit going on around them didn't kill the bond they shared. She was prepared to die with all of her secrets, but she prayed that they would remain hidden long enough for her to erase anyone who threatened to unveil them.

Ca$h & NeNe Capri

Chapter 8
Confirmation

Kiam opened his eyes and looked over at the empty spot next to him and his heart began to pump quickly in his chest. He reached out and rubbed his hand over the cold sheets and the sting of her absence hit his stomach. Faydrah's laughter was replaced with tears and her smile was replaced with a permanent scowl on Kiam's face that he vowed to maintain until her killer's body lay cold in the ground.

He forced himself to sit up then he planted his feet on the hard-wood floor. His pain worsened when he looked around the room at the many boxes that contained her things. He didn't like having to pack up and move because this had been their home, but the enemy knew where he laid his head and it would've been foolish of him to remain there.

As he moved to the bathroom he kept his gaze forward trying to dismiss the emotions that overloaded his mind.

Before going into the bathroom he grabbed his tool off of the dresser and carried it to the shower with him. *I'm not playing no games with these niggas.*

Kiam sat the semi-automatic .45 down right outside of the shower and stepped inside. He turned on the hot water in an effort to rejuvenate his spirit. His mind flashed to the day he stepped out of prison with a mission in mind. He had always known that when you played at this level of the game it could go either way; sometimes you murder the game and sometimes the game slayed you. But damn, it hurt like hell when you lost the ones you loved most.

He took a few deep breaths then lathered his cloth and ran it over his body. "I'ma kill all them muthafuckaz," he vowed as an evil gleam settled in his eyes.

He put Faydrah's memories in a sacred place in his heart then turned every other part pitch black. His new motto was, *No mercy.*

Even death needed to be afraid of him and the devil himself was getting a new name—Kiam Adkins, to be exact.

He washed and rinsed then stepped out to start his day. Once he was fully dressed he moved about his house packing the last of his things in boxes. He was on a serious mission and he wasn't letting nothing stand in his way.

Buzz. Buzz.

Kiam sat the tape down and picked up his gun and moved to the window and looked outside. His eyes settled on Lissha who had her arms folded battling the cold as she waited for him to open the door. Kiam took a good look up and down the street before leaving the window and heading to the door.

Lissha raised her finger to the bell to ring it again just as Kiam clicked the locks.

Kiam stared at her with a suspicious eye then looked past her to check the area again.

Lissha looked down at his shiny black tool then up into his eyes. There was coldness that she had never seen before. The Kiam she had grown to love and care about had checked out and there was a beast ready to devour its prey dead or alive.

"Am I coming in or do you want me to wait for you in the car?" she asked lowly, being careful not to say the wrong thing.

"Nah, come in. I have to do a few things real quick." His voice was stern and unwavering.

Lissha moved through the small space he provided and as her body passed him, his scent rose in her nostrils causing her mouth to water.

Kiam locked the door then followed her into the living room.

"You need me to do something?" she asked, looking around at the boxes then taking off her leather jacket.

"Nah, just chill. Let me handle something real quick then I'll be ready to go to the other house." He turned and headed up the stairs.

70

Lissha took a seat on the couch and continued to eye all the packed items in the room. Death was all over the place; the room was cold and dark. She thought about Gator, Waleek and Donella and now Faydrah. It seemed like death was on her heels and she wondered how long she would be able to keep it off of her ass. After a few moments of sitting there being tormented by her thoughts she got up and headed upstairs.

Lissha stood in the doorway of Kiam's bedroom and watched as he slowly placed the last of Faydrah's items from the dresser in a small box.

Kiam held a photo of him and her tightly in his grip, staring down at it as if his gaze could bring her back. He took a deep breath and placed the framed picture in the box and closed it up.

"You okay?" Lissha spoke in a soft and comforting tone.

"No. But I gotta do what I gotta do." He sat the box on top of several others then grabbed his jacket from the bed.

"Kiam. Do you ever think about getting out?" She threw it on the table.

"Getting out of what?" He paused and gave her a raised brow.

Lissha again chose her words carefully. "Can I just talk to you for a minute?" she asked, walking towards him.

Kiam took a seat on his bed and Lissha sat down next to him. Her mind raced with several thoughts; so many things wanted to fall from her lips but she knew that she would be added to the death toll if she uttered them. She quickly checked herself and began.

"Look. I understand your loyalty to Daddy and your own convictions. But you have your whole life ahead of you. Is this shit worth dying over?" She looked at the side of his face.

Kiam heard her but getting out was the furthest thing from his mind.

"At one point I thought that getting out was an option, but I buried both of my reasons," he stated coldly.

Chills went through her whole body. "Kiam..." she said then paused as she thought better of it.

Kiam looked over at her wondering what had ahold of her tongue. "Say what you gotta say," he prompted.

Lissha wanted to let her tongue run eighty miles per hour. She had to calm herself and speak right.

"You are a determined man. I know you will get each and every one of them. But on the way they are going to get some of us. I don't want any of us to have to bury someone else that we love." She put her hand on his leg.

Kiam looked down at her hand then up into her eyes. "I don't either, ma, but the reality is they touched and destroyed the best part of me. I can't leave this muthafucka without their blood on my hands."

"Just promise me that if shit starts to stack against you, you will get out," she pleaded as tears formed in her eyes.

Kiam felt a lump in his throat as he heard the words from her lips that mirrored Faydrah's. "I will try. But on the real I don't give a fuck if I die trying. Life don't mean shit to me no more. I will do my best to protect you and the crew but I will not stop until my mission is complete."

"I understand. Just be careful," she said, putting her hand on the back of his head.

Kiam stared in her eyes then pulled her close to him. "I got you, ma," he proclaimed as Lissha rested her head on his chest.

"I love you, Kiam. I wish I could take away your pain," she said as tears of regret slid down her face.

"I love you too. But we gotta tuck that shit. I can't let them get to no one else that I love." He held her firmly in his grasp.

Lissha lifted her tear stained face and as they got closer, she pulled him to her and attempted to kiss him.

Kiam jerked his head to the side dodging her lips. The frown on his face warned her not to try that shit again. Lissha lowered her eyes and the pain of rejection stabbed her in the heart.

"Let's go," he said, rising to his feet and reaching down to help her up.

Lissha allowed him to pull her to her feet. Placing her hands against his chest she looked at him, wanting to say so much but knowing that he was not in the mood for forgiveness. She tore her eyes off of him and walked out of the room.

Kiam looked at her as she exited his room and a strong thought came to his mind. She was hesitant with her words but quick to offer a kiss.

Don't you trust that bitch.

Ms. Combs warning rang loudly in his head and he couldn't shake it out. He was nobody's fool, something didn't feel right and he definitely needed to keep Lissha as close to him as possible.

When Kiam got to the bottom of the stairs Lissha was standing over an open box staring inside.

"Whats up?" he asked, coming up behind her.

"Nothing." She seemed lost in thought, but he figured that his rejection had dimmed her mood.

Moving a step closer, Kiam peered over her shoulder and saw what held her attention. "That's Miss Charlene, the woman who raised me. She was like a grandmother to me." He reached out and took the picture from her and stared at it wistfully. Had he paid closer attention he would've felt Lissha's body tremble against his.

"Is she still alive?" Lissha forced herself to ask, although she knew the answer better than anyone.

"Nah, she died while I was in prison." He ran his hand over her face then laid the picture back in its place and put the lid on the box.

Vomit rose in Lissha's throat as the full weight of her deceit stared her in the face. "What happened if you don't mind me asking?"

"Somebody beat her to death and that slimy muthafucka is at the top of my kill list," he spat, walking to the door.

Lissha took in some air as she tried to calm her nerves. Kiam had just confirmed what she had pieced together right before killing DeMarcus. She shook her head as she wondered what the fuck else Big Zo hadn't told her.

I gotta go see Daddy immediately she thought as she walked closely behind Kiam.

Chapter 9
Defiance

Big Zo strolled into the visitation room stepping with more life in his stride than he had exuded in years. He could see his master plan coming into fruition and freedom would soon follow. Because he absolutely couldn't see spending the rest of his life behind bars.

He turned down the collar of his khaki shirt and ran his hands over the creases in his pants. His short 'fro was cut evenly around with just a touch of gray near his temples. A newly grown goatee added to his masculine appearance.

The mothers of other prisoners in visitation eyed him with salacious appetites, but he paid very little attention to them other than a curt nod or a quick insincere smile. He was more than used to a woman's attention.

His eyes searched the room for his woman. When he located her, he moved quickly to the back where she was seated, looking as delectable as ever. Big Zo stopped in front of the table and took in her appearance. Lissha's hair was pinned all to one side and very curly. The light makeup that she wore highlighted her attractive features perfectly, making her eyes and cheekbones stand out.

Big Zo's eyes traveled down pass her pouty lips and her sleek neck to the swell of her breasts. The green and bright Juicy Contoure top snuggled against them like a pair of hands.

He stood there waiting for Lissha to stand up and greet him with a deep kiss and a long hug but she did neither.

Big Zo's eyes narrowed as he sat down at the table across from her. He instantly noticed that there were no snacks on the table, only a bottle of water.

Lissha unscrewed the top and took a small swig as her eyes bored into his. "Hello, Daddy," she spoke on hard breath.

Big Zo leaned back in the chair and studied her expression. He didn't speak back, instead he asked. "Do I sense a problem?"

The response he received was a face full of water. "You mutha-fuckin' right we have a problem!" she spat after dousing him.

Big Zo calmly wiped his face with the palm of his hand and looked around to see if anyone had saw what happened. The people at the next table turned their heads, refusing to meet his glance.

They didn't matter, he was more concerned about the officer at the desk. He looked toward the cracker and saw that he had gotten preoccupied with incoming visitors so he returned his attention back to Lissha.

Big Zo looked at her with a tight mouth and a hard stare. His jaw twitched with anger. "You must want me to snap your muthafuckin' neck," he said in a hushed tone.

"If I was scared I wouldn't be here, now would I? You should be worried about me snapping *your muthafuckin'* neck."

Big Zo smiled. "Is that what that nigga's dick do to you? When he fucks your pussy it damages your brain?"

"You muthafucka. I told your ass I haven't fucked him," she hissed, bringing the bottle up again.

Big Zo grabbed her wrist and squeezed until she let the bottle fall from her grasp. Water spilled out at their feet, making a small puddle on the floor.

He released her wrist. "Go get some napkins and clean that shit up. Right fuckin' now!"

"Hmph. Don't hold your breath." She folded her arms across her chest defiantly.

Big Zo stood up and went to get something to wipe up the water. He had already determined her penalty for defying him. A dead bitch was much better than a disobedient one.

When he had cleaned up the spill, he threw the wet paper towels in the trash can and returned to his seat. Neither one said a word for ten minutes. They only stared until Lissha broke the silence.

Leaning in close to him and speaking low, she said, "Why do you have me working with Kiam knowing that the woman you had me *visit* on Miles Road a few years ago was his grandmother?"

Big Zo figured that she would eventually find out. Obviously her and Kiam had been having intimate conversations. The thought of that nigga laying up in *his* pussy put a bitter taste in the back of his mouth, but he swallowed it for now.

"Don't forget that back then we needed the money because you had ran through most of what I left with you. So don't come in here questioning me about it now."

Lissha couldn't say shit.

"Anyway, how was I supposed to know that his grandmother would rather die than open the safe for you. Still, I didn't tell you to kill her. That blood is on your hands literally and figuratively."

Lissha narrowed her eyes at him as she bristled inside.

"We do what we gotta do," Big Zo went on. "Anyway, the nigga should've kept his business to himself. Back then he didn't know shit about me. He killed the old bitch himself when he told me about his stash."

"Daddy, that's cold." She shook her head at his callousness towards Kiam.

"Life is cold and then they got a cold ass hole to put you in on your way outta this bitch," he reminded her. "Ain't no muthafuckin' love for the next nigga."

"But what about me? Do you have any love for me?" Tears welled up in Lissha's eyes as harsh reality slapped the shit out of her.

"You don't have to ask me that. Everything I'm doing is for us. The question is 'do you still love me or has Kiam stole your love'?"

"Yes, I still love you," she answered without pause. It was true, she loved him dearly, but Kiam had infiltrated her heart without even trying to and continuing to betray him was becoming harder by the day.

"Daddy, what do you think will happen if Kiam finds out that I did it? Are you concerned about that?" she asked in a whisper.

"He won't find out because you and I are the only ones that know, everyone else believes it was Wolfman." He smiled at the thought of how masterfully he had orchestrated that.

Lissha told him what had happened at Kiam's when she looked inside the casket and realized who DeMarcus was. "It was a close call, Daddy," she said. The anguish in her voice was more for the pain she had unknowingly caused Kiam than it was for her own safety.

Big Zo hunched his shoulders like *so what, you handled it. So what the fuck you tripping on?* And in that moment Lissha realized that he would truly sacrifice anyone for himself, including her.

"Daddy, I'm done," she said. "I'll hire you the best lawyer money can buy but I will no longer do this to Kiam."

"Bitch, yes you will!" he said, scowling. "Or you'll die with that nigga." He sat up in his seat and leaned in no more than two inches from her face, grabbing both of her wrists, pressing them against the table out of plain sight. "Don't forget your arms are too short to box with god."

"Maybe they are, but you're not Him." She snatched away from Big Zo and stood up to leave.

He stood up too and pulled her into a close hug, placing his lips against her ear. "Lissha, I may not be God but if you defy me I'll call your ass home," he whispered.

Lissha struggled to free herself from his cold embrace, but Big Zo held her tightly. With one hand he reached up and clenched her face firmly in his grip, forcing his tongue in her mouth.

When he pulled back and unwrapped his arms from around her, he glared a stare that could freeze hell over. "Stick to the game plan, baby girl," he said softly.

But there was no doubt it was a threat.

Lissha met his cold gaze with an icier one. She pursed her lips and hawked a glob of spit dead in that bastard's face. "Fuck you, I hope you die in here," she said as tears began pouring down her face.

Ca$h & NeNe Capri

Chapter 10
The Crossover

Lissha drove with tears and makeup running down her pretty face. Until now she hadn't regretted much of anything that she had done, but she had come to loathe the day she allowed herself to be manipulated by Big Zo. With an anger towards him that was quickly turning into animosity, she realized that the mind control he exerted over her had been going on for a long time.

She thought back to when she was a young gullible teenager and he was an older and refined man with an intoxicating style and a gift of gab unlike anyone she had ever experienced.

Big Zo's well thought out plans were formulated right there under her mother's unsuspecting brow. Tracey, Lissha's mother, was Big Zo's number one side piece. She knew that he had a family somewhere but since her position came with benefits, she played it without complaints.

When Big Zo was out of town with his family, Tracey wasn't just sitting at home waiting for him to return. She was a dime piece that attracted the eye of some of Cleveland's top ballers, and she was not the type to turn down every advance.

Big Zo wasn't a fool, he knew that she possessed the potential to creep. He couldn't watch her 24/7 so he gradually recruited Lissha to report her activities to him. It began with a gift here and there, a cute ankle bracelet or a small diamond necklace, disguising his intentions by giving Tracey something too. He would send Tracey on drug runs out of town leaving him plenty of time alone with Lissha. They would go out to dinner or to clubs where Lissha was clearly too young to get in, but Big Zo's influence opened all doors. She quickly became enraptured with the respect that he commanded.

One night they were out at a bar when a young nigga pushed up on Lissha. He was drunk and all touchy feely. Big Zo snatched him by the back of the collar and pistol whipped him close to death. That shit turned Lissha the fuck on, and she told herself that she was going to get her a nigga with a gangsta that mirrored Big Zo's.

Being game tight, he quickly picked up on her infatuation with him. First he maneuvered his way into Lissha's heart and mind then in between her legs. The first time it was more like love although they both knew it was wrong. Every time after that, now that she looked back on it, was more like game. The careful way he made sure to begin and end each session with money, gifts, and praise.

When he had her securely in his devious clutch he turned her into a willing spy against the woman that had birthed her. Eventually it was her reports that destroyed Tracey's position in Big Zo's life. Later, when Tracey discovered that she had been replaced by her own daughter, her whole life went into a downward spiral from which she had yet to recover from.

Big Zo had always taken joy in Tracey's demise; he was a vengeful man that would stop at nothing to even a score or to one-up an adversary. Tracey had fucked Wolfman, Big Zo's fiercest rival, what better revenge against her than fucking her daughter? Not only fucking her but *cuffing* her.

Lissha felt sick to her stomach as she realized how masterfully Big Zo had played her. *That muthafucka hadn't ever loved me.* He had purchased her morals and used her to avenge what Tracey had done to him.

The raw truth assaulted her like a putrid scent invading her nostrils. Lissha slightly swerved as she pulled over to the shoulder of the interstate, jumped out of her car and ran close to the wooded area to release the evil that rose up from her gut. She thought about the ruined relationship with her mother that was left in the wake of her betrayal and the many lives that she had taken, all to please him.

Vomit continued to force itself through her lips like hot lava while the pain of her deceit grabbed ahold of her heart and squeezed. She was still heaving even when there was nothing left in her stomach to regurgitate.

She rose up, wiped her mouth with the back of her right hand, and turned her head away from the puddle in the snow at her feet. A chilling gush of air blew across her face like a cold slap of reality. It was then that she realized she needed to turn all this shit around. Everything Daddy had taught her was now going to be used to destroy him and to make sure his ruthless, narcissistic ass never tasted freedom again.

She couldn't respect the ho ass nigga that he had become behind bars, plotting a loyal nigga's downfall to regain his freedom. A true boss would never make moves like that. In her eyes Big Zo was no longer worthy of her loyalty. The nigga that deserved her total dedication was Kiam. Lissha made a vow to herself to do everything in her power to protect him and see that he rose to the top.

She looked down at her wrist and saw the platinum and diamond Tiffany watch that Big Zo had bought her a month before he got knocked and it made her skin crawl. She gritted her teeth, took it off, and slung it as far as she could.

Tears flowed down her face and her chest heaved in and out as she removed rings from her fingers and false illusions from her mind. Together she dropped them on the ground and crushed them in the snow. She pulled herself together and moved back to her car, walking with a new purpose.

Pulling the passenger side door open she reached in and grabbed her cell phone and a bottle of water. She took the water to her mouth, gargled and spat, then dialed Big Zo.

"Yeah, what's up?" he answered sourly.

"I'm sorry, Daddy," she cooed.

There was no response for a minute or so but Lissha could hear him breathing. Finally, he let out a long sigh. "I knew my baby girl wouldn't let me down," he said. "Now tell me the truth, did you fuck that nigga?"

"No, Daddy." *Not yet.*

"Okay. Do I still have your loyalty?" he asked as he looked out of the window of his cell at nothing but tall razor wire fences and guard towers.

"Yes, Daddy, always. Just tell me what you need me to do and it's done."

"Baby girl, just stick to the plan. I promise when this is all over Daddy is going to make you real happy." He paused. "I know it's hard on you, I can't hold you and make love to you, but it's almost over. Just ride with me on this. That nigga is about to do the type of shit that will seal his fate and unlock ours. That's what this is all about, right?"

"Yes, Daddy. Whatever you need I got you," she confirmed.

"Alright. Hit me when you get in. I love you."

"I love you more," she said then disconnected the call.

Big Zo hurriedly dialed a number.

"Hello?"

"Hold up on that, I think she's back in the fold," he said.

"Are you sure, Daddy?" the female asked.

"Yeah."

"Ok, but if that bitch wavers again I'm putting two in her head. We're too close for her bullshit."

"Yes, baby we are. And I promise you that if she gives me another reason to doubt her loyalty I'll give you the go ahead and next time I won't call it off."

"Please don't," she replied with disappointment. Killing Lissha would be more fun than a day at the park.

"I won't," he assured her. "Now take that clip out of your gun and let this play itself out. I love you."

"Love you too, Daddy. Bye."

"Bye, baby."

Big Zo hung up and sat down on his bunk, envisioning freedom that he hoped wouldn't be too far away.

Lissha was back on the road with a plan fermenting in her mind. She hit Treebie up but was sent to voice mail. She hung up and called right back. The phone rang several times before Treebie clicked over.

"Speak," she slurred as she inhaled deep on her blunt.

Lissha got straight to the point. "I need to see you as soon as I get back to the city."

"A'ight. What time you pulling in?" Treebie asked, looking down at her watch.

"In about three hours," she said, taking her speed up to ninety miles per hour.

"Okay, I'll be here."

Lissha pushed her whip hard until she hit Treebie's door. When she stepped out the car, her master plan was intact. *From now on niggas better do more than watch their backs.*

When Treebie pulled the door open and saw Lissha with puffy red eyes she knew that the visit with Big Zo must have gone very wrong.

"You good, LiLi?" Treebie asked.

"Yeah, I'm straight. I just had a hell of an epiphany," she stated, moving towards the couch while removing her coat.

Treebie locked the door and set her alarm. "So what's up?" She pulled her sweater closed and sat in the lounge chair and grabbed her wine glass.

"Bitch, what you in here doing? Having a date with yourself?" Lissha looked around at the candles and the wine glass in Treebie's hand.

"Sheeitt. A bitch been in here horny and regretful," Trebbie chuckled.

"Well, you and that happy ass trigger finger," Lissha laughed then reached in and grabbed the blunt and lit it up.

"I know, right? I should have at least bronzed the dick and tucked it away for kitty fun."

Lissha choked on the blunt as she busted out into laughter. "You need help," she said, grabbing the wine bottle by the neck and taking it to the head.

"So what's good?" Treebie was interested in what Lissha had cooked up.

Lissha took a deep breath then went in. "Tree, we been in this shit for a long time. We've seen the best come and the hardest fall." She paused, took another swig, and then continued. "I don't want to die over no bullshit." She looked up into Treebie's eyes.

Treebie nodded.

"We need to do those last licks that Spank had set up. Get that loot and get the fuck outta here." She brought the blunt to her mouth and inhaled deeply.

"Yeah, I think we done fucked Cleveland raw. Pussy won't even get wet no more."

"We need to make this pussy cum a few more times before we blow though," Lissha stated.

"So what's on the table?" Treebie asked as her wheels started churning.

"Spank gave us these niggas out in Warrensville Heights. It's supposed to be a big lick but we need the whole team on deck." Lissha gave Treebie a stern eye.

Treebie took a sip from her glass. "I been feeling a certain way about Bay. That bitch been up in that little nigga ass so tight if he shit, it gotta pay her a toll on the way out," Treebie slurred.

Lissha looked at her with a wrinkled brow then they burst out laughing. "Bitch, you stupid," Lissha blurted as the visual played in her mind.

"I'm serious as hell."

"I know and on the real she ain't been right since you killed Donella. We all gotta be on point. We got niggas gunning for us on all sides," Lissha reminded.

"Yeah, I know. It's only a matter of time before Riz pops up and gets shit going," Treebie said, sitting up and taking the blunt from Lissha's hand.

"Treebie, I know we have had our fallouts and we don't always see eye to eye but just know I have always been one hundred with you and regardless of how this shit may end up falling I love you." Lissha professed.

"I know LiLi. I love you too and I got your back." She looked over at Lissha with a probing eye. She sensed that her girl was conflicted and, if so, that could only involve Big Zo and Kiam.

Lissha could feel Treebie trying to read her. For a fraction of a second she thought about revealing everything but she recalled what that had gotten Wa'leek. The words that had been on the tip of her tongue slid to the back of her throat.

Treebie locked eyes with her. "Whatever you have going on just make sure that while you're planning the cross you don't end up crossing the wrong muthafucka," she warned.

Lissha took a deep breath and laid her head back on the couch. After a pregnant pause she sighed heavily and said, "I am trying to make shit right, Treebie. I just pray that I haven't gone too far to turn back."

No words spoken were ever more prophetic.

Chapter 11
Where Angels Sing

Prophecy was playing out in abundance. Big Zo had predicted that Faydrah's killing would set Kiam off and no truer words had ever left the mouth of a fake ass nigga. Only two weeks had passed since Faydrah was laid to rest and already the death toll had reached frightening proportions.

Kiam, JuJu and the twins were leaving bodies sprawled out in the snow, slumped over in vehicles, and stinking inside of warm houses that would never be a home again. With each new kill, Kiam personally delivered to Ms. Combs a copy of the story in the local section of the newspaper, confirming that the streets were indeed bleeding for what they had done to her baby.

Nobody was immune from Kiam's guns, he hit known enemies as well as their associates and anyone else that may have had a reason to cause him pain. Wolfman had lost a soldier or two to Kiam's vengeance but he had struck back quickly, ordering the gas bombing of one of Kiam's drug spots on Hayden Road in East Cleveland. The sudden rash of killings had sent the meek into hiding and the mighty into a huddle to strategize on how they were going to withstand his fury.

At night, the streets looked like a ghost town as Kiam's wrath caused a collective tremble from downtown to the suburbs, and daylight wasn't much safer. The sun didn't stop true killahs from lying in wait.

Kiam followed the black Buick Enclave as it left the Mentor Mall. He was holding a conversation on the phone with Dontae but his focus remained fixed on the SUV which was two cars ahead of him. "What's up, Bleed?"

"We need to have a sit down," said Dontae, sounding very serious.

"About what?" Kiam's tone was even. As far as he knew everything was supposed to be good between them.

"Not on the phone. Let's get together soon; someplace we'll both feel safe," offered Dontae.

Kiam lifted an eyebrow. "Do we have some type of problem, bruh?" he asked as he stopped at a red light that had caught him and the Enclave.

"I hope not but we'll talk like men, face to face. Where would you feel comfortable?" asked Dontae.

Kiam chuckled. "Bleed, I'm comfortable anywhere I go but that's just me. I'm not a scary nigga. Since you seem to be shaking over there, you pick a place and time and I'll be there."

"Hmph," Dontae remarked but otherwise ignored the slight insult. He gave Kiam a date, time, and place for them to meet.

"I'll be there," said Kiam.

After they hung up he drummed his fingers on the steering wheel and quickly replayed the short conversation in his head. Why in the fuck would Dontae feel threatened? he asked himself as dime-sized snowflakes fell from the sky and melted on his windshield.

In the passenger seat JuJu slammed a 50 round clip in his Calico and housed one in the chamber. His visage was hard, but his body was relaxed. Murder was set in his eye and his heart wasn't the place for pardons. Killing was like brushing his teeth, he didn't have to give it a second thought.

JuJu glanced over at Kiam. "Is everything a'ight, Boss?" he asked.

Kiam kept it one hundred. "Nothing will ever be a'ight again, not ever. But the other side won't win, I promise you that," he mumbled.

JuJu didn't doubt that for one second.

The light turned green and they drove off, keeping a car or two between themselves and the Enclave. The frigid temperatures and heavy snowfall had kept most motorists inside so traffic was sparse.

Kiam followed the truck for another few miles before it turned into a gas station. He slowed down and made the left turn too, parking at an opposite gas pump.

JuJu was halfway out of the car, ready to let that Calico act the fuck up until he felt Kiam's hand on his elbow. "Not yet young boy," cautioned Kiam, scanning the area for Jakes. "Let them go in and come out."

JuJu slid back inside the vehicle, holding the deadly assault weapon across his lap and tapping his foot on the floorboard. Kiam maneuvered the car so that he could not be boxed in. They both watched the driver of the Enclave get out and head inside with his head ducked down against the chill. The passenger got out wearing a thick coat with a fur hood that was pulled tightly around his face. He looked around causally and began pumping gas into the truck. Little did he know that in a few minutes he would have a story to tell, but he would have to tell it at the pearly gates.

A short while later the driver came back outside moving briskly with his hands shoved his pockets. It only took a glance to realize that the two boys were brothers, but Kiam already knew that. Just as he knew that they were not street niggas. *But neither was Eyez.*

He guessed that they both were in their early to mid-twenties, too young to die yet too old to spare. "Muthafuckin' guilty by blood," he uttered under his breath.

Kiam surveyed the area one last time before nodding to his young killah. JuJu sprang into action without hesitation. As soon as his boots hit the ground, he quickly moved towards the Enclave and the Calico came up spitting irrevocable vengeance.

Tat tat tat tat tat tat tat tat tat tat tat!

The boy at the pump body jerked back and forth on impact as the bullets ripped through his heavy clothing and entered his torso, spinning him around and pinning him against the side of the truck. The gas nozzle slid out of his hand to the ground a second before his body followed.

His brother let out a shriek and bolted back towards the store on unsure footing. His legs and arms pumped furiously and his mouth let out screams for help. His boot hit a patch of ice and his feet flew out from under him sending him flying in the air. Kiam was all over that ass even before it smacked the ground.

"What did I do to you?" the boy cried as he looked up into the unforgiving face of death.

"You came out of your daddy's dick," Kiam spat, aiming his Nine down at the boy's chest.

"Nooooo!" the frightened boy reached up and grabbed Kiam's arm.

"Fuck off of me!" Kiam gritted as he fired two shots into the boy's chest. Boc! Boc!

Still the boy clung onto the sleeve of his coat. Kiam put his foot in the boy's chest and pushed him off of him. Blood leaked out of the boy's body turning the snow beneath him red. Kiam bent over and placed the gun against the center of his forehead. "If there's a next life come out of a different nigga's nut sac and you won't have to pay for his choices."

Boc!

When Kiam looked up a woman, a potential witness, was ducked down in a car a few feet away. He walked over to the car, lifted his gun and aimed it at her through the window, and sent her to where angels sing.

Chapter 12
Ice Cold

The news that his sons had been murdered hit Wolfman like a stake in the heart. He had kept them far away from the game so that its savagery didn't touch them. Now he sat trying to comfort their mother who was beyond hysterical.

"No! Don't you put your fuckin' hands on me!" she cried as she buried her face on the kitchen table and wept.

Wolfman drew his arm from around her shoulders and sighed heavily. He had made a crucial mistake thinking that Kiam would only come after those in the life. His mind was confused as to how Kiam knew that the boys were his offspring; he hadn't really known them himself until a few years ago.

"I know this had something to do with you. Giles and Man Man didn't have any enemies. This is your fuckin' fault! My babies blood is on *your* hands," Sharon accused.

Wolfman absorbed that blow with a tight mouth and resignation born from the truth. There was no doubt in his mind who had so brutally murdered his sons; there was only one crew in the city brazen enough to kill like that in broad daylight.

"Sharon, I'm sorry. I—"

"You're sorry?" she cried, raising her head up off of the table and standing to her feet. She glared down at Wolfman through her tears with an intensity that was hot enough to light a furnace. "You're sorry? Is that going to bring them back, huh? Is it?" she screamed at him.

"I promise you I'm going to make the man that did this to them pay with his life," he said.

"No, muthafucka, you should pay with *your* life!" She broke down again. Regret grabbed her throat and it choked hard. For twenty years she had raised the boys on her own in Detroit, never contacting Wolfman for anything after their breakup. A few years ago she had given in to their pleas to know their father and because she had fallen on hard times she had allowed Wolfman to move them back to Cleveland, although she knew that he was still involved in drug dealing.

I'll keep the boys far away from it, he had promised. Now her babies were in the morgue.

Sharon looked at Wolfman and everything that he had ever done wrong to her came rushing to the forefront of her mind, adding to what she already felt. Hate for him emanated from every pore in her body. Her tears dried and her mouth formed into a slash in her face. "I hope your ass die in the streets just like you caused Giles and Man Man to die over something you did." The encumbrance of her grim reality almost collapsed her footing but she regained her stance and continued, "I hope the same people that killed them blow your head off and piss down your muthafuckin' neck!" She slammed her hand on the table that supported her. "That's what you deserve for getting my babies killed," she gritted.

Wolfman stood up from the table and locked eyes with Chino who was leaned against the sink. No words needed to be said. He moved his eyes from his lieutenant to his bitch and straightened his shoulders. No matter the weight of his troubles he was not the type of man to allow a woman to see him weakened. "Go warm up the car," he said.

Xyna moved on command. Before reaching the door she slid her ratchet out of her coat pocket in case Kiam was outside lurking. The only slipping she planned on doing was slipping up in a nigga's spot and knocking the gravy out of his biscuit.

A whoosh of cold air blew through the door as Xyna left out, but it was not as chilling as Wolfman's heart. "Sharon, if the police ask to talk to you again don't tell them your suspicions just let me handle this. I don't want them prying around in my affairs. I promise you I'm going to handle this," he said.

"Muthafucka, my sons are dead because of you. Do you really think I'm going to protect you? Did you protect *them*?" she snarled.

Wolfman looked down at her and sighed.

Sharon fell back into her seat, laid her head back on the table and sobbed as memories and regret fought for space in her mind. Both would soon have to scoot over and allow room for something far more eternal.

Wolfman nodded his head just a tad and his message was crystal clear. Chino snatched his whistle off of his waist, stepped forward, and blew Sharon's memories all over the table mats.

"She would've been a problem," Wolfman said as he stared at her noodles hanging out of her head.

Ca$h & NeNe Capri

Chapter 13
On The Brink

"**N**oodles? For real shorty, that's what you gon' feed a nigga for breakfast?" Kiam smirked as he looked inside of the bowl that Lissha had placed in front of him.

"Why are you trying to eat when you're about to meet Dontae at a restaurant? Why can't you eat there?" she asked, shrugging her shoulders. Her attitude was turned all the way up since she got to his house.

"I'ma eat there a'ight. I'ma eat that nigga's face if he comes at me sideways," said Kiam, pushing the Ramen noodles from in front of him.

Lissha glared at him and went to the cabinet and grabbed a box of Captain Crunch cereal. She placed it on the table and then grabbed a big salad bowl and a half gallon on milk out of the refrigerator. "Satisfied?" she asked, moving her bangs out of her face and looking at him real sassy.

"If that's the best you can do," he replied. "But no wonder you can't get a nigga to wife ya ass."

"Forget you, Kiam. I usually let a nigga eat and then I feed him." She crossed her arms over her chest.

"Well he won't eat again if you keep feeding him this bullshit," Kiam chuckled as he began going in on his big bowl of cereal.

"Whatever." She flicked her hand at him and took a seat across from him at the table and watched him devour the whole box of cereal. She shook her head in wonderment.

"What, shorty?" he asked, putting the bowl to his mouth and drinking the milk. When he was done his thin mustache was white. He looked up at her like a rebellious adolescent and smiled.

Lissha grabbed some napkins out of the holder and extended them to him but Kiam wiped his mouth with the back of his hand and widened his grin.

"Seriously, Kiam? That's nasty." She turned her nose up in disgust.

He made a face at her causing her to smile despite the serious disposition that she had brought with her when she showed up at his house a half hour ago.

"I'm just saying, what you want me to do? Ask you to pass the Grey Poupon?" he joked, effecting an English accent and all.

Lissha shook her head at his silliness as she stared into his thuggishly handsome face. When she saw him trying to read her, she stuck her tongue out him.

Kiam balled up a napkin and threw it at her; laughing when it struck its target.

"Stop. You play too much," Lissha pouted, picking the napkin up off of her lap.

"Aha, I hit you in that big ass forehead," he teased.

"Oh, you got jokes?" she said. "Like your shit isn't big as hell too. But you like throwing shit?" Lissha picked up a hand full of noodles out the bowl.

"You better not, I'll whup ya ass," Kiam threatened.

"I better not what?" She broke a piece off and flung it at him.

Kiam blocked it. "Throw something else and watch what happens."

Lissha held her arm back and twisted her lips as she tried to contemplate how far she could get after she threw it. "You think I won't?" she said, pushing her seat back a little.

"I know you won't," Kiam dared.

Lissha couldn't back down, she tossed what she had in her hand then tried to jump up. Kiam grabbed her leg pulling her back in the seat then grabbed his bowl and tossed the little milk that was left in her face.

"Kiam," she cried out. "You got that shit in my hair."

"I told yo ass. But here's a napkin," he teased.

Lissha grabbed the napkin and dabbed at the milk that dripped from her bangs. "Okay you like to play." She jumped up from the table and grabbed his cell moving quickly to the other side.

"Don't play with my phone. Put my shit back on the table," he warned.

"I'll throw this shit in the toilet. Dare me." She taunted.

"I double dare yo ass," Kiam looked stern in her eyes.

"I got yo phone," she teased like a little girl.

"Play if you want to," Kiam chuckled.

Lissha teased a little more then bolted towards the steps, laughing. Kiam took off after.

They were both cracking up as she flew through the living room and took the stairs up, two at a time. Her booty bounced as her legs pumped and her hands flew out wildly.

Reaching upstairs, landing a step ahead of Kiam, Lissha darted down the hallway screaming like a kid at the amusement park. Just as she reached for the knob on the master bedroom door, she felt Kiam scoop her up from behind.

"I got your ass now," he said.

"Ahh. Kiam, put me down." She kicked and screamed laughingly.

"I'ma put your ass down a'ight." Kiam carried her over to his bed and dumped her on her side.

Out of breath, Lissha rolled over on her back and looked up at him.

"Gimme my phone," he demanded, holding out his hand.

"Nope." Lissha clutched the phone tightly against her chest.

"Okay, that's how you doing it? I got something for that ass," he threatened, looking down at her with mischief in his eyes.

Lissha breath caught in her chest as he straddled her. All that dick was so fuckin' close now. She closed her eyes, anxious to go with the flow, but he had something different in mind.

Lissha felt his hands slide under her shirt. He began tickling her as she held out her arms keeping him from getting what he was after.

"Nooooo, Kiam," she cried out.

"Gimme my phone," he repeated.

"Okay, just stop. Please." She was laughing like crazy as he found all of her ticklish spots.

"Give it to me," he commanded.

"I said okay," she screamed.

Kiam stopped tickling her sides and Lissha dropped the phone over the edge of the bed. When he climbed off of her and reached for it, she jumped on his back and bit him on the neck.

"Ouch!" Kiam yelped and tossed her off of his back onto the bed again. He dived on top of her and they wrestled around for some payback, knocking the covers and pillows off of the bed. Kiam pinned Lissha's arms above her head. "I'm biting your ass back," he said.

"Noooo! I'm sorry," pleaded Lissha. "I promise, I'll never do it again."

"Fuck that," he said and sunk his teeth into her neck and bit the shit out of her.

Lissha screamed at the top of her lungs and tears flowed from her eyes. "That shit hurt!" she cried, punching him I'm the chest.

Kiam laughed but felt bad when he saw the bite mark that he had left on her neck. "Sorry about that li'l mama," he apologized.

Lissha had tears running rapidly from her eyes as she rubbed her neck, playing the moment for all that she could. She wanted him to take her in his arms and make it up to her in a way that they both desired.

"You want me to kiss it and make it feel better?" asked Kiam.

"Yep," she said, nodding her head up and down theatrically.

"I got you, ma."

Kiam grabbed her leg and pulled her across the bed. He towered over her then placed his soft lips against Lissha's neck and kissed the bite mark. He reached up and wiped her tears and her eyes filled with desire, while his lowered from the guilt that whispered to him from within his soul.

They stared at each other with much different feelings mounting, but their needs were the same. Their mouths came together, their tongues explored, and their hands got busy. Before they knew it, they were both stripped down to their underwear.

"Wait, Kiam," said Lissha, putting her hands against his chest just as he was about to cover her nipple with his mouth.

"Fuck it, it is what it is," he said. He felt bad but he had to have her to help him deal with his grief.

Lissha thought that he was referring to breaking his promise to Big Zo. "No, Kiam, it's more than that," she uttered as her eyes became misty. Heat rushed through her body as she felt the head of his dick resting against her wet panties.

"Just let this shit happen, we'll figure out the rest later." He gave in and covered her nipple with his mouth as his fingers reached below, slipping into her panties and tracing her moist lips.

"Ssssss," she moaned, wanting him to just put it in before her tongue spoke a truth that would forever end his yearning for her.

Kiam pushed his fingers deep causing her back to arch with every thrust. Lissha's hot pussy released liquid pleasure as she gripped him tightly around the neck. Kiam closed his eyes and enjoyed how good she felt but a picture of Faydrah flashed through his mind and jolted him back to reality. He opened his eyes looking down at Lissha full of heat and passion but he was conflicted by honor.

Lissha pulled up towards him and nibbled his neck as she rode his fingers. Both of their hearts filled with guilt-ridden cravings and the urge to put each other out of the miserable place they were suspended in.

Kiam rose up on his knees and pulled out that steel and stroked his thickness. Lissha glanced down at all of that blood engorged beef and her heart sunk with anticipation. She hurriedly lifted up and pulled her panties off and tossed them across the bed.

Kiam leaned back in and kissed her deeply. Each taste of her lips and touch of her hands caressed away memories that were hard for him to bury. He still ached for Faydrah but he needed to feel human again. He grabbed Lissha's leg in the crook of his arm and prepared to go deep.

She gripped him around the neck with one hand and grabbed the sheets tightly with the other. "Kiam please," she moaned as she felt the head at her entrance.

Just as Kiam got ready to give her some heat he looked past her head to see his phone lit up with JuJu's name and number. He had told him to call only if shit went wrong and seeing him calling was confirmation.

"Shit," Kiam yelled out as he released Lissha's leg and reached out for the phone. He sat on the edge of the bed and dialed JuJu back. "What's up?"

JuJu's response was heavy with grief and unbridled anger as he reported the somber news. Kiam listened then let out a long sigh.

Lissha grabbed her panties and slid them back on then looked around for her other clothes. From the look on Kiam's face she knew that shit had become critical.

"We on our way," he said then disconnected the call.

Lissha was already up off the bed gathering her clothes and putting them back on. Kiam moved to his drawer, grabbed some fresh boxers and some black sweat pants and a hoodie to match. He went into the bathroom and closed the door. When he emerged Lissha had left the room. He grabbed his tools and phone and headed down the stairs.

Kiam looked around the living room then darted his eyes into the kitchen; Lissha was already strapped up with her fo-fifth in her hand checking the clip.

"You ready to roll?"

"Always," she shot back.

Kiam acknowledged that with a respectful nod of his head; if nothing else he knew that Lissha would bust a nigga's ass. What they had been on the brink of doing upstairs was pushed out of mind; the hour called for a different kind of kill. His meeting with Dontae would have to wait too. Blood needed to be shed and graves needed to be filled.

Chapter 14
The Price of War

When Kiam and Lissha arrived at the address on Parkview that JuJu had given them, he was waiting outside without a coat, hat and gloves on, impervious to the sub-zero temperature. He held an AK-47 with an extended clip down by his side as the wind howled around him like an angry lion. His face was as hard as the ice beneath his feet and his eyes were mere slits.

A team of six heavily clothed goons were posted around the yard, packing mad arsenal up under their thick coats. They were not worried about neighbors calling the cops. On this street in the heart of the hood people minded their own business because they knew that the penalty for snitching came swiftly and without mercy.

One of the goons hurried up to the car to open Kiam's door while a second one did the same for Lissha. Their feet touched the ground almost simultaneously. Lissha's scarf blew in the wind as she tucked her hands in her coat pockets and waited for Kiam to come around to her side and together they walked up to JuJu.

"Take me to the girls," Kiam said. There was no time for greetings and chest bumps, every single minute was critical. Isaac was missing and his abandoned truck had been found a few blocks away with blood stains on the driver's seat. He had spent the night with one of the girls that lived here and Kiam was there to get some answers or to leave a crime scene behind in his wake.

As soon as they stepped in the house the heat blasted them in the face. They looked around the nicely furnished living room where Isaiah stood over a girl that looked to be in her early twenties. She was hog-tied, with blood running down her face. A few feet away a second girl was seated on the floor, sobbing, with her head down in her hands. A young enforcer named Dirty drew his foot back and violently kicked her in the ribs.

"Y'all bitches gonna talk or die," he spat.

The girl coughed up blood and whimpered loudly.

Kiam turned to JuJu. "Which one of them was Isaac here to see?" he asked.

"This ho right there." JuJu pointed to the girl that was hog-tied. "Cut her loose."

When JuJu cut the rope from around the girl's hands and ankles, she cried tears of relief. But that would quickly change.

Kiam walked straight up to her, grabbed a hand full of her hair and snatched her head up. "Dry those muthafuckin' tears and tell me what happened. And if you stutter one time, I'ma make it your last. Do you understand me?" He immediately took control.

"Yes," she sniffled.

Whap! He slapped the dog shit out of her.

"Talk!" he commanded.

The girl dried her eyes and began telling her story from the time Isaac had picked her up and taken her out to dinner last night to when they came back to the house and spent the night together. "The last time I saw him was this morning when he left," she swore.

Kiam studied her face and saw that her jaw was twitching. He turned to Isaiah who was now pacing back and forth. "Twin," he called, "how long has your brother known her?"

Isaiah stopped and looked down at the girl with disdain. "A few months," he replied.

"That's all?" Kiam confirmed.

"Yeah, and I don't believe this bitch. She's hiding something."

"No, I'm not, Twin. I swear," she cried. "I would never do anything against your brother, I *loved* him."

"Bitch you lying," JuJu cut in. "My fam ain't even know you like that! And what the fuck you mean you *loved* him? Did y'all hear that fuck shit?" He looked from Isaiah to Kiam.

Lissha stepped up with her tool already out. "I heard it," she said and shoved it in the girl's mouth. "This grimy bitch just said she 'loved' him, like she already knows he's not coming back."

"Yep." JuJu nodded his head.

Isaiah kicked her in the face and she toppled over on her side. "You set my brother up!" he gritted. "You slimy ass rat." He snatched his banger off of his hip.

Kiam walked up on him, placing his grip at the fold of his arm then Isaiah reluctantly eased off of the trigger but the blood that pumped from his heart was hotter than fish grease.

"Lift her up," Kiam said.

Isaiah stepped back, he wasn't touching that bitch unless it was to dump her body in a deep, deep hole. Kiam understood it for what it was; he looked at JuJu as he snatched shorty up into a seated position. Her mouth was busted and the left side of her face was swelling fast.

Kiam didn't mince words. "The people that paid you to set Isaac up can't protect you now. You're going to die and there's no way to change that. Do you understand?" His voice sounded like Satan's.

"Y—eah." Her whole body trembled. The greed that had led her to cross Isaac was now replaced with regret. Tears ran down her face and mixed with the snot that ran from her nose and the blood that poured from her mouth. She looked at Kiam pleadingly but it was in vain.

Kiam's eyes were merciless.

"Tell me who approached you and I promise you they'll die worse. Was it Wolfman?" he interrogated.

She shook her head side to side, fearfully. "No. It was Chino. Her swollen lips trembled, "He promised me enough money to make a better life for myself."

"By selling a nigga out?" The boom of Kiam's voice reverberated throughout his body. He despised a disloyal bitch.

The girl dropped her head in shame.

"I'm sorry. Please don't kill me," she begged.

Kiam fought off the urge to shoot her in between the eyes. *How in the fuck she gon' plead for mercy when she had none for my nigga?* He didn't even respond to her pleas. "What about your girl over there?" he pointed. "Did she have anything to do with it? If she did, don't spare her ass. Take that bitch to the grave with you."

She looked over at her friend who was pleading with her eyes not to get exposed. They went all the way back to grade school together, but that didn't matter now.

"That bitch brought Chino to me," she spat. "I kept saying no but they talked me into it. It's all her fault. I swear I didn't wanna do it." Her sobs rendered the rest of her plea unintelligible but Kiam had heard enough.

He nodded his head and stepped over to her co-conspirator. Without uttering a word he shot her in the center of the forhead, sending her brains spraying out of the back and blood soaking up on his and Dirty's pants legs.

Dirty looked down at his crisp new True Religion jeans; they were soiled with the blood of a trifling ass bitch. He started to strip out of those muthafuckaz right there on the spot before the tainted blood seeped through and touched his skin, but it was too gotdamn cold to go outside in his boxers. He looked down at the dead girl at his feet and gritted, "Punk ass bitch."

He click-clacked his whistle, pumped three shots in her chest then pulled out his dick and pissed all over her. "When you reach hell don't forget to wash ya ass," he spat.

Out of habit Lissha pulled some money out of her pocket and took a step toward the body before she caught herself and let her hand fall to her side.

Kiam walked back over to the other side of the room and looked down at the bitch whose future was shorter than a mosquito's dick. He contemplated delaying the kill in hopes that he could barter her life for Isaac's but he knew the answer to that. Chino was a killah just like them; Isaac was probably dead already. And the bitch that set him up had already lived too gotdamn long.

"Y'all cut this bitch up in little bitty pieces and deliver them to the muthafuckaz that bought her soul," he directed as he turned and headed for the door with Lissha in tow.

Ca$h & NeNe Capri

Chapter 15
Weary

Bayonna stood beside the bed staring down at JuJu with worry in her heart. He had been running with Kiam nonstop for the last month and the strain of the streets had caught up with him. Along with the search for Faydrah's killah he also carried the burden of Isaac's disappearance. Weeks had passed and everyone knew he was dead but not finding his body to give them all closure was killing JuJu. He had brought him back in and the reality of being responsible for him was tearing JuJu up inside. Bayonna's heart was aching with every passing day watching the blame weigh heavily on his soul.

JuJu was laid out and exhausted from throwing up all night. Bayonna had been up with him every hour trying to help him back and forth to the bathroom. His head had finally been on the pillow for a couple of hours and she was more than relieved.

Bayonna moved to the bathroom and cleaned it from top to bottom, hopped in the shower and changed clothes then went to prepare him some homemade chicken noodle soup. When she came back in the room he was laying on his back with his eyes open staring at the ceiling.

"Hey, baby. You feeling better?" she asked, sitting next to him on the bed.

"I feel a little better. I need you to help me get ready." He tried to sit up but got dizzy and laid back down. "Fuck," he yelled out.

"Baby, you gotta rest. You can't go out like this."

"I got shit to take care of, ma. I gotta get up and handle my business."

"Look I understand all of that but you gonna be laid out next to the nigga if you are not right when you step out of the door. Kiam will understand," she tried her hand at reason.

JuJu tried to accept her words of wisdom but her logic was conflicting with the beast in him and his will to not let Kiam down.

Bayonna could see in JuJu's weary eyes that he was not going to accept failure on any level.

"Baby, I'ma help you into the tub and get you straight and then we can see how you feel after that." She rubbed her hand up and down his back then left the room and ran him a hot bath. While the tub water cooled she got him a small bowl of soup.

JuJu sat up in the bed while Bayonna fed him small spoons of broth and hot tea. He had to admire how she stood strong by his side. Unlike most females he had dealt with in the past who mostly were trying to come up on a young nigga's trap. Bayonna was very different, indeed. She had her own shit; she understood the streets and being able to support him without all that extra complaining about the game taking up all of his time made her the whole package.

JuJu forced a little smile as she took him by the hand and pulled him up to his feet. "You know I love you, right?" he reconfirmed.

"Yes baby and I love you back. But don't talk because that breath is kicking like old Timbs." She joked.

JuJu chuckled. "My bad," he covered his mouth.

"It's all good but I need my hair line so be easy until we bust this toothpaste open."

"Oh, shit," he burst out laughing and grabbed his side because he was sore from all the vomiting.

Bayonna helped him down into the warm water then ran a little more hot water and began rubbing the soapy cloth over his body. JuJu put his head back and enjoyed her gentle touch. She allowed him to soak while she put fresh sheets on the bed, vacuumed the carpet, and laid out his clean clothes. When she was done, she helped JuJu out of the tub and carefully dried him off.

Proceeding into the bedroom, JuJu laid across the bed in his towel and closed his eyes as Bayonna's oily hands attended to every inch of his body. "You better be careful before you wake up my little nigga," he affectionately warned.

"Boy, please. That's the Nyquil talking. If I get up on that little nigga you gonna need an IV and a heart monitor, you are in no position to fuck with ya girl," she joked.

"You ain't never lied. Once that pussy get wet you might as well get my pinstripes ready," he chuckled. "Because you be killing me."

Bayonna laughed as she continued to rub his aching muscles. JuJu closed his eyes and soon drifted off again. Bayonna covered him up and lay next to him with her arm around his stomach and she dozed off too.

When she finally opened her eyes the room was dark and she realized that they had slept into the night. Bayonna reached up and put her hand on JuJu's forehead, checking his temperature. He was still a little warm but it seemed that the worse was behind him. Just as she was about to get off of the bed his cell went off. She looked over at it and saw Kiam's number.

"What's up, Boss?" she answered, walking into the bathroom.

"Where's JuJu?"

"He's fucked up," she said, peeking back in the room at him.

"What the fuck you mean?" Kiam went straight into beast mode.

"Nah, nothing like that. He got the flu or some shit. He's been throwing up all night and he has a fever."

"Damn. Well, me and Lissha are about a half block away. Get ready to open the door," he said then disconnected the call.

Bayonna sat the phone on the dresser, threw on her stretch pants and a t-shirt, and headed to the door.

Kiam and Lissha pulled up, eyed the area and jumped out with their guns firmly in hand. Kiam looked up the block and nodded at security who deaded their lights and got on point just in case a nigga wanted to get stupid. Dirty and two others that had tailed Kiam nodded back as him and Lissha moved up the walkway.

When Bayonna opened the door they piled in quickly. Kiam had a lead on Chino's whereabouts and he was ready to get at that nigga.

"Where JuJu at?" Kiam asked.

113

"He's in the bedroom," Bayonna responded.

Kiam didn't even wait for an invitation, he walked off toward the room with Bayonna on his heels. Stopping in the doorway, he stared at JuJu laid up and he felt bad for him. But Kiam's mission didn't change, he needed to get at Chino, ASAP. That nigga didn't deserve another hour on this earth.

JuJu must have sensed Kiam's presence because his eyes fluttered open and he tried to come to attention. "What's up, Boss? You ready to roll?" JuJu asked, pushing himself to sit up.

"Nah, li'l bruh. You gotta sit this one out," Kiam responded.

"Nah, just let me get my shit, I'm good."

JuJu's spirit to ride regardless brought a slight smile to Kiam's mouth. He knew that he had a loyal nigga on his side but he also knew that you never overwork your strongest arm because when you needed the muscle it might fail you. With Isaiah still rocked by his twin's disappearance and not really on point. Kiam couldn't afford to have JuJu down for too long but he needed him well, first.

"Chill, Youngin. Get your rest. I got it. But when you feel stronger go check on Isaiah, I think he's going through it right now," he said.

"Yeah, he is. But I'm ready to ride, it don't—"

"Kiam, me and Bay will roll with you," Lissha cut in from behind him.

"Nah, I got it," JuJu insisted, as he tried to sit up and get off of the bed. But dizziness took over and he was forced to lay back down.

"JuJu get your rest. I got Dirty and 'em outside, we got it," Kiam confirmed.

"Kiam, you know good and well I handles my shit and you need to have people in the room with you that you can trust to not bitch up if shit goes wrong." Lissha said, pulling off her jacket. "Bay give me some shit to throw on."

"Hell yeah, you know I'm down." Bay moved to the closet and grabbed two pairs of black sweat pants and two black hoodies.

Lissha and Bay stripped down and began suiting up. Kiam sat back and watched as the two of them got into killah mode. Bayonna click-clacked her guns and began tucking them. She handed Lissha her two spares. Lissha checked her ammo and tucked one gun securely in her waist and strapped the other one on in an ankle holster.

When they threw on their hoodies and turned around Kiam didn't see the face of two beautiful women, he saw the invitation of death and he was ready to help them deliver it.

"We ready," Bayonna said on a low grimace.

Kiam looked between Lissha and Bayonna, the cold fearless look in both of their eyes charged his own killah instinct.

JuJu laid back on the bed feeling satisfied; he knew that even the bitches on their team had bigger balls than most niggas.

"Y'all already know if a nigga lifts his hand to scratch an itch make it his last act," Kiam spat.

"You already know," Lissha concurred.

Kiam turned to walk out of the room with Lissha right behind him.

"Hand me my shit," JuJu said, pointing at his Nine on the dresser.

Bayonna picked it up then walked over to JuJu and kissed him on the forehead. "I love you, bae."

"I love you too. I'ma be mad as hell if you don't bring my pussy back safe and sound," he joked.

"You so nasty," she kissed his lips.

"On the real be careful and keep your eyes open."

"I got it, baby. I'll be right back," she said then turned to leave the room. The smile dropped from her face and was replaced with tight lips and a creased brow.

Outside, Kiam walked over to Dirty's car and instructed one of the boys to stay there with JuJu. There was no way he was going to leave his right hand unprotected.

When Kiam pulled up to the small house on St. Clair, he deaded the engine and scanned the area. "This nigga been holding out. I know he knows what happened to the twin. I need that nigga alive and talking, is that understood?"

"Got you," Lissha said.

Bayonna just nodded her head but she was not sure if she would be able to comply.

They each exited the car and pulled their heat out. Slowly they approached the steps to the house keeping a stern eye up and down the block. Kiam approached the porch's window and peeked through the small crack to see Sonny sitting in the living room smoking a cigarette, watching television. Kiam tried to look around the room to confirm that what he was told about ole boy being alone was true.

He moved back and whispered in Lissha's ear then stepped to the side pulling Bayonna next to him. Lissha pulled back her hood, purposely messing up her hair then she rung the bell and started banging on the door.

Sonny looked out the window with his face balled up. "What the fuck you knocking on my shit for?"

"I need that shit," she started scratching and moving around.

"Go the fuck up the block," he yelled back.

"Ain't nobody out there. Please just let me get a hit real quick," she begged, pulling some money from her pocket.

"Bitch, get the fuck on." He yelled through the window as he watched her scramble to get the money straight.

"Please. Please. Please. I'll even let you get your dick wet real quick." She dropped to her knees and put her hands together.

Sonny looked into her pleading eyes, sucked his teeth then closed the curtain. When Lissha heard the locks clicking she reached around her back and rose to her feet.

As soon as the door cracked Lissha kicked it open and put her gun in his face. "Put your hands up and don't you muthafuckin' move. Stupid nigga ain't nobody giving yo dirty ass no pussy."

"Bitch, you must be crazy," he said, backing up with his hands in the air.

As he got ready to hurl some more venom in her direction his eyes grew wide when he saw Kiam and Bayonna coming at him with their heat drawn. Bayonna kicked the door closed as Kiam and Lissha backed Sonny up to the couch.

"What the fuck is this about?" he asked, falling back onto the sofa.

"Shut the fuck up, nigga, you ain't asking the questions," Lissha barked, lowering her weapon to point right at his chest.

Kiam stepped around her and looked down at Sonny menacingly. "Before I begin, look in my face nigga." He forced eye contact then continued. "Do I look like I came here to play games?"

Sonny didn't respond.

Kiam chuckled then cracked his head open with the butt of his gun. "We're gonna try this shit a different way, but if you fuck with me you'll get the same result." He stared down at Sonny's bloody face. "I want that nigga Chino and you're gonna deliver him to me or your pastor is gonna deliver your eulogy." Kiam spoke low but demanding.

"I ain't got shit to tell," Sonny mustered the resolve to answer calmly, ignoring the blood that leaked from his busted brow.

"You hear this muthafucka?" Bayonna looked over at Lissha.

"Yeah, I think this nigga's memory needs to be jogged." Lissha smirked, knowing that all niggas talked once that steel touched that dome.

Bayonna moved past Kiam and smacked the shit outta Sonny with her gun, busting his mouth and loosening two of his front teeth. "Muthafucka, lie again." She grabbed him by the throat and pressed the gun against his nose.

"What the fuck is wrong with you," he spat, looking up into Bayonna's eyes.

"Where the fuck is Chino?" Lissha yelled out then fired a shot an inch above his head.

Sonny jumped high enough to dunk a basketball. When his ass touched back down on the cushion he had lost some of his bravado. "Hold up. Please. I ain't got nothing to do with this shit." Amazingly, he looked from the girls to Kiam for mercy. "Bleed, you know I do my own shit. What's going on between you and Wolfman ain't my business."

"Nigga, you made it your business when you let him duck off at your crib for a few days. Now where is he?" Lissha turned up the heat.

"You right. You right. I saw him. But I swear to God I don't know where that nigga at."

Lissha's blood started boiling, she stared him in the eyes hard then slapped him with her steel. "You think we playin' nigga?" she growled then gave Bayonna the nod.

Bayonna pulled a knife out of her pocket, knelt before him as she drew her arm back and drove the rigid blade into the plate of his kneecap.

Sonny's body jolted mid-way from his seated position but the jammed blade enabled him from standing at full range. His arms flailed as he jerked backwards and forward from the intense suffering. He balled his hands into fists and bit down on his knuckles breaking his own skin. "Fuck." Sonny cried out.

"Talk nigga," Bayonna barked back as she pulled the blade out of his knee and pressed it against his throat.

Sonny kept still despite the urge to punch one of them in the fuckin' mouth. The sharp razor reminded him not to move though. His lips were tightly repressing his reply of any kind and silence wasn't the right recourse. Lissha double slapped him. "Bitch nigga, start yapping," she demanded.

"What the fuck is wrong with you bitches." He blurted in distress.

"Oh, I'ma bitch?" Lissha asked then shot him in his dick. "Well, now you're one too," she mocked.

Sonny fell to the side grabbing the crotch of his pants as blood poured between his fingers. An animalistic sound escaped his lips and his body began to shake uncontrollably.

"Do this muthafucka dirty," Lissha ordered Bayonna.

An evil smile formed on Bayonna's lips as she raised the knife over her head. "Where. Is. Chino?"

Blood poured from Sonny's wounds and his eyes rolled up in his head as he tried to form a lucid thought. The vicious bitches standing over him had turned him softer than tissue.

"He's staying on East 114th and Kinsman." Sonny mumbled out defeatedly.

"Who helped him snatch up my mans?" Kiam asked.

Sonny's answer came out on low breath strained by the excruciating throb in his groin. He whimpered and groaned with each word. "Two brothers," he panted, "Doral and Hawk from The Valley."

The names didn't register with Kiam but he stored them in his memory.

"That's all you had to say in the first fucking place. Bitch ass nigga," Lissha spat as she aimed the gun at Sonny's head.

"I gave y'all Chino. Why I gotta die?" he squeaked. Blood gushed freely through his hands as he tried to staunch its flow from between his legs.

Bayonna stepped back breathing heavily. She looked down at the blood dripping from her blade and her coochie got wet. To her the kill was better than a full blown orgasm. "Let me finish him LiLi," she said as her chest heaved up and down.

"Make this nigga respect you, Bay," Lissha stepped back.

Bayonna moved to where his head lay in blood, sweat and tears. She grabbed him by his short 'fro and stuck the knife into his throat, dragging it from one side to the other. Blood gushed out onto the carpet as he gurgled and gasped for his final breath. She dropped his head back to the sofa and looked on with low eyes and flared nostrils.

"Punk muthafucka," she spat then wiped the blade on his shirt.

"He should have spoken up sooner," Lissha said, looking at Bayonna with a proud gleam in her eye.

They both watched his body twitch one last time and their hearts jumped widely in their chests. The smell emanating from Sonny's pants filled their nostrils with a scent that was satisfying due to what it confirmed. His bowels had released and the sorry muthafucka was on his way to hell with a one-way ticket.

Kiam looked on as the murderous glint in Lissha's and Bayonna's eyes defied their femininity and beauty. He was elated that he had real riders on his team but he sensed that what he had just witnessed wasn't new to them. They had to have killed like this before and obviously their specialty was torture.

As they rode across town to follow up on Sonny's lead, Kiam's thoughts were fully on his adversaries. If they found Chino tonight, he was going to cut off that nigga's head and hang it from a light pole by that prissy ass ponytail. As for Chino's boss, Kiam was going to make him and his family's next generation feel his wrath.

Chapter 16
Losing It

Kiam didn't find Chino where Sonny said he would be. Wolfman's ponytailed assassin was as smooth as butter and he never remained in one spot too long. Being a certified body snatcher himself, he knew how important it was to change your habits when trying to stay a step ahead of the enemy's guns. By the time Kiam kicked in the front door of Chino's last known whereabouts that night, he had seemingly vanished into thin air.

Weeks went by with no word on Isaac's whereabouts. His body hadn't turned up anywhere frozen and Wolfman hadn't called demanding any type of ransom for his return. But Kiam wasn't under the false illusion that Isaac would suddenly appear unharmed. He knew that the other side was just as ruthless as his team and that they would never snatch a nigga up just to set him free later. He figured that Isaac's body wouldn't turn up until the snow melted and the ice thawed. All he could do was hope that his souljah hadn't suffered much before he died.

Isaiah and JuJu had accepted the bitter truth too. But Isaiah wasn't the same since losing his other half; his hustle had slacked tremendously and every night he tried to wash away his pain with liquor and cocaine. And his hate of women became damn near misogynistic overnight. He had murdered a girl that he'd been seeing for the small transgression of not being able to account for an hour of her time.

"For all I know she could've been somewhere planning to set me up," he had reasoned.

Kiam and JuJu tried to understand, though neither of them knew about his recent indulgence with cocaine. What caused discord was that now Isaiah was suspicious of Lissha and Treebie too. And for some reason that he couldn't explain, other than a hunch, he absolutely didn't trust Bayonna as far as he could throw her bony ass.

"Cuz, let's take that bitch off somewhere and split her mutha-fuckin' wig before she ends up crossing you," he'd urged JuJu.

"Bleed, is you crazy, nigga?" JuJu snapped.

"Nah, *you* are if you trust that ho."

"Hold the fuck up, fam!" said JuJu. "My bitch is official. If you can prove otherwise I'll be the first to send her ass up out of here with slow music playing. But if you're just talking out the side of your neck, you can kill that noise."

Sitting at his kitchen table, Isaiah recalled that conversation as he shoveled more coke up his nose. He had been snorting all day and a half empty bottle of Jack sat at his elbow next to his fo-fo. Plies *One Day* played on repeat on his cell phone.

God give me my nigga for twenty-four hours
So we can ride and laugh at these pussy ass cowards
Hit the liquor store, park, and just talk for hours
Show him half the niggas die when they lose they power
Nigga forget about you dog after they give you them flowers

After another toot Isaiah pinched his nostrils together and leaned his head back. The coke rushed to his head at the same time that he felt a drain from his nose trickle down his throat.

I'm sittin' right here homie, eyes full of tears
Never thought that pain last these many years
One thing I learned from all this shit, life real
Rep yo name 'til I die homie dats how I feel
Watched how everything changed since u got killed

Isaiah closed his eyes and thought about his brother, they had been together since the womb and now he was disoriented without him. What hurt him most was that he had introduced Isaac to the bitch that ended up crossing him out.

"Fuck!" He slammed his fist down on the table sending the coke and the small silver spoon that he used to shovel it up his nose flying in different directions. "Why the fuck did I hook him up with that ho?" he lamented.

He covered his face with both hands and felt the tears wet his palms.

After a minute or two, Isaiah put both palms on the table and pushed himself up, toppling over the chair in the process. He stepped over it and went and opened the refrigerator door. Peering inside, he found what he was looking for on the top shelf. He carefully picked it up, carried it back over to the table and sat it down.

Blood trickled from Isaiah's nose from the damage that the raw cocaine had done and fresh tears poured from his eyes. He grabbed his gun and stared at the human head that he had placed on the center of the glass table. The eyes were gauged out and with the passage of weeks, the features barely resembled the dirty bitch that had crossed out his brother but the head was definitely hers.

"You lowdown trifling, ho," Isaiah spat as he raised his gun and fired two shots into the severed head. It flew off of the table and rolled around on the floor. He went and retrieved it and hurled it against the wall as memories of him and Isaac as far back as the cradle came rushing back in amazing clarity.

The head hit the wall, fell to the floor, and bounced around before settling up against the bottom of the stove.

Isaiah aimed his gun down at it and was about to squeeze off more shots until he felt someone grab his arm.

"Yo, what the fuck are you doing?" JuJu asked, looking at him like he had lost his mind.

Isaiah snatched away from him and walked over to where the head laid. "Fuck that shit, cuz. I hate this bitch." He drew his foot back and kicked the head, sending it flying across the kitchen floor into the pantry. Boc! Boc! He fired two shots in that direction. "Punk ass bitch," he cried out from the depths of his soul.

"Cuz, you gotta pull yourself together," JuJu said from the door-way where he watched on, feeling a pain in his chest.

"Man, she didn't have to do my brother like that. He was a good nigga, he would've gave her sheisty ass anything she asked for," Isaiah spewed.

He walked over to the table, looked down at the evidence of what his brother's disappearance had done to his psyche and he let out a pained cry that sounded like a wounded animal. "Argh."

The sound rattled the dishes on the counter. Isaiah bent down and flipped the table over with one hand. It crashed down on the floor with a bang and the bottle of Jack landed next to it and wasted on the tile. Isaiah looked down at the mess at his feet, amongst it laid his cell phone. The music coming from it wrung his heart and sunk him to his knees in a flood of tears and deep sobs.

Wish I could bring my nigga back for one day
Take him by the daycare to see his son play
And go to show him how his baby mama done went astray
And how the fuck niggas claimed they loved him walked away

As JuJu stood in the doorway painfully looking on, he didn't take the lyrics to heart because he knew that there was no way Isaiah believed that he or anyone else in the crew had forgotten about Isaac. Bodies were being left around the city in record numbers as they avenged what they all knew had happened but no one wanted to come out and say.

He understood Isaiah's pain for what it was. It was grief like none he had ever felt in his lifetime. There was no words that could ease his hurting, only time could do that. And perhaps if they could find Isaac's body and send him away properly.

Isaiah's sobs rung in JuJu's ears and squeezed his heart like a pair of vise grips, but JuJu could not break down. This was street war at its unforgiving cruelest and the only way to avenge him was to remain strong in the face of all casualties.

JuJu was powerless to erase Isaiah's pain or to give him his unbreakable strength, but he did what family does for one another in times of sorrow. He went and sat down beside Isaiah and held him until his cries subsided.

Ca$h & NeNe Capri

Chapter 17
A Touch of Comfort

JuJu's head was fucked up after seeing Isaiah like that. He had begged him to come home with him but Isaiah wouldn't bulge. All he wanted was to be left alone with his liquor, cocaine, and that bitch's head.

Walking out of there and leaving Isaiah sitting on the floor wallowing in grief was one of the hardest things JuJu had ever had to do. When he got home, Bayonna noticed the stress on his face as soon as he walked in the house.

"You okay?" she asked, meeting him at the door with her piece in her hand.

"Not really, shorty." He walked straight back to the bedroom, removed his banger off of his waist and sat it on the nightstand. Sighing heavily, he sat down on the edge of the bed and stared at the wall.

Bayonna slid her gun under the pillow then sat down beside him and wrapped her arms around him. "What's wrong, bae? Did you find him?" she asked.

JuJu couldn't respond.

"Talk to me," said Bayonna, rubbing his neck.

He removed her arms from around him and laid back with his hands behind his head, looking up at the ceiling. The words came out slowly. "This shit has Isaiah real fucked up and I don't know how to help him. He has started putting that shit up his nose and drinking all night and day."

"He's grieving, bae. You have to give him time," she offered in Isaiah's defense.

JuJu didn't have the heart to tell her what Isaiah thought of *her*. There was no need for that. He sighed again then told her about the severed head.

Bayonna listened without comment as he described Isaiah firing shots into the head and kicking it around the kitchen. "And he won't get rid of it," JuJu said with exasperation.

"That's dangerous, bae. What if somebody had called the police after hearing those gunshots, and they come there and find that shit?" said Bayonna.

"I know," he agreed. Then he became silent again.

Bayonna laid her head on his chest and listened to the beat of his heart. In the dim light of the bedroom their silhouettes danced across the wall but the only music playing was the silent cries in JuJu's head.

"Is this what it's about?" he wondered aloud. "Killing, dying— dying inside like cuz even though you're still walking around? Is that all the game offers muthafuckaz like us?"

"It's not too late to get out," Bayonna wisely reminded him.

JuJu chuckled, sounding just like Kiam. "Nah, shorty, the only way out of this shit for a nigga like me is in a box. Nah mean? Muthafuckaz started the beef and I'ma finish it."

"And I'm going to be right there by your side," she vowed, draping a thigh over his leg.

"I know you will," he acknowledged and pulled her on top of him.

"You want me to ease your troubles?" she asked, looking down at him with hunger in her eyes.

"Yeah, baby," he said. "Put your nigga to sleep."

Bayonna didn't have to be told twice. She knew exactly how to comfort him and make his ass snore when she was done.

JuJu awakened in the morning with his thumb in his mouth, literally.

When Bayonna saw that shit she started cracking up. "I told you your ass can't handle this," she teased once he opened his eyes.

"Girl please, I was just fuckin' with your head, you didn't do shit." He tried to burst her bubble.

"A lie don't care who tell it, nigga." She snatched the pillow from under him and hit him over the head with it. "I had your ass crawling up the headboard then as soon as you got that nut you went out like a light." She laughed.

JuJu cracked a little smile. "Like I said, you didn't do nothin'."

"Hmph. I handled my business, I bet you that." She stuck her tongue out at him.

"Yeah you did," he conceded. "You got that shit that'll fuck around and make a nigga drop on his knees and propose."

Bayonna was cheesing mad hard. "I know something that I can do on *my* knees?" she cooed. "You want me to show you?"

"I do but I need to get up and go holla at Kiam."

"Awww." Bayonna exaggerated a pout.

"Fa real, ma. I gotta go tell my nigga what the business is." JuJu leaned over and placated her with a kiss.

"Okay, I guess I'll go hang out with my bitches today." Bayonna reached for her cell phone while JuJu got up and jumped in the shower.

Chapter 18
I Got Your Back

When JuJu arrived at Kiam's new house Lissha let him in wearing a serious mean mug. Behind her Kiam slid his fo-fifth back in place and stepped around her to greet his boy with a pound.

"What's good, Boss?" asked JuJu cutting his eyes at Lissha.

"We'll talk in a minute," said Kiam.

"Hmph!" Lissha huffed as she grabbed her coat off of the coat rack and put it on. She looked at JuJu and said, "Try to talk some sense into your *Boss Man* because I damn sure can't."

JuJu wrinkled his brow.

"Oh, trust, it isn't that," Lissha quickly clarified. "On my worst day I'm not that hard up." She turned her head just in time to see Kiam grinning.

"You want to be in charge so bad it's killing you," Kiam teased.

"Do you know what your problem is Kiam?" she asked.

"Nah." He shoved his hands down in his pockets. "But I'm sure you'll tell me," he replied flippantly.

"I sure fucking will," Lissha spat. "Your problem is you're too cocky. Look in the mirror, nigga, ain't no '*S*' on your chest."

"I love you, too," quipped Kiam.

Lissha was hot. "That's what I get for caring about your ungrateful ass." She snatched the door open and stormed out, slamming it behind her. Kiam got on her damn nerves with his stubbornness.

Knowing what she did about Big Zo's plot, Lissha had been trying for hours to get Kiam to take a calmer approach to the war in the streets and to think shit out a little more. But Kiam was set on hitting niggas hard.

Even though she didn't agree Lissha refused to turn her back on him. She had so many things to make amends for and there was no better time to start than now.

As she backed out of Kiam's driveway, Lissha commanded her phone. "Call Treebie," while she continued to fret over Kiam's bull headed attitude.

"I'm making sure his ass is safe. Niggas can't be trusted," she mumbled to herself as she waited for her girl to answer.

In the warmth of his den, Kiam sat in his Lay-Z-Boy with the fire cackling in the fireplace behind him. His expression remained unchanged as he listened to JuJu's reports on last night's episode with Isaiah.

As JuJu told the story, he made sure not to omit anything. His love for Isaiah had compelled him to offer him comfort last night but it did not force him to compromise his loyalty to Kiam. They were at war with a muthafucka that made niggas disappear if they weren't on point, and Isaiah was definitely slipping.

Kiam knew that if it came out of JuJu's mouth it was official. He understood Isaiah's pain better than anyone—he had lost a part of himself too—but he could not overlook him fuckin' with cocaine. That was the number one rule: don't get high on your own supply.

Isaiah had put in mad work for the team so Kiam didn't want to just cut him off cold, but he could no longer rely on him. If Isaiah was slipping that bad he was a danger to all of them. A chain is only as strong as its weakest link, Kiam reminded himself as he tried to decide what to do about Isaiah.

It didn't take long.

"I want you to fade Isaiah into the background until this war is over. Put Dirty in his place, let him handle distribution to our street team and make him head of security. I like his gangsta."

JuJu nodded his head. He liked Dirty's get-down too.

Kiam continued, "Put someone else over the houses that Dirty ran, and shut down the spots that we have on the Westside until further notice. I don't feel good about our protection over there, those boys are sitting ducks for Wolfman."

JuJu was impressed with how in-tune with all aspects of the operation Kiam remained in spite of everything that he had to deal with. He rattled off one instruction after another, addressing even the smallest matters.

"I'll take care of it all," JuJu assured him.

"Oh," Kiam remembered. "I want you to pay Isaiah the same as he was being paid when shit was good. And if he pulls himself back together we'll put him back in his position."

"That's love."

Kiam turned around and stared at the fireplace, its heat was nothing compared to what was building up in the streets. "We're going to come out on top," he promised.

"I know we will. I've never once doubted it," said JuJu.

Kiam turned back around and saw the confidence in his mans' eyes. JuJu's loyalty was rock hard. As concrete as Kiam's was to Big Zo.

Satisfied with the look he saw in JuJu's eyes, Kiam changed subjects. "We're meeting with Dontae and his people later on this evening," he said. "I don't know what's on the nigga's mind."

"When and where is the meeting?" JuJu asked.

Kiam gave him the details and before he could instruct him to have the place put under surveillance immediately, JuJu was already dialing numbers.

A few miles away Lissha was doing the same thing.

Chapter 19
Unwanted Guest

Treebie moved around her house trying to get out of the door to meet Lissha. She had been away for a few weeks, scouting out a big lick in Akron, Ohio. With Spank gone she had to do all the foot work herself. Time was getting away from them and it was only a matter of time before the trail of death that Blood Money left behind would lead right to their doorsteps.

Treebie grabbed her keys and a small stack of money, put on her coat and ran her plan through her mind. She unlocked the front door and braced herself to encounter the frigid cold, but what she encountered almost caused her to swallow her tongue.

"I guess my threats don't mean shit to you," Riz said with his face firm and focused. Beside him Bones looked like he was primed to bust some knee caps.

Treebie looked at them with a steel gaze as she tried to calm her heart. "What's up?"

"You know what the fuck is up," Riz said, pushing past her and letting himself in.

Treebie mean mugged Bones as he followed Riz into the living room.

Riz took a seat on the couch and put his feet on her table like he was paying bills.

"To what do I owe the pleasure of your presence?" Treebie said, closing the door.

"Look, I didn't drive a million miles to play no fuckin' games. Where the fuck is Wa'leek?"

"You tell me. That nigga gave me his ass to kiss then pulled out dropping my keys on the table," she calmly stated holding her eyes with his.

"And you haven't tried to call that nigga and find out what's up?" Riz asked, knowing that no matter what happened between them, Wa'leek was not letting Treebie go.

"Let me explain some real shit to yo ass. I love Wa'leek no doubt. But the shit between us has been fucked up for a long time." She paused and took a seat across from him. "What I need you to do for me the next time you see that nigga is tell him to stay gone."

"So you're more concerned with him leaving you than you are with the fact that the nigga done turned up missing?" Riz took his feet down and sat forward.

"I came in this world by myself and when they carry my ass outta here I promise you I will be alone. What I don't have time for is worrying about how the next nigga is eating and shitin'. Now I got mad love for Wa'leek but at this point in my life I don't give a fuck what he does or where he's at."

"Out of respect for him I'ma take that for now." He rose to his feet. "But I'ma do my own investigation and I hope and pray ain't no foul shit going on or you can add me to the top of your list of problems."

"I solve all my problems." She stood as well.

"I'm counting on it," he responded.

Bones looked at Treebie with a suspicious eye but he held his tongue. He knew that time was the type of bitch you had to fuck slow and he was prepared to ride this shit out.

"I'll be in touch. Don't go too far because if shit don't smell right around this muthafucka yo ass is the first one I'ma be all up in," Riz threatened.

"I'ma hold you to that," Treebie hurled back.

"Let's go, my nigga." He turned to Bones who had a look on his face like he wanted to ring Treebie's neck. He didn't trust her or anybody in her crew.

Riz walked to the door and Bones reluctantly moved behind him.

Treebie watched as the two of them stepped out the door then down the walk. She slammed the door behind them then went to the window and watched them pull away from the curb. She waited a good fifteen minutes before she too left out of the door. When she jumped in the car she was on fire, not only did they have to cover their tracks with Kiam they now had Riz breathing down their necks.

Treebie walked into the restaurant looking all over for Lissha. When she spotted her in the corner sipping on a drink she moved swiftly in her direction.

Lissha looked up and saw the seriousness on Treebie's face and became alarmed. "What the fuck is up with you?" she asked.

"Man," she elongated. "We gotta make some moves and quick," Treebie said, sliding into the booth.

"What happened?"

"Guess whose nose is in our asses now?"

Lissha ran some names through her mind then the color drained from her face. "Please don't say it's Riz." She shook her head from side to side.

"That nigga was at my door asking questions and looking for answers."

"What you tell him?"

"I ain't tell that nigga shit. If he ain't see it, he ain't going to know it if he gotta wait for that shit to slip off my tongue," Treebie confirmed.

"So what did he say," Lissha was tuned all the way in.

"He's looking for Wah and since he sent him to look for Blood Money that means he's looking for our asses too." She grabbed Lissha's drink and downed it.

"How long that nigga been here?" Lissha asked as she waved for the waitress.

"I don't know, but you know he ain't trying to leave until he finds some shit out."

"Well you know what that means." Lissha paused and ordered them four shots of Patron. "We gonna have to toe tag that nigga."

"You already know." Lissha looked towards the door. "Damn, where Bay at? I swear that little bony ass bitch is going to be late for her own funeral," she said affectionately.

"I know, right?"

Lissha shook her head in vexation.

"Anyway, on some other shit," said Treebie. "That thing that I went to Akron to check on isn't going to work out. Those niggas are too deep. But we should move on them niggas from East Cleveland that Spank set up before that shit get cold. I've been tracking them niggas too and they getting sloppy, if we're gonna strike it gotta be now." She looked up to see the waitress coming back with their drinks.

When the waitress was out of earshot Lissha went in. "We gotta get the fuck outta here. Kiam is killing everything moving and it is only a matter of time before we all get busted or laid the fuck out. I'm ready to make this move on these niggas but it gotta be quick and clean."

"We really need Bay ass here to plot this," Treebie said with venom on her tongue. She was running out of patience with her girl lately.

"I don't know what her problem is; I think that young boy be fucking her brain at the same time that he's up in her coochie." Lissha lifted her glass to her lips.

Treebie grabbed her glass as well and sucked it down. They both stared at each other trying to plot their next move. They had to make sure to keep them niggas off their ass long enough to get that money. Lissha was juggling Big Zo and Kiam, Bay was in love, and Treebie now had Riz and Bones sniffing around her door.

"Treebie no matter what happens we can't fold," Lissha confirmed.

"The only way they gonna get shit outta me is if they question my corpse. Fuck them niggas."

"A'ight then we ride on them niggas in a few weeks." Lissha smiled as she brought her glass to the middle of the table.

"Blood Money," Treebie said on a low but firm tone.

The glasses clinked and the deaths were set in motion.

"On a more urgent note, we gotta protect Kiam. That nigga think his ass is bulletproof," Lissha said as she stirred her drink with a straw.

"Hold up," Treebie stopped her. She had just noticed Bayonna come through the door.

They waved Bayonna over to their table. She was glowing like somebody had stuck a flood light down her throat.

"Hey, ladies," she spoke.

"Bitch, sit your ass down and catch up," said Treebie.

Bayonna took a seat and waved for the waitress as Lissha began telling them about Kiam's plans to meet with Dontae.

"Tonight?" Treebie asked.

"Yep," Lissha confirmed. "We gotta make sure that if Dontae is cooking up some bullshit, he gets fed it himself."

Before the last word left her mouth she was up and putting on her coat.

Treebie and Bayonna rose up too. As they headed towards the door Treebie remarked, "LiLi, you fucked Kiam didn't you?"

Lissha stopped and looked Treebie in the eye. "Nah, bitch, I didn't fuck him," she stated truthfully. "But I'm about to fuck a nigga up *about* him. You can bet that."

Ca$h & NeNe Capri

Chapter 20
Piece by Piece

Dontae, the nigga that Lissha was talking about fucking up, was having serious regrets about forming an alliance with Wolfman against Kiam.

The more time that Dontae had to think about it, the less convinced he became that Kiam was the force behind Blood Money. He realized that out of anger over the murder of his right-hand man, Two Gunz, he had allowed Wolfman to manipulate him. But as long as Kiam didn't know about that short-lived allegiance, things could get back tight with them. He wasn't even going to mention the Blood Money thing.

What Dontae wanted was peace and he was determined to press Kiam to agree to squash the beef with Wolfman. The war had the streets on fire and money was hard to get with niggas getting slumped with every misstep. Nobody knew who to trust and the slightest noise sounded like the patter of enemies coming to serve retribution. That was no way for a nigga to live, thought Dontae as he looked over in the rearview to make sure that his bodyguards were still behind him.

"You sure this place that you're meeting him at is safe?" asked Foxy from the passenger seat.

"Yeah, it's my man Lug's restaurant and neither of us can go inside strapped. That's the agreement." He smirked, knowing that Lug had some shit planned for Kiam if the nigga acted stupid.

"You trust that shit, nephew?" she asked, checking the clip in her tool as they neared their destination.

"I don't know if I trust anything anymore, Auntie," he said.

"You can trust that if Kiam walks out of that door before you I'm going to empty this clip in his ass."

Dontae glanced over at her and smiled. Foxy was his father's sister and the most gangsta chick that he knew. She had just came home from doing her third bid up in Marysville and was already itching to light a muthafucka up.

"You do that," Dontae said as he turned into the lot and parked behind the restaurant. He passed the keys to Foxy and stepped out of the truck, feeling naked without his heat on his waist.

Dontae ordered himself something to eat and settled in his seat waiting for Kiam to show up. As his meal arrived so had his enemies. Kiam and JuJu jumped out with caution and approached the double glass doors.

Dirty sat behind the wheel with a firm eye on every move, ready to jump out and light up the night.

Dontae looked on as Kiam and JuJu were patted down by Lug and given the okay to enter the restaurant.

Kiam stepped hard as he moved to Donte's table. JuJu moved just as rigid as he eyed the room, looking at everything he could quickly turn into a weapon.

Dontae and his two bodyguards stood up to greet them. Dontae extended his hand out to Kiam. "My nigga," he greeted him warmly.

Kiam looked down at Dontae's hand like that shit was a serpent. "JuJu, pat them niggas down," he said.

JuJu checked them for weapons but they were clean. He ran his hand under the edges of the table and the back of the chairs, finding nothing. "They're good, Boss," he announced.

Only then did Kiam shake Dontae's hand.

"Thank you for agreeing to meet with me. Please have a seat." Dontae offered as he sat back down and brought the tender well done meat to his mouth.

After everyone was seated around the table, Kiam looked across at Dontae. "It never cost a nigga to listen, it's when he doesn't that causes his demise," he said.

142

Dontae nodded and continued to stuff his mouth. He swallowed hard then put his shit on the table. "Bruh, I heard about what happened to your girl and you have my condolences. But Wolfman swore to me that he had nothin' to do with her murder."

"So you're holding counsel with Wolfman these days, huh? Nigga, pick a side and stay your ass put," Kiam purposely disrespected.

Dontae's mans started moving around in their seats.

JuJu started whistling *I'm Going Home to Jesus.*

"Everybody just calm down and let me and this man talk," said Dontae. His people settled down but their eyes were locked on Kiam and JuJu. Dontae continued, "Kiam, I know that you lost somebody that can't be replaced but Wolfman has too; he lost two sons. And he still maintains that he had nothing to do with your girl's death."

Kiam scoffed.

"Whether he did or not," Dontae went on, "the lives that were lost will never be paid for no matter how much blood y'all shed." He paused and brought his drink to his lips.

Kiam was ready to leave.

Dontae sat the drink back on the table and went on. "Bleed, y'all gotta get past this shit so we can all eat again. I know you ain't trying to die in the street and neither is Wolfman."

Kiam couldn't stomach listening to another word of that fuck shit Dontae was saying. "Unlike you. I live and die for mine," he snarled. "I don't give a fuck about money when my family has been touched." Kiam sat forward. "I came here tonight to look in the eyes of the man that can give his word then turn into a bitch."

"You got the wrong nigga. I have been on the up with you from day one. This shit you got going with Wolfman is between you and him. I called you here to try to mediate this shit," Dontae said, cutting into his meat looking down as if Kiam was the new kid on the block.

Kiam looked around the small restaurant at the few tables. There was one with a young couple giggling and enjoying the moment. Two old ladies sat sharing a dessert at a second table, and next to them a chick with a long blond wig had her face glued to a book. Near the back was a middle aged couple who appeared to be in a slight disagreement.

Kiam tried to assess which of the patrons would show up in court to testify against him if he snapped Dontae's bitch ass neck.

When Kiam's eyes settled back on Dontae, the nigga was still talking.

"The way I feel about this shit y'all muthafuckaz need to let it go," Dontae concluded and continued to eat and suck his teeth.

Kiam had to chuckle, this muthafucka was entertaining if nothing else. "Nigga, you don't know shit about me. The only reason you're still alive is because I haven't finished justifying why I should kill you." Kiam rose to his feet.

Dontae's bodyguards rose up too. They tensed up for a confrontation.

"Relax, we'll meet again," warned JuJu.

Kiam glared down at Dontae and spat, "I came here because I wanted to see if you was a real nigga but I see you're a bitch. So meeting adjourned."

Dontae laughed but it didn't hide his nervousness. Kiam put fear in him even though he was talking like his balls hung down to the floor. "Just as I thought. Pride is going to be your downfall," he predicted in a low voice.

The air around the table was thick with murderous breaths, but no one was strapped. Dontae looked up at his goons and said, "Hawk and Doral, y'all have a seat and finish your meals. I'ma let this arrogant nigga bury himself."

Hawk? Doral?

144

Kiam's brow damn near folded in half. Those were the names that Sonny had given him. "What the fuck did this nigga just say?" he asked JuJu.

JuJu nodded his head, he had caught it too.

Dontae thought Kiam was referring to his comment that he would end up burying himself. He said, "You heard me, nigga. I don't repeat myself." He sat back and crossed his arms over his chest.

Kiam tilted his head to the side, rotated his eyes around the restaurant then looked at JuJu. When he looked back at Dontae's smug grin he grabbed the steak knife off the table and lunged forward, stabbing him repeatedly in the throat.

Dontae grabbed at Kiam's hands as life began fleeting his body.

"What the fuck?" Hawk came running at Kiam and jumped on his back.

JuJu sprang into action throwing blows and connecting with every swing. Doral rushed Kiam and ran into a two piece that rocked him back on his heels. They started hooking like Tyson and Holyfield back in the day.

All of a sudden, a voice belted, "Pussy muthafuckaz," and a big bald headed nigga jumped over the counter and ran towards them with a banger in his hand, firing off shots.

JuJu dove one way and Kiam dove the other taking cover under a nearby table.

"Get them niggas," Lug yelled out as he reached under the counter and grabbed a pump.

The two old ladies seated at the far table popped up with youth in their bounce and bangers in their hands. "Y'all niggas don't want nothing," Lissha yelled, losing her gray wig as she ran around the table letting loose. *Boc! Boc! Boc! Boc! Boc!*

Next to her Treebie was making her shotgun show the fuck out. *Kaboom! Kaboom!* Hawk caught a blast in the chest that flipped him over a table backwards.

"Bitch muthafucka!" Treebie yelled.

Bayonna had pulled her face out of the book and her ratchet out of her bag. She dropped down to one knee and lit Lug's ass up like a Christmas tree.

Doral tried to run for the door but Lissha wasn't having that. She trained her gun on him and sent ass and glass flying everywhere.

The innocent diners were screaming and scrambling for cover. Kiam squinted his eyes and realized that the grandmas were Treebie and Lissha.

Two other men came out of the back of the restaurant sending heat Lissha and them way, but they got chopped down by more experienced gunners.

To Kiam's left, bald head was injured but not dead. He tried to crawl to the gun that he had lost when Lissha put some of that hot shit in his life. She looked at Kiam and slid him her ratchet.

Kiam quickly hopped to his feet and ran over to the man just as he reached the gun. He kicked it out of the man's reach and stood on his hand.

"I give, nigga." Baldhead surrendered.

Kiam chuckled. He put the gun to the man's dome and painted the wall with it.

Lissha walked up to him. "What about the witnesses?" she asked.

Kiam didn't even have to think about it. "We're not leaving any."

One by one everything breathing, besides their own, was executed. JuJu looked around at all the slumped bodies and was satisfied. Kiam gave him the nod and they moved swiftly to the door.

Lissha and Treebie moved fast in their gray haired wigs and knitted sweaters. And Bayonna trotted beside them in her plaid wool skirt and blonde wig. JuJu moved to the car opening the door for Kiam.

Kiam turned to look in the direction of a brown skin woman approaching him and his gun instantly came up. Then, for a reason only he understood he allowed his arm to fall to his side.

As Kiam turned his stare away from her, the smile quickly dropped from Foxy's face and something long and silver came up with her hand.

Boc!

The gunshot echoed loudly in the still of the night. A spray of brains and blood splattered against the car and the body smacked the ground.

Dirty stood over Foxy and hit her with two more shots. "Boss, you good?" he asked.

Kiam nodded and they jumped in the car and pulled out.

Chapter 21
The Shit Flows Downhill

"That's it!" Mayor Thaddeus Brown's fist came slamming down on the desk sending papers flying all over the floor. "I have had enough! Do you hear me Simon? Enough!" He stood up with his palms flat down on the desk and scowled down at his Chief of Police.

The mayor was so livid his whole face shook even though his head was still. He was fed up with the recent outbreak of violence in his city and he blamed the man who sat before him for not being able to stop it.

"Sir, my men and I are doing everything that we can to solve the rash of murders that have occurred recently, and I'm very confident that we will do so," said Chief Simon Hubbard.

"Listen." the Mayor wagged a finger at him. "Don't you come in my office giving me that bullshit press release response or I'll toss your black ass out of here on your goddamn head."

"Sir—"

"Fuck that shit!" Mayor Brown cut him off. "Don't get my dick hard if you're not going to put out. I want concrete fuckin' answers. Like these young folks say—real spit!"

The Chief had to suppress a laugh. He and the mayor went all the way back to grade school at Wade Park. They had both worked their way up from the hood to become men of prominence in the city. In front of the public and amongst constituents the mayor was as proper as an English teacher but behind closed doors Thaddeus Brown could go hood on a muthafucka real quick.

"Do you find something funny, Simon?" The mayor's light brown face was red.

"No, sir."

"Because I'm not playing with your ass. I'll have you back on foot patrol helping little old ladies across the street."

"Yes, sir." Simon replied, keeping a straight face.

The mayor tossed a copy of the morning edition of The Plain Dealer onto his lap and sat back down. "The governor is all up my ass about this and do you know what happens when shit rolls downhill?" he asked.

"I do, sir."

The paper was already folded back to the article on last night's mass murder at the restaurant. The Chief had been to the crime scene already but he pretended to be reading the article to appease the mayor. After an appropriate amount of time had passed he looked up.

"Have we made any arrests?" Mayor Brown fired.

"Sir, several motorist saw a group of people hurrying out of the restaurant to their cars. We have strong reason to suspect that these individuals perpetrated the crime but we're still trying to identify them."

The mayor exploded up out of his chair and pointed his finger at the door. "Get the fuck out of my office! Didn't I tell you I wanted straight yes or no answers?"

Simon rose to his feet with his braided service hat in his hand. "I'm sorry, sir. If I—"

"Get to steppin'!" Mayor Brown shut him down. "You're incompetent. I'm calling in those federal boys." He reached for the phone as his Chief of Police left out of his office with his head down.

Wolfman didn't have to read about the murders in the newspaper because the ghetto grapevine was buzzing with wild reports. Rumors had last night's death toll at fifty, although the small restaurant's seating capacity was no more than thirty-five.

The one thing that wasn't inaccurate was the fact that a lot of muthafuckaz were dead, including Dontae, but Kiam wasn't one of them. Wolfman tossed back a shot of Hennessey and shook his head in disbelief. He sat the glass down on his desk and looked at Xyna and Chino who were both sitting across from him in the office of his club. "I never would've thought that Dontae was such a fool. I tried to tell him that there's no compromising with a man like Kiam. He wants to rule but he doesn't know how," remarked Wolfman.

Chino nodded in agreement and poured Wolfman a refill. Wolfman lifted his glass to his mouth but left it suspended in air. He appeared to be contemplating his next words. When he spoke it was with the wisdom of having seen many come and go.

"Chino, I want you to promise me one thing," he said, speaking low but firm.

"Anything," Chino agreed without question.

Wolfman sat the glass down on the table. With both hands wrapped around it he held his lieutenant's stare. "If I shall somehow succumb to this reckless muthafucka that calls himself a boss, I want you to promise me that in my place you will not move foolishly like Kiam does."

"Never," Chino spat on the floor.

"No man is an island all to himself," Wolfman continued. "In this dog eat dog game that we're a part of everybody needs friends. Some of my friends are my worst enemies. I assure their loyalty by the fact that they need me. But this Kiam nigga thinks he can stand alone, and in trying to do so he's a threat to everyone else. Do you understand what I'm saying?"

Before Chino could reply, Wolfman's private line rang. Xyna picked up the phone and handed it to him.

"Hello?" he answered.

"The mayor has called in the feds. With all of this killing going on I will no longer be able to provide you with any assistance. It's about to get hot in the city if you know what I mean."

"I do."

"I know you've heard about the restaurant murders last night."

"I have," Wolfman admitted.

"If you can tell me who was involved I may be able to keep the heat down some."

Wolfman didn't even have to think about that. He was many things, most of them bad, but the one thing he wasn't was a stinking ass snitch. "I have no idea who's responsible for that. And if you ever again ask me something like that, I'm going to cut your tongue off and shove it up your tight ass," he threatened.

"I'm sorry. No disrespect intended. I'm just trying to keep some heat off your ass."

Wolfman ignored the apology. "Thanks for the information," he said. He disconnected the call and sat the phone back down on the table. Then he tossed back his drink and held counsel within his own mind.

Chino and Xyna sat quietly.

After a brief silence, Wolfman said. "We're closing down all of our spots. I don't want any more retaliation against Kiam's people. It's time that we move with a single purpose. Let's cut off the head and the body will die."

Chino stood up. He was itching to get after Kiam's ass. Fuck waiting for that nigga to find him.

Wolfman put his hand up and Chino sat back down. "I just thought of something," said Wolfman, stroking his beard. "Find out where Faydrah's mother lives. Sooner or later Kiam is bound to visit her."

He leaned back in his chair with a wicked smile across his face. *Kiam is about to find out why I am who the fuck I am in this game.*

Chapter 22
Just Chill

JuJu had taken his fifteenth trip to the window and was on his way back to the couch when Bayonna yelled out. "Baby, you gonna wear a hole in the carpet." She frowned at his paranoia as she dusted the wooden shelf with the pictures on it.

"You know I have to be on my toes. That fuck shit them niggas pulled at the restaurant got me ready to turn this whole fucking city red." JuJu said, plopping down on the sofa.

Per Kiam's orders he had been in the house for a full week and it was driving him crazy.

"I gotta get the fuck outta this house," he said, running his hand down his face.

"Baby, it's too much heat and with the descriptions they gave on the news you need to just relax and let shit play out," Bayonna stated as she sprayed Windex on her paper towel and prepared to clean the glass frames.

JuJu didn't respond he was used to being in the streets and sitting in the house hiding was not how he rocked.

Bayonna shook her head as she ran the towel over a picture of her and the girls. Fond memories took over her mood as she reminisced about the night they had at the club. Donella's laughter rung in her head causing her chest to hurt.

So much has been going on lately, sis, but I have not forgotten you. Bayonna brought the photo to her lips and planted a single kiss on Donella's face.

JuJu looked over at her and saw the sadness that washed over her face. He got up and walked over to her and wrapped his arms around her waist. "I'm sorry, baby," he said, holding her tightly.

"I miss her," she confessed as water pushed itself out of her eyes and down her cheeks. "And I'll never believe that she was in violation. That bitch Daphne lied on her."

"But why would she do that?"

"I can't answer that yet, but I'll never stop searching for that answer." Bayonna sniffled.

"I feel you, baby. We took some big ass hits this year and the souljahs keep falling." He kissed her on the neck then nuzzled his nose behind her ear.

"I don't want to die, JuJu," she said as she brought her hand to her eye to catch the tears.

"Don't none of us want to die, Bay. But the reality is that we signed up for death the day we took our first breath. We're all gonna go. Our demise will be much sooner though. We guaranteed that on the day we took our first life."

As the words left JuJu's lips Bayonna tried to recall her first victim but she had stolen so many souls they now ran together in a jumbled collage of horror.

"The die is already cast, ma. We just gotta make the days we have left and all the sacrifices we made to be at the top worth every second," JuJu said as if he was reading her thoughts.

Emotion took over Bayonna's whole body and the tears cascaded down her cheeks fast as small sobs left her lips. The weight of her decisions had finally caught up with her.

JuJu held her close and allowed her to let it all go. She put her head back against his chest and released what felt like years of pain. JuJu turned her to face him, he placed his hand under her chin and softly stated. "Baby, we were born G's. And gangstas don't live long. Being able to share a part of my life with you means that I will leave this muthafucka with no regrets." He kissed her passionately on the lips.

Bayonna opened her mouth and allowed their tongues to sensually dance. The honesty in his kiss guilted her, but the things he didn't know that she could not tell him made her sadder.

Bayonna knew that JuJu's love for her was real but *she* wasn't exactly who he thought she was. She slid her hand in his and tenderly caressed the hideous scar that confirmed her deception. One day soon it would all come out, she was certain of that. Circumstances would not allow it to remain hidden for much longer.

Bayonna's heart ached for what she knew the truth would do to him. At the same time, his arms around her made her want the charade to go on forever because it felt so good. "I need you to make love to me." she whispered through her tears.

JuJu pulled her close and walked her toward the bedroom removing her clothes along the way.

When Bayonna's body settled between the sheets she reached up and grabbed him behind his head as his thickness rested against her pussy, causing instant wetness.

"I love you, Bay," he whispered as he fed her an inch at a time.

"I love you too," she moaned as his slow stroke set her on fire.

Soft kisses and slow deep strokes sent chills all throughout Bayonna's body. Tears rolled from the corners of her eyes as JuJu answered the call from her soul. She held him tightly as he gently ran his tongue over her nipples. With every stroke she released a painful piece of her spirit. It seemed like she had been running for so long, but today she was going to be still and let JuJu have every part of her.

Lissha moved around her kitchen loading the dishwasher and preparing the plates for dinner. Kiam had been at her house the past two days just laying low and she was happier than a preacher watching the collection plate spill over with tithes.

Lately she had kept herself attached to him like a third arm, trying to protect him and make up for the bullshit that she had helped initiate. She looked in the oven and the aroma of her baked Ziti with spicy Italian sausages invaded her nostrils, causing her stomach to growl.

"I am about to fuck this up," she said, sliding on her oven mitts and pulling out her dish resting it on top the stove.

She placed a few pieces of garlic bread in the oven then put the salad into two bowls. Lissha danced around the kitchen snapping her fingers to *Drunk in Love* as she prepared the plates.

Kiam came down the hall in his baggy shorts and a t-shirt rubbing the creamy lotion on his arms. A smile came to his face when he saw how clean and organized the house was coupled with the aromas from the kitchen almost made life seem normal.

Unconsciously Kiam's eyes glued themselves to the back of Lissha's tight boy shorts as she bent over to pull the bread from the oven. He quickly checked himself for lusting before entering the kitchen. "You need to put some clothes on," he said half seriously. He roughly moved her aside.

"Stop, boy," Lissha shouted, hitting Kiam's arm as he took a seat at the table.

"What you in there hooking up?" he asked, propping his feet up in a chair across from him.

"Something that will make your mouth water. I have to show you how a real bitch get down since you were talking shit the last time I had you in the kitchen." She sauntered over to the table with his plate of Ziti, garlic bread and a bowl of spinach salad with homemade dressing.

"Yeah 'cause you were trying to feed a nigga oodles of noodles. Then gave me some cereal." He leaned forward allowing the delicious steam to caress his nose. "This smell good as hell." He picked up his fork.

"You better not," she scolded.

"What?" he wrinkled his brow.

"Don't be rude. Let me get mine and you gotta say your grace, you heathen," Lissha joked.

"God has been done with me for a very long time," he spoke matter-of-factly.

"Don't be like that Kiam. Even though most of the time we be on some bullshit, I believe He still loves and protects us." She looked in his eyes as she sat her plate on the table.

Kiam's face was stone. *He didn't protect Eyez.*

"I'll say it." Lissha took Kiam by the hand and bowed her head. "Lord, we pray that you bless this meal and protect the hands that prepared it as well as the one that it is shared with. We thank you for all of your many blessings. Amen." She released his hand and smiled at him. "See that didn't hurt." She grabbed her fork and began to dig in.

"Sometimes you shock the hell outta me," Kiam said as he too began to dig in. As soon as the flavors collided on his taste buds he closed his eyes and chewed slowly.

"Yeah, say my name, don't even front I got that ass open now." Lissha rocked her shoulders.

"It's a'ight," Kiam said, taking another big mouthful.

"You are so full of hate," Lissha joked, shaking her head.

Kiam laughed as he continued to dig in. Lissha was content chomping away with her feet up in the chair. She got up and retrieved them a glass of Sprite and gin on ice.

"Your conniving ass is up to something," Kiam gagged, taking a few swigs of his drink as she collected their dishes.

"Ain't nobody thinking about you." Lissha moved from the table back to the kitchen.

Kiam downed his drink and sat the glass down and asked for another one. Lissha filled his glass then went to put up the food and load the rest of the dishes and start the dishwasher. Kiam downed his second drink then moved to the living room and turned on the television. He kicked his feet up resting his head back. He was full and beginning to feel the slight effects of his drinks.

Lissha walked over and took a seat beside him still nursing the first drink she poured herself. "I wasn't going to bring this up but I think I need to." She paused and sat her glass down.

"What's up?" he turned the volume down on ESPN and looked in her direction.

"That was a real close call at the restaurant. We all could have been laid the fuck out. What happened when you came out? Why did you freeze up like that with that lady?"

Kiam took a deep breath and reflected on the events of that night then he weighed in on them. "I didn't thank you but I know I owe you. You, Treebie and Bay really came through for a nigga and I'm grateful for that. I still can't believe how y'all was up in there disguised and shit," he chuckled.

"Thanks Kiam but I asked what made you freeze up like that with ol' girl? That wasn't like you."

"I saw something in that woman's eyes that I have not seen in almost twenty years." He stopped his tongue before all of his emotions came rushing back.

"What did you see?" Lissha spoke softly.

"I saw my mother," he confessed then turned back to the television.

"Do you want to talk about your mother?" she offered.

"Nah, I'm good," he declined.

"Okay, Kiam, I didn't mean to pry," Lissha comforted as she rubbed his arm.

"It's all good," he said before having a change mind. "I always wanted to know what happened to her. I use to stare at every brown skin woman that resembled her in any way. I kept hoping that the next one would be her but it never was so I gave up looking. That night was the first time I saw eyes that looked just like hers," he said then got quiet.

"It will be fine, Kiam." Lissha tried to comfort him. Her heart was breaking for him, it seemed like he had lost everyone that he ever loved.

Being alone with him had allowed her to see inside of the beast that the streets demanded that he be. She saw that when he put his banger on the shelf he was so much more than what met the naked eye. He could be silly, caring, introspective and witty as hell.

Lissha wished that she had a giant eraser; in one smooth stroke she would expunge everything that had ever hurt him, including her transgressions against him.

Her guilt slammed into her stomach like a fist. "I'ma let you watch your game," she spoke tenderly then stood up.

"Nah, chill with me for a little while." Kiam looked up at her glossy eyes. "I know you ain't getting soft on me, killah." He smiled trying to ease her mood.

Lissha reluctantly sat back down. "I'ma stay for a minute but I ain't trying to watch no damn game." She tried to switch the mood.

"What you want to watch? Some crybaby shit?" he teased.

"No, I got Scandal saved on my DVR." she brightened up and reached for the remote.

"I'm not watching that bullshit." Kiam tried to grab the remote from her hands.

"Stop if you want me to stay you have to compromise." She held the remote out of his reach.

Kiam continued to grab at it and before long they were laughing and tussling. Kiam pulled Lissha on his lap as he tried to get the remote from behind her back. Kiam bit into her arm causing the remote to fall to the floor.

"Ouch, boy. Oh, you wanna fight dirty?" Lissha grabbed Kiam by the back of his head and bit hard into his neck.

"Stop, a'ight, let got," Kiam tried to get Lissha off of him.

"Move your hands," Lissha said through clinched teeth and bit a little harder.

Kiam put his hands up as if he was under arrest. "A'ight let go."

"Say sorry." She squeezed his skin between her teeth.

"I'ma fuck you up."

As Kiam reached towards her face Lissha bit harder. Kiam's hands shot back up in the air.

"What you gonna do?" she taunted.

"Nothing, let go."

"Nope. This is payback, baby boy. Say you're sorry." She clenched her teeth tighter.

"A'ight. Damn, sorry, now let go," he relented.

Lissha eased up a little then sucked gently on the spot to lessen the pain.

"You better run when you let me go," Kiam warned.

Lissha took full advantage of the moment and positioned herself perfectly on his dick as she continued to suck on his neck.

Kiam felt his boy waking up but he wasn't quite ready to give in to his lust. Every time he thought about it memories of the true love that he'd shared with Eyez made him pull back. "Why are you always tryna start trouble?" he asked, resting his hands on Lissha's thighs while he fought an internal tug-of-war.

"I wanna be in trouble," she moaned as she felt his dick rock up between her thighs.

Lissha released his neck from her grip then began nibbling on the other side. Kiam closed his eyes and tried to block out the guilt.

It had been months since he had felt the velvety softness off a woman's center; that warm place that could hold a man and allow him to release his worries. Kiam knew that no woman on Earth could ever welcome him into her essence like Eyez had, but he could not remain celibate forever. Life had to go on.

It took everything in him to accept that but he did. And when Lissha felt him giving in to his desires she pressed her soft body against his and whispered what she truly felt. "I want you so bad, baby."

Kiam ran his hand between her legs. When he slipped his finger in the side of her shorts and felt her wetness, Lissha let out a cry.

"Lift up," he whispered.

Lissha was already dizzy but she moved to his command, allowing him to pull off her shorts.

Kiam looked at how fat and juicy her pussy looked in her panties and his mouth watered. He nibbled on her erect nipples as he placed his middle finger on her clit and circled slowly.

"Kiam I need you," she moaned just as his fingers pushed inside of her.

"I know. We both need this right now." He lifted her up and laid between her legs.

They were both on fire and wanted to be free of everything that was going on around them. Their hands and tongues were all over the place. It was like they were teenagers sneaking and dry humping while their parents were away from home.

Kiam pulled out and prepared his mind to handle his business. He was ready to drill and her pussy was welcoming him with wet lips.

Lissha pulled her thong to the side and awaited his intense push. Kiam grabbed his dick firmly in his hand and put it right where she so badly wanted him.

Lissha tensed up as she felt the swollen head entering her opening. Kiam pulled back and pushed in sending heat from her toes to her eyebrows.

"Oh, baby," she cried out in ecstasy.

Kiam pulled all the way back ready to play in her tightness but his stroke was stopped by a familiar ringtone. Lissha and Kiam's heads snapped to the side simultaneously. They looked over at the coffee table breathing heavily and feeling like they were busted.

"Hell no, I'm not answering it," she said. She wrapped her thighs around Kiam and tried to hold him there but the moment was lost.

"This is like the third time a call has stopped us," Kiam recollected. "It must not be meant to be." He unwrapped her legs from around him and sat up.

"Ughhh," Lissha screamed. She snatched the phone off of the table and hit the call button. "Hello!"

"What's up? Is that the tone I get from you now?" Big Zo's stern voice boomed through the speaker.

"No, Daddy." She quickly adjusted her attitude.

"Listen closely because it's time to make our move. Do you hear me?"

"Yes, Daddy. I'm paying attention."

Lissha looked over at Kiam and turned her head away while Big Zo gave her instructions that she had no intentions on following.

"Once we set this in motion you're going to have to fall back so you won't go down with that nigga. Do you understand?" Big Zo concluded. There was not a trace of regret in his voice and that made Lissha sick to her fuckin' stomach. She wanted to spit through the phone dead on his face but she had to play it cool.

"I understand everything perfectly well." Sarcasm dripped off of her reply. Wanting him to face the man that he had mentored behind slimy intents Lissha said, "Daddy, Kiam is right here. Would you like to speak to him?"

"Bitch, don't play with me!" he snapped, but Lissha was already handing the phone to Kiam.

"What's good Pop?" Kiam asked as Lissha got up off of the couch.

"I saw the city on the national news." Big Zo remarked as thoughts of Kiam fucking Lissha caused his voice to tremble with suppressed rage.

"Yeah, but things are quiet now."

"That's not the right move. Keep it hot and strike while those other muthafuckaz are tucking their tails. Men like us never let up."

Kiam lifted an eyebrow and sat listening to Big Zo as he rattled off several instructions and coded directives to the way he wanted him to carry out the next phase of the mission.

Lissha pulled her shorts back up and put her breast back in place as she sat down trying to read the stone look on Kiam's face.

"Yeah a'ight, let me give you back to Lissha." Kiam passed the phone to her and stood up and walked down the hall to the bedroom.

Lissha put the phone to her ear. "What else, Daddy?" she asked dryly.

"What else?" he mocked. "I'll tell you what else. Kiam is not a boss. I control that pussy nigga without him even realizing it. So don't get it in your head that he can replace me. I told you a long time ago that I'm often imitated but never duplicated." His arrogance spilled out in torrents.

Lissha couldn't say what she wanted to. *You ain't no boss, you're a bitch ass nigga that can't do your time like the true gangsta I used to think you were.*

"I hear you," she mumbled.

"Good," Big Zo roared. "Now spit that do-boy's dick out of your mouth and handle your business or I'm gonna have a muthafucka bust something down your throat other than Kiam's nut." Big Zo hung up the phone.

When Kiam returned, Lissha was just holding the phone staring at it.

"You straight?" Kiam asked, coming from the back suited up in all black. He threw on his thick goose down.

"Yeah, I'll be fine. Where you going?" Lissha asked, rising to her feet.

"I gotta make some runs," he moved to the door. "Stay in the house and be on alert."

"Let me go with you. You don't need to be out there alone Kiam," she pleaded

"I got this." He needed time to think.

"Kiam call me when you're on your way back," Lissha said, sounding worried beyond reason.

"Stop tripping. I told you I got this." He grabbed his whistle off of the table and checked the clip. It was fully loaded. "I got sixteen muthafuckaz rolling with me tonight," he boasted.

"Just be careful," she said as he turned to walk out the door.

"You too," he replied as the door slammed closed.

Kiam checked the area then jumped in his truck and pulled out.

Chapter 23
Sirens in the Night

After running through the trap spots Kiam parked a block over from Bayonna's and stopped in on JuJu. He gave him some information and just like that he was out again.

JuJu did the same song and dance Lissha did but Kiam turned him down as well, he needed to be alone with his thoughts. Plus he knew if it was his time to go it didn't matter if he was alone or with a crowd. His ticket would get punched.

Kiam drove in silence as he headed to see Ms. Combs. He hadn't been to check on her in close to two weeks. Riding down East 131st Kiam turned onto Benwood. The street held many memories of him and Faydrah hustling on the block. He could almost see her holding her strap down by her side, ready to clap a fool, while he served them through the window of their car.

I miss you, ma.

Kiam pulled up in Ms. Combs' driveway and stepped down from his truck with his hand inside his coat and his eyes alert. As usual cars were parked up and down the street but he saw no danger lurking from behind them.

The sky was as dark as coffee without cream and the moon looked down on him like an one-eyed man who had seen it all. The worst of winter had passed and the snow had begun to melt. Kiam moved quickly to the door and rang the bell.

Once he was inside Ms. Combs hugged him tightly and looked up in his face with a loving stare. "How have you been?" she asked sincerely

"I'm fine, Ma," he said as he began removing his coat.

"I saw the news. I was so worried about you," she said, taking his coat.

"Don't worry I am just handling my business and delivering sad hearts to the families of our enemies." He took a seat.

"Baby, I think I may have been wrong about that," she said, sitting down in her lounge chair. "Faydrah would want this, Kiam," she stated, causing a hard thump in his chest.

Kiam looked at her. "Ma, they brought this to our door. I'm just stamping it *return to sender.*"

"I know, baby. But I don't want nothing worse to come to our door. I believe we have been paid back for our lost." She put her hand on his knee.

"I owe her all of their pain." He placed his hand on top of hers.

"Don't lose your soul, Kiam. You are a beautiful man. You have a whole life ahead of you. My daughter would want you to live it." She looked at him with pleading eyes.

Kiam internalized her words and the weight of them dropped into the pit of his stomach. "Can I have something to drink?" he asked, feeling the saliva drying on his tongue.

Ms. Combs patted his hand then got up and headed to the kitchen.

Kiam's eyes darted around the living room and in every corner of the room were several pictures of Eyez. On every wall was a reminder of her life and her smile. Her eyes stared back at him and tore into his soul.

Kiam stood up, put on his coat then reached in his pocket.

"You leaving already?" asked Ms. Combs, returning with a glass of orange juice.

"Yes, I have something to take care of." He accepted the juice and downed it in one gulp.

"You want more?" She took the glass out of his hand and turned back towards the kitchen.

"No, Ma, I'm good." He pulled his hand from his pocket and handed her a stack of crisp one hundred dollar bills.

Ms. Combs clutched the money in her hand then pulled Kiam into her embrace. "I love you. Please don't be another news article in my book." She sobbed against him.

"I love you, too. Just pray for me." He looked down and saw Trapstar peeking out from behind the couch with his bright eyes as he pulled back from Ms. Combs and headed for the door. The whole experience was haunting.

"When will I see you again?" she asked, following him to the door.

"Soon. Lock up, Ma, and turn on the alarm. I'll call you in the a few days."

"Okay," she said and then did just as she was told. She took a deep breath then felt down in her pocket for the .22 Kiam had given her weeks ago.

Ms. Combs picked up Trapstar and sat on the couch stroking his fur. She hated that her daughter was gone and she worried that Kiam would die avenging her. "Lord, please protect that boy. I can't live with myself if he dies giving me what I wanted," she prayed out loud.

But the universe was already in motion.

Kiam drove away from their feeling down. He had lost Faydrah and had yet to be able to move on. His crew had taken hits and all of the grand plans he had when he walked out of prison less than a year ago seemed unimportant now. Big Zo was telling him to make more noise but Kiam knew in his heart that could not possibly be the smartest move right now.

Why? Kiam wondered.

He was lost for an answer and his head pounded from trying to come up with one.

He drove around aimlessly as he reflected on each move that he had made. Victories seemed short-lived in comparison to how long the losses remained with him. No amount of loot, expanse of drug territories or even vengeance could make up for Eyez. Not even for

Isaac or the other fallen souljah's. All of their lives were loss riding for him; all of their blood was on his hands.

"Real muthafuckin' talk," Kiam said to himself.

Most nights he could shoulder the blame on those proverbial broad shoulders of his that made him a force to be reckoned with. But tonight that weight had him in a head lock.

Kiam decided that he wanted a drink. He needed to toss back a few shots amongst strangers and numb his mind for a minute. That or maybe some stray pussy wouldn't leave him feeling like he had betrayed Faydrah's memory.

Liquor won out over pootang and a short while later Kiam pulled up at a bar out in Mayfield Heights. He steered into a parking space and deaded the engine. After checking his mirrors he secured his weapon and got out.

The wind whipped around his head as he hurried to the entrance. Kiam located a seat back in the corner then ordered something tall and strong and headed to the unoccupied table against the back wall. Just as he settled into his seat he looked up and saw something tall and sexy walking through the door. He guzzled half his drink while watching the dark haired, light skin woman with ass for days move to the bar and place her order.

The woman took her glass by the stem and sipped slowly as she turned down a few dudes that came her way.

Kiam chuckled at the lame dudes trying to approach her just to get shot down, one by one.

Slim got up on the stool and pulled off her fur jacket then continued to enjoy her drink. Kiam waved the waitress over to his table and ordered himself another round. Then on second thought he also sent something to the woman at the bar.

When the drink was put in front of her she looked in the direction that the waitress pointed and smiled when she met eyes with Kiam. She grabbed the drink and her fur and headed to his table.

"Can I drink this and look at the sexy muthafucka that sent it?" she asked, sitting down not waiting for a response.

"You spittin' some hot shit. Can you fuck with a real nigga?"

"Can you fuck with a real bitch?" She challenged bringing her glass to her full lips.

"You alone?" Kiam asked, taking his drink down and slamming the glass.

"I am now but I don't want to be." She locked gazes with his.

"I got something for a bitch that will make her pant loud, reach and grab," he said, looking at her breast sitting high in her shirt.

"And I got something that makes a nigga dig long and deep," she tossed back.

"Then why we're having this conversation vertical when we should be having it horizontal?" Kiam stood up. He was in an *I don't give a fuck* mode and some pussy to go along with it would top off his evening.

"What you driving?"

"A dark grey BMW," she responded.

"Can you keep up?"

"You better hope *you* can keep up," she said, pulling her coat back on. When she was ready she held out her hand. "My name is Khandi, I'm exotic and tasty."

"You can call me Daddy 'cause I'ma take care of that pussy tonight," Kiam spat that hot shit as he took her hand.

In the light above the table his eyes settled on the ink on her wrist. "What does that tattoo represent?" he asked out of pure curiosity.

"Oh this?" She held it up. "It's a Black Mamba. It just means I know how to hold on tight when I ride for a nigga," she smiled.

"Well, I hope you're not afraid of heights."

"It's like that?"

"Worse. You ready?"

"Sure am," she said, turning around and heading to the door.

Kiam saw her to the car then jumped in his truck. When he started the engine his phone vibrated in his pocket. He didn't even check it. Whatever was going on was gonna wait until he did some shit to erase the feelings that was fucking with his head. Tonight he was going to bury all love and welcome hate. He wanted his heart cold. He knew that once he climbed up outta ol' girl he would be a different man.

He sped through the streets looking in his rearview mirror making sure she was still close behind.

When they got to the light the woman picked up her phone and made the confirmation call.

"Hello," Wolfman answered as he brought a blunt to his lips.

"I got him," Xyna said, sticking close to Kiam's bumper. He finally showed up at the old bitch's house just like you predicted and I followed him to a bar out in Mayfield Heights.

"Where are y'all headed? I'm on my way!"

"I don't know, baby, but you can relax. I'll call you after it's done."

"Xyna, don't fuck around with that nigga. Remember he's a killah too so don't slip. As soon as he lets his guard down take his ass out and get out of there. You hear me?" Wolfman cautioned.

"I got you, baby," she said then disconnected the call.

When they pulled in front of his condo Kiam looked around then jumped out. Xyna quickly jumped out her car as well. She hurried up his walkway and stood behind him as he fumbled with his keys. Her gun was halfway out when the headlights of an approaching car lit up the area. Xyna eased the gun back inside her purse. Damn, she would have to go inside and rock his ass to sleep.

Kiam opened the door then hit the alarm. Xyna came inside and pulled her coat closed, it was just as cold inside as it was outside. She eyed all the boxes that were still scattered about the living room and hallway.

"Make yourself at home," he said, turning up the heat.

"Thank you." she took off her coat and shivered a bit.

"Don't worry that ass will be on fire in just a few minutes," he said, throwing off his coat and taking her by the waist.

"You don't want to have something to drink first?" She was still hoping to get a chance to murk him without having to put out.

"I'ma give you something to drink but it's going to be from a kneeling position," he said, continuing to push her up the stairs to his room.

Again, his phone went off and again he ignored it as he pulled off his hoodie and stepped out his boots.

Xyna played it cool when she saw him take the gun from his waistband. She resigned herself to sleeping with him but as soon as he nutted he was going to be coming and going at the same time.

"Take your clothes off," he rushed her.

She pulled her shirt off and slid her pants down while keeping her eyes on his steel. She swallowed her spit and took in a little air then smiled. "You only need one piece of steel when you fuck with a real bitch," she said, releasing her breast from her bra.

Kiam placed his gun down on the nightstand. "I thought you were thirsty," he said as he whipped out that grown man.

Xyna cut her eyes over to her purse which she had sat on the bed. She thought about reaching for her heat now but decided that it was too risky. She would get him good and comfortable first.

She went to her knees, wrapped her hand around his girth and guided the head into her mouth. Kiam peered down on her as she took him to the back of her throat. That shit felt so good he rose up on his toes.

Lissha zipped through the streets tracing all of the steps she thought Kiam would take but every spot she went to turned up empty. She kept calling his phone but got no answer. She was beyond worried at this point.

By the time she got to Bayonna's house Lissha was near hysterics. "Kiam left and I don't know where he's gone to. He's not answering his phone or nothing," she nervously reported.

JuJu jumped up and got dressed. Bay was putting on her clothes too, getting strapped. "No, li'l mama, you stay here and hold shit down in case he comes here," instructed JuJu.

When they drove off Lissha went in one direction and JuJu went in the other. Lissha drove looking everywhere she thought he might have gone. When she kept striking out tears started to run down her face; her worst fear seemed like it was coming true.

Out of options, Lissha decided to go look for him at his house again. She made a U-turn in the middle of the street and took off towards Brentwood where Kiam had moved.

Kiam looked down on Xyna as she tried her hardest to make him come. Her jaw felt like it was about to lock. She moved back and let him slip from her mouth.

"I wanna make you come," she whined, stroking his dick in her hand.

"Then let me finish talking to your tonsils," Kiam said with his brow wrinkled and nostrils flared.

Xyna realized that the man she thought was going to be an easy mark was going to be hard to make bend. She wanted him flat on his back with his eyes closed before she dared reach in her purse for her gun.

She took Kiam back in her mouth and began trying every trick she knew.

172

Lissha sped down the blocks close to his house praying all the way. When she pulled up and saw his truck she was slightly relieved until she saw the grey BMW parked behind it. *This muthafucka laying up in some pussy while I'm worried sick about his ass.*

She chided herself for thinking like that. What if a nigga had him duct taped up in there?

Heat surged through her body and her palms started sweating on the steering wheel. Lissha grabbed her gun, clacked one in the chamber and jumped out. She moved swiftly and with caution as she walked up to Kiam's door then began ringing the bell.

"Fuck," Kiam scoffed when he heard the doorbell ringing. The way shit was going he wondered if he would ever get to bust a nut.

Only close members of his team knew where he rested so it had to be one of them at the door and it had to be urgent the way they were leaning on the bell.

Letting out a sigh of frustration Kiam pulled back, but Xyna grabbed his ass with both hands and defied her gag reflexes as she tried to keep him deep in her throat.

"Hold up," he said, pushing her head back and trying to force his steel in his pants before grabbing his banger off of the nightstand and going to the door.

Xyna stood up and slipped her clothes back on. She quickly grabbed her purse and tiptoed behind him down the steps.

When Kiam opened the door Lissha's eyes went from his smug face down to what had his zipper poking out like a tent. She bit down on her lip trying to stop herself from slapping a spark out of his no good ass. Here she was worried to death over him and he was laid up in some ass for real!

Not only that, she was doing everything she could to make things right and to show him that she truly loved him and—and. The thought was too much to bear. Lissha looked up at him with teary eyes and gritted teeth. "You trifling ass muthafucka!" she spat as she raised her gun.

"Fuck you talking about?" He reached for her arm while Lissha looked over his shoulder and saw concrete proof of what had him rocked up.

As she peered at her competition, recognition sat in and her eyes grew wide. *Xyna!*

The Black Mamba had just slipped something long and shiny out of her purse and it was aimed at Kiam's back.

"Watch out!" Lissha screamed and pushed him out of the way.

In the next instant gunshots shattered the quiet of night. Lissha's whistle whirred and Xyna's banger hummed. *Boc! Boc! Boc! Blocka! Blocka! Blocka!*

A bullet parted Lissha's hair and another one slammed into the door frame just inches from her head. Her shots missed Xyna entirely but she was a pro and Xyna was not. Lissha's trigger finger remained steady while Xyna panicked in the heat of return gunfire. Her aim faltered worse as she frantically hopped from side to side trying to dodge steel jacketed bullets that came at her in a burst of accuracy. And now it was two guns against one because Kiam was letting loose on her ass from the floor.

Boc! Boc! Boc! Boc! Boc! Boc! Boc!

Xyna's head burst open like a pinatã as some of that heat from Lissha's fo-fo struck her in the center of her forehead. Two successive shots from Kiam's whistle hit her high in the chest and knocked her backwards as blood splashed all over the furniture and her body smacked the floor.

"I'm fuckin' LiLi, bitch!" Lissha exalted.

Kiam tattered Xyna's body with three more shots then he climbed to his feet and snatched Lissha all the way inside the house and slammed the door.

"What the fuck?" he said, looking from her to Xyna's bullet riddled body sprawled out in his living room.

Lissha dropped her gun and slapped the shit out of him. "Do you know who that was?" she cried.

174

"Fuck is your muthafuckin' problem," he spat.

Lissha pushed him in the chest. "That bitch is Wolfman's girl." Blood trickled down her face and mixed with her tears. "You could've been dead." She broke down crying.

"A'ight, ma, calm down." Kiam wrapped his arms around her and let her bawl against his chest as he thanked her for saving his life.

The all too familiar sound of police sirens nearing drowned out her sobs and snapped her back into rider mode. "Kiam, you have to go. Hurry, grab all of your guns and go out the back door. You're a convicted felon, they'll send you back to prison. I got this," she said.

Kiam looked at her. "I'm a G about mines. Fuck it, I can do another bid." He spoke through drunken lips.

"Kiam go!" Lissha yelled at him. "Please."

The sirens were getting closer. Kiam snapped out of his moment of insanity.

Kiam grabbed her face with both hands and kissed her hard. "Much love, ma," he said. Then he dashed through the house snatching up the guns that had bodies on them. By the time the police knocked on the front door Kiam had vanished out of the back.

Ca$h & NeNe Capri

Chapter 24
Murder Was the Case

Kiam hiked almost ten blocks before finding a 24 hour convenient store. His feet and hands were nearly frost bitten and on top of that he was worried about Lissha. Not only had she saved his life, she had remained at the house willing to take a body charge. He had to give Lissha her props, she was a down ass bitch.

Shivering a bit, Kiam headed straight to the coffee machine and fixed himself a large steaming hot cup with no sugar or cream. With both hands wrapped around the cup he began to thaw out a little. He walked up to the counter and paid the old white woman who had been watching him like a hawk since he entered the store.

Kiam pulled out his cell and hit JuJu as he walked to another section of the store.

"Yo, Boss. Where you at?" JuJu asked before Kiam could get a word out.

In a whisper, Kiam told him the business.

"Goddamn. You're a'ight, ain't you?" JuJu asked.

"Yeah, just cold as fuck and worried about shorty."

"I feel you. She's gangsta." Their respect for Lissha was now off the rack. "I'm on my way," said JuJu.

JuJu arrived in record time. As soon as Kiam got in the truck he made some phone calls letting the crew know to meet him at JuJu's where Bayonna was already waiting.

When they arrived Bayonna greeted JuJu with a hug and they sat down on the couch next to one another. Treebie was already kicked back in an overstuffed chair nursing a glass of 1800. She sat the glass down on the table and blazed a blunt.

"Put it out," Kiam ordered as he sat across from her in an arm-chair.

Treebie lowered her eyes at him in defiance.

"Not tonight," he warned in a serious tone.

For once Treebie didn't test him. She put the blunt out and picked up her drink. "Is a bitch allowed to drink around this piece?" she asked sarcastically.

Kiam ignored her, he did not have time for the bullshit. The scowl on his face matched the perpetual mean mug that Dirty, who was on post by the door, wore.

Clearing his throat Kiam commanded everyone's full attention. When he was sure that they were locked in he gave them a short version of what had transpired.

"That's my bitch," Treebie exclaimed proudly. She could picture Lissha letting that tool pop.

"I could've told Wolfman's bitch she wasn't ready," Bayonna chimed in. She jumped up from the couch and whipped out her banger. "Fuck a diamond, this right here is a bitch's best friend."

"Fuck she think our girl was a duck?" Treebie tossed back her drink, stood up and high-fived Bay. "Tell Xyna to get it how she muthafuckin' live! Oh, hold up," she clowned. "The bitch *dead*."

Kiam let them act up for a minute then he told them to sit their asses down. "This is serious," he reminded them.

"No, it's not. It was self-defense," said Treebie.

Kiam wasn't so sure that it was going to play out like that. He was familiar with the court system and he knew that those dirty bastards didn't play fair.

"Don't worry, LiLi will come bursting through that door any minute," Treebie predicted.

But she was wrong.

After being taken to the emergency room and treated for a superficial head wound Lissha was taken to jail and charged with murder, possession of a firearm while in commission of a felony and possession of marijuana.

One week later...

Kiam smiled as Lissha entered the small phone booth-sized cubicle where he sat separated from her by a thick Plexiglas partition. She was wearing blue jailhouse scrubs that fitted her loosely. Her hair was pulled back into a ponytail and her eyebrows needed arching but she looked like new money to him.

He stood up so that she could check him out then they both sat down. Lissha smiled as she picked up the black telephone, wiped it down with the sleeve of her shirt then put it to her ear.

Kiam picked up the receiver on his side of the glass and spoke into it. "What's up, ma? How are you holding up?"

"Hi, baby. I'm a rider so you already know," Lissha replied cheerfully as she looked in his eyes. "You look good, man," she complimented.

Kiam had gotten a fresh haircut and was rockin' all Burberry, an icy watch and a platinum chain. Stuntin' a little so that people at the jail could see that she had a boss nigga on her side.

"You look good too," he remarked.

"No, I don't," she laughed. "My hair is jacked and it feels like I've lost all of my booty."

Kiam chuckled. "Nah, that ass is still on swole."

Lissha started cheesing mad hard. "I'm going to need you to tap it for me whenever I get out of here," she said, crossing her fingers that he didn't reject her.

"I got you, baby girl."

Lissha couldn't believe her ears. She did her little happy dance on the hard metal stool and when she sat still her pussy was still jumping. "I can't wait," she said. "And this time I'm turning off both of our phones. Muthafuckaz be blocking like a mug."

Kiam couldn't help but feel a stronger connection to her now. In the game it was all about show and prove. Lissha was doing both.

"Shorty, I'ma have you out of here in a few days. I talked with the lawyers yesterday and they assured me that the murder and gun charges will be dropped. You did the right thing by not giving a statement that night. One thing for sure, Big Zo taught you well," he acknowledged.

Lissha's smile melted at the mention of Big Zo's name but she quickly forced it back onto her face.

"You a'ight?" asked Kiam.

"Yes, baby, I'm fine. What have my bitches been up to?"

"Everybody miss you. Treebie is about ready to come bust you outta this bitch. Bay threatening the bondsman and shit even though he can't do nothing until the judge sets a bond. JuJu can't wait to put one in the air with you."

Lissha was cracking up.

"What about you, do you miss me?" she asked Kiam, holding his stare with soft eyes that communicated her love for him.

"Yeah, I miss your big headed ass. Fa real, shorty. That's why those lawyers better have you up outta here by the weekend or I'ma go ham?"

Lissha blushed so hard she turned two shades lighter. "Tell me what you're going to do to me the first day I come home."

Kiam whispered something real hot into the receiver.

"Oh, my, god!" She wiggled around on the stool. "These mutha-fuckaz gots to hurry up and free a bitch. I need some of that heat."

They exchanged freaky promises back and forth until it was time for Kiam to go. Lissha pressed her thighs together to calm her pussy down before she stood up.

Kiam put his palm to the glass and Lissha touched hers to his. "Love you, shorty," he said.

"I love you too, Kiam," Lissha professed as her eyes became misty. "With all my heart and soul." She returned the phone to the hook and moved to the doors afraid to look back, she didn't want to ruin her happy moment with tears.

Kiam watched as they cuffed her and lead her out. He had been on the other side many times but this was the first time he experienced what it felt like seeing someone he loved in chains.

JuJu and Dirty was waiting out in the truck for Kiam when he came out of the jail. "How is she?" asked JuJu as soon as Kiam got in the car.

"Shorty is a real trooper. She's not tripping nothin'; she's just kicked back, keeping her mouth closed, and letting those Jew boys do what I'm paying them to do. She'll be out in a few days."

"That's what's up," said JuJu.

Dirty nodded his head but otherwise his focus was on security.

Kiam turned on some music and Chief Keef blasted out of the speakers. He turned the volume down some so that they could discuss drug business. The streets were dry and Kiam wanted to fuck the game until its pussy got wet again.

In the middle of the discussion Kiam's phone vibrated in his pocket. When he answered it Big Zo's voice belted in his ear. "What the fuck are you doing out there? Tell me why my daughter is locked up for protecting *you*."

"It's a long story, Pop, but don't worry, it's nothing. I'll—"

"Don't tell me it's nothing!" Big Zo yelled in his ear. "You're fuckin' up out there. If you quit trying to fuck everything in a skirt you might learn to make the right muthafuckin' moves."

Kiam took the phone away from his ear but Big Zo's voice continued to boom out. JuJu and Dirty looked away, embarrassed by what they were hearing.

"Weak men follow their dicks. I should've never put you in charge!"

Kiam waited until his mentor calmed the fuck down then he put the phone back to his ear and spoke in a low and respectful tone. "Pop, you're overreacting. I got this. Lissha will be home any day now. And if you didn't think I could run this you would've never turned it over to me."

"Now I wish like hell I hadn't."

"Pop, like I said everything is fine. You gave me the keys to the car now let me drive."

"Drive?" Pop shouted. "Fool, you can't even *walk* straight."

Kiam had heard enough. "Look, old man, you're not talking to no bitch. I respect you but I'm not your ho."

"Muthafucka, you're whatever I want you to be," Big Zo exploded.

His remark crushed Kiam.

"That's how you feel, huh?" Kiam asked.

For a minute there was nothin' but silence on the phone. Biz Zo was the first to break it. "I'm sorry, son," he apologized. "It's just that my daughter is all I have. I told you that."

"And I told you you have me."

"I know that I do."

"A'ight Pop, it's all good. I'ma charge that one to your mind not your heart. I'll talk to you later." Kiam hung up the phone and looked out of the window. The heat coming off of his brow was hot enough to melt steel. Never had any man talked to him like that and lived to tell it.

Chapter 25
Bitch'n Up

Big Zo was cooler than a summer's breeze as he was escorted to the attorney/client interview room by the captain. Only he knew the bitch move that he was about to make.

He spoke to the homies as he passed by and said over his shoulder, "These muthafuckaz trying to give me some more time. Ha! I already got life, what can they do to me? Hot ass niggas out there telling shit that's ten years old."

Nobody suspected that Big Zo was about to officially become a confidential informant because he was thought to be the last of a dying breed: a man of principle who would rather spend the rest of his life in prison than turn state.

"You can take the handcuffs off of him," said the DEA agent as soon as the captain led Big Zo into the interview room.

The captain removed the handcuffs and stepped outside, closing the door behind him.

"Have a seat," said Special Agent MacArthur, a tall broad shouldered man in his late forties. He introduced himself but didn't offer Big Zo a handshake because he hated a rat too. But informants were the Bureau's best investigative tool.

Big Zo sat down and bounced his leg up and down as he calculated what he would reveal and how it would work in his favor.

"Alonzo Wilson," MacArthur addressed him.

"Yeah, that's me."

"Your daughter contacted our office in Ohio on your behalf and we're very interested in how the two of you might be able to help us."

"We can help you, alright. We can help you get some big names off the streets. I'm talking *big*," Big Zo boasted. "Kingpins and drug gangs that move hundreds of kilos of cocaine a week and who are responsible for hundreds of murders over the years."

The agent had done his homework on Big Zo before agreeing to meet with him. He knew that Big Zo had dealt with some powerful people in the drug world before his incarceration. They had tried to flip him back then but he had refused to cooperate. MacArthur figured, correctly, that the time had finally broken Big Zo. "Who can you give us?" he asked as he picked up a pen and prepared to jot down the names.

Big Zo rattled off some heavyweights.

Agent MacArthur let out a long whistle as he wrote. The agency had been after one of the men Big Zo named for years.

"And I'm going to help you get the person that is most responsible for the increase of murders in Cleveland, Ohio, including the mass murder that happened at that restaurant a month ago."

MacArthur's head snapped up and he looked Big Zo in the eyes to determine if he was being forthright. The restaurant slayings was a case that the mayor of Cleveland really wanted to solve.

Big Zo returned his look with one of sincerity and MacArthur read just that. He sat his pen down on the notepad and folded his huge mitts on the desk. "And what is it that you want in return?" he asked.

"My freedom. And I want immunity for my daughter. I don't give a fuck about nobody else."

"How deeply is your daughter involved with these people?"

"She's involved very deeply. But she has to receive full immunity and I have to walk out of prison scot-free or it's no deal."

"Will she agree to become a confidential informant too?"

"Yes. She'll do whatever it takes."

MacArthur smiled. If Alonzo Wilson and his daughter could deliver as promised he would be looking at a huge promotion. "Let me clear this with my superiors and get with your attorney off record and I'll get back to you."

Big Zo stood up. "Don't drag your feet on this. I'm getting old. I want to get the fuck out of here."

Back in Ohio, Kiam was having lunch with Riz at a restaurant in the warehouse district. At a table next to theirs sat Bones, JuJu and Dirty.

Kiam put a fork full of tilapia in his mouth and chewed as Riz voiced his concerns in a low tone. "Kiam, I'm suspicious of one of the people that's on your team," he began.

"And who might that be?" Kiam looked up from his plate and took a sip of water.

"Treebie," Riz replied without hesitation. "A little over a month ago I sent one of my most valued men here to search for Blood Money. That man's name was Wa'leek and I loved him like a brother. The last time I spoke with Wa'leek he indicated to me that he had found out the identities of Blood Money. He was supposed to deliver their bodies to me but now Wa'leek, for some unexplainable reason, has disappeared off the face of the earth." Riz stabbed a shrimp with his fork and held it up to his mouth but didn't put it in.

"I'm sorry about your man but what does Treebie have to do with it?" asked Kiam, taking another bite of his fish.

"I see you don't know," said Riz. "Wa'leek was Treebie's husband."

Kiam was surprised to hear that Treebie was married but he still couldn't make the connection that Riz was inferring. "Okay," he said. "But what reason would Treebie have to make her husband disappear? Did he violate her in a major way? You know Treebie ain't the bitch for a nigga to cross."

"Or trust either."

"I'ma have to respectfully differ with you on that," Kiam defended her. "But if you can prove it, I'll gladly listen."

"Nah, I can't prove it but my instincts are seldom wrong. There's something real foul going on within your crew and it all revolves around that bitch Treebie and probably Lissha too. Bayonna is the only one of them that can be trusted." The shrimp disappeared into his mouth followed by another one.

"Well, we will let history unfold, but if I find out you are the one sewing evil intent in my house we will definitely have a problem," Kiam warned.

"Fair enough. But if we find out you live in a den of thieves then the problem will be mine to solve." Riz spoke firm as well.

Kiam nodded his understanding then changed the subject to business. He was damn near out of product and there was too much money out there to be made to let it go into another nigga's pocket.

Riz told him that he wished to continue doing business with him but he was concerned about the heat that was coming down over Kiam's beef with Wolfman. "I wouldn't want your problems coming to my front door," he wisely stated.

"I'm tryna bring a mil' and some change to your front door. Then two weeks later I'll double that. So I'm talking three point-five. How does that sound to you?"

Riz pushed his half-eaten seafood platter away from him and wiped his mouth with a cloth napkin as he weighed Kiam's proposal. Finally he said, "Everything in me tells me that you're as official as they come, yo. So I'm going to continue to fuck with you. But I need one promise from you before I leave here today."

"Ask it," said Kiam, pushing his plate away too and looking Riz in the eye.

"Kiam, I had decided to have Bones kill Treebie. But I'll cancel that now. Just promise me, man to man, that if it turns out that Treebie is foul you'll kill that bitch yourself."

"On my word," vowed Kiam.

Riz reached his hand across the table and Kiam locked it with his. No other words were necessary. They agreed on the next shipment and Kiam and his mans departed.

Kiam dropped JuJu and Dirty off then headed home to start getting things ready for Lissha. The murder and gun charges were going to be dismissed tomorrow and she could bond out on the weed charge.

Kiam's phone rung as he neared home. He looked at the screen and saw that it was Big Zo calling. He allowed the call to go to voicemail because after the way Big Zo had talked to him he was cool on that nigga. Kiam was unsure how that would affect him and Lissha, but if she planned on fucking with him she was going to have to choose a side and ride.

As Kiam turned onto his street a police car came up behind him and turned on its flashing lights. He smoothly slipped his banger into the hidden compartment on the door and pulled over, figuring that he must've made a turn without coming to a complete stop.

All of a sudden cop cars swarmed in out of everywhere, uniformed and plainclothes police jumped out with their guns aimed at his head. "Get out of the car with your hands up! Don't move or I'll blow your fuckin' head off!"

Kiam looked to both sides and saw that he was surrounded. His hand itched to reach for his banger but before he could follow up on it, he was snatched out of the car and thrown to the ground facedown.

When he heard clink clink and felt those steel cuffs around his wrist he regretted surrendering peacefully.

"You're under arrest for murder in the first degree. You have the right to remain silent. You have the right to an attorney. If you can't afford an attorney the state will provide one for you..." recited a pale faced white boy as they snatched him up and roughly hauled him to a police car.

"Save that shit, cracker," said Kiam then he hawked a glob of spit in his face.

Chapter 26
Shit Don't Stop

It didn't take long for the streets to hear about Kiam's arrest for the restaurant massacre or for rumors to spread as to who had fingered him. Some said Lissha had ratted on him to get out from under her murder charge but most fingers were pointed at Wolfman.

Niggas that didn't know any better believed that Wolfman had dropped dime because Kiam's gun smoke had sent him into hiding and he could not withstand the losses that he was suffering as a result of having to close down shop.

Kiam's crew was just waiting for him to give the word and they were getting booted and suited to go knock a muthafucka's head off. In the meantime, JuJu and Dirty was going to stay on top of business to make sure that the streets didn't get shit twisted, thinking that they were to be fucked with because Kiam was in jail.

Treebie and Bayonna had hit a lick the other night and left a nigga with his dick in the dirt. And just as casually the next day Treebie was dropping Bay off at the airport to go visit her mom.

"Bitch, don't be acting up while I'm away," warned Bayonna as Treebie pulled up to the Delta Airlines entrance.

"I'ma act however niggas make me act," said Treebie. She popped the trunk and they got out and met at the rear of the car.

Bay reached in and grabbed her bags. "Seriously Tree, lay low for a minute in case we're next on the list to get snatched up by those boys."

"Ha!" Treebie laughed. "Before I let them put my pretty ass in cuffs I'll die with my finger on the trigger."

Bay shook her head. They hugged and touched cheeks. "I'll call you, bitch. Tell LiLi I love her and I'll see her when I get back."

"Okay, have a safe trip."

Bayonna stood there for a second and her eyes started getting misty. "Girl, your acting like you're not coming back," remarked Treebie.

"I know right?" Bayonna smiled then headed for the entrance.

Treebie watched her disappear inside then she hopped back in the car and headed to the bondsman's office to post Lissha's bond.

Treebie left out of the bail bondsman's office and jumped in her car headed to the county jail to pick up Lissha. She was more than focused; recent incidents had put everything on the table. Blood Money needed to hit and hit hard.

When she pulled up she put the car in park and lit a blunt; at this point she was way past giving a fuck.

Treebie sat and pulled hard as she thought about all the shit her and the crew had been through the past year. Donella had to be executed for disloyalty, Bayonna was dick whipped, Lissha was team Kiam one hundred percent, and there was no telling when Riz and Bones would pop up at her door again on that brolic shit.

The writing was on the wall, Blood Money could not last much longer. Her mind flashed back to the day she had to live by the code and kill the only person that had ever loved her unconditionally. With regret she remembered how they had dumped his body in Lake Erie as if it was nothing more than refuse.

Although he had been controlling, Wa'leek had walked into her life and made her feel again. Before him she had been misused by men to the point that she had turned cold. Wa'leek's love had warmed her heart for a while but once she suspected him of creeping with Donella she slowly began to turn cold again.

Every time Blood Money went on a lick and Treebie aimed her ratchet at niggas, the faces that she saw was of the men that had hurt her. Pulling the trigger became payback for all that was done to her. But she didn't even want to think about that now because it would take her back into a dark place that would cause a whole lot a mutha-fuckaz to feel her pain.

Treebie stared out the front window and thought back to when shit was good and easy; when all they had to do was knock a few niggas in the head and count that money. But now everything had changed. Everything was out of place and if Kiam didn't beat his charges things were going to go from bad to worse.

I need to hit these last licks hard and get the fuck out of Ohio.

"Damn, bitch, open the door," Lissha yelled out, jolting Treebie out of her reverie.

"Bitch, don't bang on my shit," she said, popping the locks.

"It's damn near forty degrees and you got me standing in the cold like a homeless bitch begging for change," Lissha joked, strapping her seat belt.

"Smoke this and shut up before I put yo ass on the bus." Treebie passed the blunt and pulled away from the curb.

"Shittin' me. You will have to drag my jailbird ass out this muthafucka kicking and screaming." Lissha pulled hard on the blunt and put her head back. Those three weeks felt like a year.

"So what now?" Treebie asked as she bent the corners.

Lissha took a deep breath. "First of all, I'm going to see Kiam tomorrow and find out what he wants us to do. With him off the scene niggas are going to get funny. Damn, a bitch was looking forward to him picking me up instead of your ass."

Treebie rolled her eyes and pulled to the curb. "I'll holla, bitch. Your bus should be coming in an hour or so."

"You stupid," laughed Lissha.

"I'm just saying, ho. I know that nigga got that ass open but remember who got your back from day one to day none." Treebie checked her side view and pulled back into traffic.

"Bitch, you know I love you but until you grow something thick, long, hard, and move around this muthafucka with swag your ass is playing second," Lissha said, passing the blunt back to Treebie.

"See, I knew you fucked Kiam. You a ho," Treebie laughed and put the blunt to her lips and pulled hard.

"Trust me, I haven't fucked him yet but when I do you'll know it because I'll come floating over the roof of your house in the middle of the night."

Treebie shook her head as she pulled onto the expressway and checked her rearview for a black truck that had been behind them since they'd left the jail. "LiLi can you take your mind off of Kiam for a minute? Shit don't stop. We need to hit these last licks I have set up and add that to our stash for relocation."

"Bitch, you ain't saying shit. Just let me go check on my man and after that it's whatever."

"I'm ready but it's just me and you," Treebie looked over at Lissha with her lips pursed.

"Where the fuck Bay at?" Lissha asked as her mood switch from relieved to pissed.

"Her mother is sick, she went out of town to visit her. I just dropped her off at the airport a little while ago." Treebie glanced in her rearview mirror again and saw that the black truck was no longer behind them.

Lissha thought about how neither of them knew much about each other's families. Big Zo had always discouraged the sharing of personal information. She had never met Bay's mother but she prayed that she would be okay.

Lissha pulled even harder on the blunt as she shifted her thoughts to those niggas that Treebie was talking about hitting. Those boys were strong. Ideally, Blood Money needed all the muscle they had to run up on those nigga's spot. *Fuck it*, she thought. They had already wasted enough time. They needed to do this shit soon.

"Well, we started this shit with us and we will end it with us. I got your back. You got mine?" Lissha questioned.

"Hell yeah. We roll on them niggas hard. No questions. Just come in that bitch blastin'." Treebie nodded her head up and down. She was ready for the kill.

"Let's do it next Friday." Lissha put her fist out and Treebie bumped it.

Treebie pushed through the streets headed to her house. In another week it would be time to put in those blood read eyes and wreak havoc.

Chapter 27
Contemplation

When Kiam stepped into the visitation booth he was totally surprised to see the person on the other side of the screen. He sat down and picked up the telephone and stared at Isaiah for a full minute without either of them saying a word. It was hard for Kiam to believe what a couple of months had done to him.

Isaiah looked like a powder monster. His hair was long and matted, his clothes were filthy and there were sores around his nose.

"How you doing, Boss?" he asked, breaking the silence.

"I'm maintaining, nephew. But you're not looking so good yourself."

"I know but it don't even matter. Nah mean. I don't give a fuck about living no way so why I gotta care how I look?"

Kiam didn't know what to say to that. When he was in the feds he had seen many men give up but he had never understood it. As long as he had breath in his body he was going to always fight. But he knew that he couldn't give another man his unending will to persevere.

"Don't worry about me, Boss. This might be the last time you see me because I'm on some *I don't give a fuck* type shit. All I do is hunt and stalk all day." Kiam furrowed his brow and Isaiah went on. "I'm real close to finding that nigga that touched my brother. When I do find him you'll hear about it."

"Nephew, hold up." Kiam put his hand up to stop him from talking recklessly on the prison phone.

"It's all good." Isaiah understood. He wiped his runny nose with the sleeve of his coat. "I just wanted to come see you and let you know that I got love for you. You're a real nigga."

"I got love for you too. I want you to try to get yourself together. You—"

"Fa real, Bleed," Isaiah cut him off. "Fuck this life. I ain't got shit to live for no more. When they took Isaac, I died that day. But I'm gonna handle my business before I check out of this bitch. And I'm gonna prove to you and JuJu that ain't none of those bitches no good. Treebie, Bay or Lissha. I'm all over their ass, Boss." Isaiah pulled a bloody handkerchief out of his pocket and blew his nose.

Kiam cringed inside.

Isaiah rose up and tapped his chest with his fist. "One love." And then he was gone.

Kiam had a hard time sleeping that night. In a way he felt responsible for what had become of Isaiah. That was the hard part about the game; the way it decimated lives and crushed a muthafucka's future.

As he laid staring at the ceiling he realized a few of his mistakes. He had come home from prison trying to wife the game when in reality that bitch was worthy of nothing but a one night stand. *Smash the pussy and keep it moving.*

Kiam wondered why Big Zo hadn't given him that advice. He had to know that the longer a nigga fucked with it, the harder he was going to fall. He sat up on the bed and looked out of the bars at two older men playing chess out in the day room with only a sliver of light illuminating the chessboard.

Kiam stood up and walked over to where they were playing and watched the game quietly. He loved chess and he was pretty good at it. Big Zo had been the best on compound when Kiam was there. In fact, he recalled, he had never beaten Big Zo a single time.

As he watched the men maneuver the pieces for command of the board, it occurred to him how every single piece would get sacrificed to save the king.

"Life is like a game of chess," Big Zo had often said.

So who is the king? Kiam asked himself.

The answer was crystal clear. Big Zo was. Or at least he considered himself to be. And Kiam would've been cool with that because in order to lead, a man had to first learn to follow. But as he thought back on everything he saw that Big Zo was leading him off of a cliff. And it had to be for some reason other than incompetence because if nothing else Big Zo was astute.

Muthafucka, you're whatever I want you to be.

Kiam chuckled. Had Pop really disrespected his gangsta like that? Nah, it could never be *Pop* anymore. From now on he was Big Zo.

"Checkmate," the older gentleman on Kiam's left called.

Kiam looked down at the board and saw that the other man's king was trapped.

That's what I gotta do, Kiam told himself as he went and sat back down on his mattress. Locking him up was the worst thing they could have done because it had given him time to sit back and think.

If he ever touched freedom again he was going to move on his own command and show Big Zo who the true king was.

Muthafucka, you're whatever I want you to be.

He was going to make the old man eat his words.

Ca$h & NeNe Capri

Chapter 28
Tears and Treachery

Kiam waited for the guard to remove his handcuffs then he walked to the booth, sat down and picked up the phone. JuJu and Lissha stood on the other side of the window side by side.

Lissha was looking like a star. Her hair was cut short and feathered in a sexy style that highlighted her cheekbones. Her waist length fur was open, showing off her perfect titties in a form-fitting top, and her jeans hugged her hips like they had been sculpted on her. Her jewels sparkled through the glass as brightly as her smile.

"Hi, love," she mouthed.

Kiam hit her with a sexy wink and she widened her smile valiantly although it crushed her heart to see him on the wrong side of the window.

JuJu tapped his chest with his fist and stepped into the booth. Kiam returned the greeting in the same manner and waited for JuJu to sit down and pick up the receiver.

JuJu put the phone to his ear. "What it do, fam?" he asked.

"I'm good on this end. How are things out there?"

"Everything is everything, but you know I had to come through and let you hear that face to face."

"I wouldn't expect nothin' less. How is your other half doing?" inquired Kiam.

JuJu's face brightened up. "Bay is lovely. She's out of town visiting her mother right now but she sends her love."

"That's what's up," replied Kiam. Then he told him about his visit from Isaiah.

JuJu sighed. "Damn, man, I don't know what to say."

Kiam didn't either, so he shifted the conversation to business and they spoke in code. JuJu explained that Riz refused to fuck with them until he was out.

Kiam told him in code to look for another connect for now, someone that he could trust.

"I got you, Boss," replied JuJu, tapping his chest again. I'ma let you visit with your girl before time runs out."

He looked over his shoulder at Lissha who was smiling from ear to ear. Turning back to Kiam, he said, "Til the grave, my nigga."

"Ten toes down," Kiam replied in salutation.

When Lissha accepted the phone from JuJu and sat down in the booth, tears had already begun to cloud her eyes. Kiam looked at her and said, "I thought you was hard, ma. You're softer than a baby's ass."

"I hate to see you in there." The floodgates opened and the tears poured down.

"I'll be home soon. These bitch ass muthafuckaz don't have shit on me. Dry those tears, baby girl, you know they can't hold a nigga like me down."

Kiam's confidence made Lissha feel better. But if she could trade places with him she wouldn't hesitate, she told him.

"You already proved that," he reminded her.

"And I'll do it again and again," she said from the heart.

Kiam put two fingers to his lips then touched them to the glass. Lissha's heart fluttered as she did the same. "I love you so much, Kiam."

"I know," he said, flashing that cocky ass smile of his. "And I love you too, shorty."

"Aww. You're going to make me start crying again." Lissha covered her face with her hand.

Behind her JuJu mouthed to Kiam. "Nigga, you're Charmin."

Kiam smiled. Then his expression turned serious. He asked Lissha if she had spoken to her father.

"Yeah, I talked with him the other day," she replied dryly.

Kiam said, "When I come home things will be different with him and I. You're going to have to decide where your loyalty lies." His eyes penetrated hers in an effort to read her heart.

Lissha put her hand up to the glass. "Baby my loyalty is to you. First, second and lastly. I will die for you, Kiam." Her words came out sincere and steadfast.

Kiam put his hand up to hers. "That's my bitch," he said.

"You better be knowing," Lissha exclaimed proudly.

The announcement came over the speakers that visitation was now over. Lissha's eyes immediately teared up again.

"Stop crying and tell me something good before you go," said Kiam.

"I love you so much, baby," she cried as he rose up to leave.

Kiam whispered something into the receiver and Lissha's whole body heated up.

"I can't wait, baby." She gushed.

He blew her a kiss and she watched with sadness as he walked back into the bowels of hell. When he was out of sight Lissha turned and walked into JuJu's arms. He hadn't always liked her but he had grown to respect her being official with Kiam. He knew he had to be there for her.

Big Zo almost collapsed himself when he heard that Kiam had been arrested by the state for suspicion of the murders at the restaurant. That was the last thing he needed to hear. His get out of jail free card was contingent upon the feds making a case against Kiam for the murders and other charges.

"Somebody fucked up," Agent MacArthur told him. "The problem was that the feds had not told the local police that they were investigating Kiam in a multi-defendant case that was much bigger than the state could bring against him. We're working with the state authorities to let him out so that we can build a case against his entire organization, excluding your daughter, so that we can get his supplier and the others that you supplied information on."

Big Zo looked across the desk at MacArthur with a scowl on his face. "All I know is that I've kept my word to you and it feels like I'm getting fucked with no Vaseline."

"Don't worry," the agent assured him. "We're more interested in building a multi indictment against the various organizations than we are of fucking you up your old ass."

"I hope so." Big Zo worried.

As he walked back to the cell block and headed up to his cell several inmates whispered to each other.

"I'm telling you, son," a con named Jason said. "Big Zo is hotter than a muthafucka. Watch what I tell you, that nigga talking. When you look up, that bitch nigga will be back on the streets and another muthafucka will be in here doing *his* time."

"Nah, Slim, Big Zo is one hunnid. He would never flip on a nigga," his partner disputed.

"Mark my muthafuckin' words, a caged bird will only fly from side to side so many times before he starts trying to figure out how to open the lock," Jason said, taking a seat on his bunk.

Unlike the others he was not willing to give a Big Zo the benefit of the doubt. He could smell a rat when it was in his presence.

Chapter 29
Phantom of the Night

Isaiah knew that the nigga he was hunting would underestimate him and eventually come out of hiding. He had searched everywhere leaving bodies in his wake. He was like a phantom; he would pop up and if a nigga didn't have the right answer he would push his shit back and fade into the darkness again.

When Isaiah wasn't hunting Chino, he was following one of the girls. Always moving in the shadows with a steady supply of coke in his pocket and weapons within his reach.

The other day he'd gotten lucky, a machete to the throat of the best friend of one of Chino's women had induced the proper answers. Isaiah had left the bitch mutilated anyway but at least she had served a purpose before leaving this earth, he reasoned as he stood in the darkness taking a bump of powder ever so often and watching the house across the street.

The temperatures had risen up in the high fifties as winter in the Midwest began to slowly release its grip on the climate. But Isaiah was still dressed like an Eskimo and he was sweating as if it was the middle of summer.

His eyes lit up and his blood filled with adrenaline when he saw the front door of the house across the street open and the suave figure step out into the night. He crouched down further in the darkness and retrieved his machete off of the ground.

Chino held his gun down by his side as he squinted his eyes and surveyed the block. It was a little after 3AM and his jump off's street was quiet but he remained on point. Kiam was in jail but JuJu wasn't and as quiet as it was kept Chino respected that young nigga's murder game.

Chino's head was on a swivel as he moved to his truck and hit the remote to unlock his doors. Once he slid behind the wheel he placed his banger under his seat and started his ignition.

As soon as he pulled off, he realized that something was wrong. "Fuck!" he spat, banging his hand on the steering wheel.

Chino pulled over to the curb, threw the truck in park and hopped out. One look and he saw that his shit had a gangsta lean. He walked around to the other side and noticed that both tires on that side were flat. He bent down and checked the front tire and came up cussing as he tried to figure out which bitch of his had slashed his mutha-fuckin' tires.

As he stood up he heard someone running up behind him. On instinct his hand shot to his waist but it came out empty. He spun around and saw the ghost of a muthafucka that he had killed.

Isaiah eyes bulged out of his head and foam ran out of the corners of his mouth as he raised the machete over his head and brought it down across Chino's shoulder. It landed with a sickening crunch and Chino cried out like a banshee. He staggered back against the side of the truck and threw up his other arm to try to ward off the second blow.

"You can run but you can't hide, pretty muthafucka," Isaiah gritted as he chopped Chino's arm off at the elbow with one powerful hack.

Chino cried out like a bitch, but his attacker was a bitch hater.

Blood poured from Chino's stub and he tried to run. Isaiah reached out and snatched him back by his ponytail slamming his head into the window of the truck. Whimpering, Chino looked into the eyes of a madman and screamed.

Isaiah raised the machete high in the air and brought it down with lightning speed. When it landed blood splashed all over the windows and the side of the truck. Chino's head dangled from side to side— held on to his neck by a flap of skin as his body slid down to the ground and landed against the truck in a seated position.

Porch lights came on and eyes peered through parted curtains but the darkness covered the grisly scene that was unfolding. Isaiah swung the machete once more and completely severed Chino's head from his body.

Laughing maniacally, Isaiah picked up the severed head and dashed through a yard to his car that was parked on the next street over. Inside his vehicle he placed Chino's head on the passenger seat and drove it home to add to his collection.

Ca$h & NeNe Capri

Chapter 30
Deep Regrets

Bayonna walked around her mother's hospital bed straightening up. Her visits were few and far in between but when she came she made sure to clean her mother's room from top to bottom and replace all of her gowns with new ones. Watching her mother slowly die always took a piece of her soul every time she came. She knew that it was only a matter of time before she would get that phone call.

"Mommy, you want something to drink?" Bayonna poured her mother a glass of water.

Her mom nodded and Bayonna moved to her bedside and held the cup to her lips. She held Bayonna's wrist as she struggled to drink.

"I love you so much," she spoke through the tracheal tube in her throat.

"I love you, too, Mommy." Bayonna smiled at her.

"I need you to promise me something," her mother struggled to say.

"Anything," she agreed.

Her mother tried to swallow then continued. "You have to finish school and become somebody. Life is too short to waste it," she said, looking up into her daughter's eyes and cherishing the moment because she knew that at any time it could be her last.

"I won't let you down," Bayonna said to give her comfort.

She stood for a minute staring into her mother's eyes then she turned to sit the cup down on the table and took a seat. She always felt so guilty that she had to lie to her, leading her to believe that she was attending Cleveland State University as a part-time student and holding down a full time job.

Her mom had did everything in her power to raise her right and not allow her to get caught up in the streets. It would've killed her instantly to know that her only child had grown up to be a ruthless killer.

Bayonna sat and watched a few shows with her and helped her eat then wiped her down and changed her clothes. She then combed and braided her hair.

"You know, Bay, I would give anything in the world to have your father hold me one last time," her mother confessed as tears came to her eyes.

"Me too, Mommy." Bayonna's eyes teared up too.

"I miss him so much." She reminisced. She had given up family and everything for him and though he hadn't been perfect their love had been unbreakable.

"I miss him also," Bayonna said with a pained heart. Growing up her father had always been on the road, coming and going in and out of town regularly. But one thing Bayonna could say was that he never missed a birthday or any other important event in her life.

When she heard his car pull up in the yard, Bayonna would go flying out the door to run and jump into his arms. He would scoop her up and twirl her around and around. Then he would cover her plump cheeks with kisses sweeter than candy and begin unloading the car of boxes and bags full of gifts.

Bayonna recalled that her mom would be standing in the doorway filled with love for the both of them. And her father would look back at her mother with that same love in his eyes.

As she grew older her father's love for her and her mom never changed. She didn't know what he did when he was on the road but she knew that when he came home her mom and her were the apples of his eye.

Losing him was the worst thing that had ever happened to her mother and probably the one thing that caused her to deteriorate quicker. Lupus was something many could live a long life with but for her mom, her dad was her life and strength, and without him she was just buying time.

Bayonna wiped a tear and leaned in and kissed and hugged her mom tightly. She held her as if it was her last time because she felt like after she left this time either one of them could go.

She sat back in her seat and held her mother's hand as she drifted off to sleep. Feeling a flood of emotions Bayonna stood up and walked outside to call JuJu. The weather was in the seventies in Palm Springs, Florida where Bayonna was so she enjoyed the warm breeze that blew through her hair.

"Hey, bae," she said in a dour tone as soon as JuJu answered.

"How is she?" he asked.

"Not very good. I don't think she'll be with me much longer." Bayonna leaned against the bricks of the building and broke down crying.

"Shorty, I'm on the plane in the morning," said JuJu.

"No, it's okay. You have a lot of important things going on." She sniffled.

"Bay, right now you're what's most important. I'll be on the early bird flight. Pick me up at the airport. I'm about to call and book it now. I'll call you right back."

"Okay," she said, feeling comforted by his love and concern. "JuJu, I love you."

"I love you too. I'll hit you right back."

When he hung up the phone Bayonna wept harder than she had ever cried before in her life.

Chapter 31
No Turning Back

Bayonna had been out of town for more than a week and her girls could not afford to put things off any longer. It was time to make a move before the opportunity was missed.

Treebie and Lissha moved around the basement of Treebie's condo preparing for the mission at hand. Lissha walked over to the radio and pumped up Waka Flocka's *Luv Dem Gun Sounds.*

Ring alarm! dem boys in town
Like Joc, lay dat pussy nigga down
I don't talk, I don't laugh, I just frown
From da eagle to da choppa, luv dat gun sound,
Dat gun sound, luh dat, luh dat gun sound

Lissha threw back a few drinks then began loading her weapon. The bass from the speakers moved through her body intensifying the liquor and weed that took over her system. Treebie bounced her head as she rolled another blunt then put on her Kevlar vest. When her part came she sang loud.

"Murderman Flocka what the fuck are these niggas thinking, Point blank range, do this shit without blinking."

Lissha smiled at Treebie as she too suited up. She was ready to lay some niggas on their ass.

Once they were in full gear they moved to the center of the room then poured one last drink. Tonight they wanted to be numb. They wanted to only feel the oneness with their triggers; everything else was dying with only one person left to tell the story.

"Blood Money," Treebie said with her nostrils flared and her eyes squinted.

"You already know." Lissha touched her glass. They downed their drinks, pulled up their mask then rolled out.

211

Lissha drove in silence thinking about all that was on the line. Big Zo was on her ass, Kiam was locked up, the team was falling down around them and shit was back to just her and Treebie.

Even though Lissha was down like four flat tires she felt exhausted. She had started making runs for Big Zo at the age of fourteen. At nineteen she had delivered her first soul to hell. She had lived through three different wars in the city and held Big Zo down through all of them. After he got sent away, she had helped Gator rebuild what little was left of Big Zo's empire. And when Gator began to live high off of the hog and neglect business, she had helped facilitate Kiam taking over the throne.

But on the real, Lissha said to herself, the shit had become old and the game had changed. There was no such thing as loyalty or any adherence to the code of death before dishonor as Big Zo had preached to her so often she could still hear his voice ringing in her ears. His bitch ass had proven that the only person a muthafucka was loyal to was self.

Lissha hated herself for allowing him to manipulate her into his devious plot. She had been such a fool. Before any of this happened with Kiam, she would've never thought that Big Zo would trade a real nigga's freedom for his own. For that she had lost all respect for him to the point that she hated his mark ass. The thought that she had ever loved him made her sick to her stomach.

Lissha realized that she was not without blame, because at the end of the day she had gone along with everything that Big Zo had devised. But now she was determined to right her wrongs by riding hard for Kiam until the muthafuckin' wheels fell off. She was going to do everything in her power to make sure that he came home and Big Zo's pussy ass died behind bars.

"LiLi, you ready?" Treebie's voice brought Lissha back to the here and now.

"Hell yeah," she responded as the car came to a stop.

They both looked around and were a little thrown off when they saw all the extra cars parked out front of the spot that they were about to run up in.

"I thought you said it was supposed to be a few dudes." Lissha turned in Treebie's direction.

Treebie looked over at her. "I don't know what the fuck is going on. But on the real all I see is more money. The body count will just have to increase," Treebie spat, grabbing her gun.

"That's the shit I'm talkin' about. Let's go," Lissha said, grabbing her door handle.

The two women sprang into action moving stealth-like around the house listening for voices and trying to gauge the position of where everyone was at in the room. They crotched down low and peeked through the first floor window and did a quick head count. Lissha got excited when she heard the men inside talking about major weight and serious dollars. That was the type of shit that made her ratchet go off without prejudice.

Lissha gave the signal and they made sure that their watches were synced down to the second. Treebie moved to the back door and Lissha moved to the front, pressing her body against the side of the house and stepping lightly as she summoned up the beast within.

Treebie stood with her tool cocked and locked, and her breathing increased as she waited for the seconds to tick by on her watch.

Lissha drew her fo-fo and rang the bell twice then stepped back. When a figure appeared and asked who it was, Lissha let that cannon answer for her. *Boom! Boom!* She blasted and stepped in on that suicide shit.

Treebie's fo-fifth sounded off like an explosion, shattering the lock on the back door. She kicked the door open and ran inside ending muthafucka's future in a split second of *Boom!*

Just that quickly the house was under siege as they blasted everything moving. Treebie put her back against the kitchen wall and moved low hitting knee caps and ankles. Her motto was "If a nigga can't stand, he can't run."

Lissha's hammer ripped through bones and vital organs, skulls and brains. She was not tryna spare nothing but time. She hit niggas high and low then dived behind the couch for cover.

"Y'all muthafuckaz want some of this?" A tall skinny dude yelled out from his kneeled position as he emptied his clip in her direction.

Lamps shattered and stuffing blew out of the couch as bullets came flying in rapid succession. When Lissha noticed that the nigga's gun had gone quiet she peeked around the couch to see his position. He sprang up on his feet and tried to dash up the stairs but her whistle was quicker than his feet.

Boc! Boc! Boc! Boc!

"Bitch nigga, Blood Money is up in this muthafucka," she yelled as her steel jumped with each shot.

But this time her aim was errant and the only thing she murdered had been purchased at Haverty's. Just as Lissha steadied her hand and was about to blow a hole in dude's melon, a spaghetti head came running down the stairs letting off shots in her direction.

"LiLi get down," Treebie yelled.

Lissha screamed and dove out of the way in the nick of time as Treebie made sure that the dread wearing dude didn't get off another round.

Boom!

His chest opened up and his body flew backwards, flipping over the banister, before hitting the floor. "Punk muthafucka," Treebie screamed.

Lissha scrambled to her feet. A hand shot up and grabbed her leg pulling her back to the floor. A nigga they thought they had put on his ass pressed a sharp blade to her throat. When they came up from the floor he had his forearm around Lissha's neck. With a little more pressure he could've easily crushed her wind pipe.

Lissha gagged and wiggled but the dude was mad strong. "Put that muthafuckin' gun down nigga or I'ma do your boy," he yelled at Treebie.

Treebie stood firm with her pump in place, staring at him with those blood red orbs that made her look like the devil's child. Out the corner of her eye she spotted another dude rise up and reach his hand under the tattered cushion of the couch. Treebie whirled around and sprayed his thoughts all over the furniture. "Y'all think this is a game," she spat, looking at the lone survivor of their on-slaught.

"Nigga, back the fuck up or I will end your boy's life," he threatened as he pressed the sharp blade to the side of Lissha's neck and used her as a shield.

"Bleed, I don't give a fuck about that nigga," Treebie spat as she placed a second hand on her gun to steady her aim.

"You must think I'm playing?" Dude dug the knife a little deeper, drawing blood. "Fuck with me and this nigga is dead."

"Muthafucka, all I heard was mo' money. You gonna kill him. I'm gonna kill you then walk outta here with all this shit. I don't give a fuck either way," she growled, aiming the .45 semi-automatic at his head.

He stared her in those blood red eyes and saw nothing but murderous intent. He knew that she wouldn't hesitate to do him dirty but if he was dying, he was taking somebody with him. He pulled Lissha's head back exposing her windpipe completely, but that was costly because it exposed *his* head.

Boom! Treebie shot one in the top of his head sending blood and brain splattering all over Lissha. The dude's body tumbled backwards and Lissha fell forward covering her ears with both hands as they rung from the blast.

Treebie hurried over to see about her partner in crime. She kneeled down and was relieved to see that Lissha was unharmed. "You alright?" she asked, helping Lissha to her feet.

Lissha's ears were still ringing and her heart rate was ridiculous. But she was about that life, and with it death was always right around the corner, so her brush with fatality didn't require a hug. "I'm good, bitch," she said, pouncing to her feet and retrieving her ratchet off of the floor. "Let's snatch the loot and be out."

Side by side and in step they moved through the living and dining rooms hitting anything that appeared alive with a few more shots. When nothing was left moving but their eyes they spotted a stack of bricks on the dining room table and stacks of money next to the drugs. They quickly stuffed the duffel bags that they had brought along and moved towards the door. Suddenly, Treebie came to a halting stop.

Lissha looked at her like, *what the fuck?*

"Bitch, we almost forgot to sign that nigga's check." Treebie took a Ben Franklin out of the duffel bag, bent down and rubbed it in the blood of the dead man by the front door then she stuffed it in his mouth.

"Blood Money, nigga," they said in unison.

"Tell a friend," added Treebie.

Moving swiftly and on alert they left out the door much quieter than they had entered.

As Treebie pulled off and bent a corner she noticed a car staying a few feet behind them. She adjusted the rear view mirror, grabbed her spare gun from between the seats and sped up to see if the vehicle behind them would do the same. When she saw it turn off she relaxed and continued on to her house.

When they pulled up Treebie hit the garage button and pulled in closing it behind them. They grabbed the bags off of the backseat and moved to the basement to see what all they had.

"Damn, this was a good night," Lissha said as she poured the money out on the table.

"Bitch, them niggas almost killed our asses."

"No bitch *you* almost killed me. I was like well damn."

"Well, I had to go up top on that nigga to get yo ass outta there," Treebie said, placing the bricks on the counter.

"Next time warn a bitch you almost took the side of my face off." Lissha began to count.

"I hear your crybaby ass," Treebie said with a smile.

Lissha ignored the good natured joke. "Let's split this shit up and go drop some weight on Dirty and them. The traps have been dry for almost a week."

"Damn. Can't that wait until tomorrow? I need to come down off of this high. When I took that nigga's head off, that shit got my panties wet."

"Eww. TMI." Lissha scrunched up her face.

"I'm just saying," Treebie laughed.

Lissha had to chuckle. "Tree, you stupid as hell."

"I know, that's why you love me." She did a little dance in her seat, mocking Lissha.

"Bitch you wish." Lissha smiled. "Stash the money and let's go drop this work off. Time waits for no one."

"Okay," Treebie agreed. "Let's get cleaned up and roll out." She began helping Lissha stack the dope back in the bag.

When that was done Lissha and Treebie went upstairs, showered and changed clothes, then cleaned up the basement and collected the stash. As they moved out the front door headed toward Lissha's car they heard a click clack behind them. The sound was unmistakable. Treebie and Lissha froze in place.

"I knew you bitches weren't shit," Isaiah grumbled, moving closer to them.

"What the fuck is you doing?" Lissha asked as she realized who the voice belonged to.

"Bitch, don't say shit to me. I told Kiam and JuJu they couldn't trust you thirsty bitches." He held the gun firmly in one hand and reached out and snatched the bag off of Lissha's shoulder with the other. Then he shoved her forward. "Blood Money, huh?" he remarked with disdain as he tightened his grip on the gun.

Treebie's heart started beating faster as she prepared to reach for her strap and go out bustin' back but Lissha's cry bought them time.

"Isaiah. Kiam knows all about this why the fuck is you trippin'?" Lissha said, turning in his direction.

"Don't fucking look at me with yo foul ass," he spat.

Lissha looked at his unsteady hand and dilated pupils and knew that he was an unstable nigga. "Dude like for real you need to put that shit down and let's get the fuck outta this cold," she tried to reason with him.

"Say one more thing and I'ma blow your fuckin' pretty face all over this cold ass ground."

"Bitch nigga, make another threat." Treebie couldn't hold back. She turned around and met him face to face. If she was going to die she was going to look him in his eyes.

"That's what I'm talking about. A bitch that think's she a man." Isaiah raised the gun.

Treebie grabbed ahold of his arm and held on with all of her might. He slung her from side to side until he finally shook her off of him, but in the process his gun clattered to the ground. Treebie stumbled back then caught her balance. When Isaiah bent to snatch up the gun she quickly kicked it out of both of their reach.

Isaiah straightened up, whipped out his machete and smiled like the deranged muthafucka that he had become.

Lissha wasted no more time. As Treebie back peddled away from Isaiah, she drew down on him and hit him with a back full of hot lead. Isaiah's body lurched forward knocking Treebie down and he landed on top of her still holding onto the machete. Filled with cocaine and tons of adrenaline, he choked Treebie with one hand and raised the machete over his head with the other even though his back was opened up.

As he began to bring the machete down in a vicious manner, Lissha stepped closer, put her gun to his cranium and blew the little bit of sense he had left out the top of his head.

"Get this crazy muthafucka up off of me!" Treebie said, trying to scoot from underneath Isaiah's dead weight.

As soon as Lissha helped her roll Isaiah's body off of her, Treebie scrambled to her feet and looked around to see if anyone had been alerted by the gunshots. Amazingly there was no movement but that didn't mean that there was no faces pressed to the windows of neighboring houses.

Moving quickly, Lissha and Treebie grabbed a leg apiece and drug the body inside the garage. Then they hurried back and gathered up the bag with the work in it, the machete, and the gun that had fallen out of Isaiah's waistband.

"That nigga gonna be heavy as hell," Lissha said as they covered Isaiah's body with a tarp.

"I know but so is a life sentence. We gotta get that nigga outta here." Treebie picked the machete up and swung it back and forth through the air. "We ought to chop his ass up like crack."

"No, bitch, quit playing. We're not doing no shit like that, he's JuJu's family. We're gonna dump his body somewhere it will be found so that JuJu can give him a decent burial. Now let's wash the driveway down and go drop this shit off. We'll move the body tomorrow night."

"Okay," Treebie agreed.

They turned the lights off in the garage and locked the door. Treebie dashed around to the side of the house and came back dragging a water hose. In the dark, she washed down the driveway as thoroughly as she could while Lissha trained her focus on the ground in search of anything that they may have overlooked. When the area appeared to be clean they hopped in Lissha's car and mashed out.

As they drove to the hood the evening's chain of events played heavily on Lissha's heart. Another murder of one of their own not to mention someone close to Kiam. She wanted to cry but the situation called for balls not bitch ass emotions. She tucked that shit and got herself together. This was not the time to let shit fall all outta place. Lissha had to do whatever it took to continue to hide the truth. There was no turning back.

Chapter 32
Homecoming

As soon as JuJu and Bayonna returned from Florida he had to bury Isaiah, whose body had been found on the side of the road wrapped in warm blankets. Being that Chino had been found beheaded a week before that and the streets accredited his grisly murder to Kiam's clique, it was assumed that Wolfman had Isaiah killed to even the score over Chino and Xyna's murders.

JuJu didn't buy that. He knew that vicious killahs like the ones Wolfman would send didn't take the time to wrap a body up in blankets and gently place it on the side of the road to be found. They would've wet a nigga up and left him bloody and twisted right where they caught him.

When the police searched Isaiah's condo for evidence that might lead them to his killer, what they discovered inside brought the news cameras and the gawkers out in droves. For days the two heads that were found inside Isaiah's refrigerator dominated the news as well as the talk on the streets.

JuJu and Kiam took solace in the fact that at least Isaiah had smashed Chino before somebody killed him. As the murders became less of a topic on the streets winter faded into spring. The warmer temperatures melted the ice on Lake Erie and Wa'leek's body washed up.

Treebie played the role of the grieving wife but Riz wasn't convinced. If he hadn't given his word to Kiam he would've had that bitch's head knocked the fuck off.

Treebie didn't give a fuck what Riz or anyone thought, her gun stayed ready. At Wa'leek's funeral up in New Jersey she brushed off the cold stares of Riz and Wa'leek's family just as easily as she put niggas in the dirt. And when she returned to Cleveland she was ready to bury the next muthafucka.

The dope that Lissha and Treebie had dropped off to the trap houses that night got things on and popping for a few days but it was not enough to sustain the streets through the drought that had come over the city.

JuJu had found a connect that could supply them with ten kilos a week; that kept some money coming in and made sure that the trap boys ate but it was far short from what was needed.

"Just maintain until I come home," advised Kiam. His lawyers had told him that the charges against him would be dropped soon because there was insufficient evidence to take the case to trial. The witness that had called the police hotline and initially picked Kiam out of a photo line-up had recanted her statement. In a second photo line-up she had chosen a different suspect.

Kiam and JuJu were ecstatic. But what neither of them had any way of knowing was that the feds were moving pieces around on the board to free the king so that they could checkmate him later, along with dozens of his associates.

In the meantime the streets were as quiet as a library. Wolfman had adhered to the police chief's warning and had fallen all the way back. The only crew that continued to get money was Kiam's.

Blood Money talked about laying some more niggas down but Bay's heart didn't seem to be in it anymore and neither did Lissha's. All she cared about was visiting Kiam and waiting for his lawyers to free him.

Finally after weeks more of waiting and praying, that day arrived.

History was definitely repeating itself. Lissha turned into the parking lot of the Justice Center, turned off her engine and took a deep breath. It seemed like it was just yesterday that she was picking Kiam up from prison and meeting him for the first time. She looked out of her window at the expansive grounds and her mind began racing.

Spring flowers bloomed around the lawn giving false hope to many that visited the men inside. Lissha couldn't help but wonder if she too was disillusioned. Had Kiam loss too many and had she done too much to be forgiven if the truth ever surfaced, she contemplated.

She considered the revelations that she wanted to disclose to Kiam but the repercussions were far too great to risk allowing her tongue to tell all. For a second she thought about pulling off and driving far away to someplace unknown to escape the lies that were bound to come out eventually. But she couldn't leave no more than she could continue to plot against Kiam. She had fallen deeply in love and her strong desire had set a fire in her soul that had to be quenched.

Tears threatened to rise up in her eyes as she thought about the complex scheme that Big Zo still had planned for Kiam. *How can I warn him without admitting my part in it?* she wondered. The answer alluded her.

Lissha leaned her head against the steering wheel as her deception stole the excitement that she should have felt. Even though she hadn't gone all the way through with it, the damage had been done. Once Kiam found out he would never pardon her.

And Bay will hate me for throwing Donella to the wolves to cover up my own deception. Lissha hated herself for that but Donella had almost discovered that Biz Zo wasn't her father. "Self-preservation," Lissha whispered. That was the same thing Big Zo used to justify crossing Kiam.

The idea that she was anything like him made her dizzy. Lissha jumped out the car and posted up on the hood and took some deep breaths. Just as she caught her composure she looked up and saw Kiam strolling towards her in the company of his well-dressed attorney. The two men stopped and shared a few hushed words then they shook hands and the lawyer walked off.

Kiam stared at Lissha from a distance. Lissha stared back. Neither of them moved at first then they began slowly walking towards each other until Lissha was in his arms. "Welcome home, baby," she cried. "I missed you so much."

"I missed you too, ma." He put a finger under her chin and lifted her head. Then he covered her mouth with his and took her breath away.

Lissha wanted that moment to last forever. She was in his arms enjoying his kiss with his hands palming her ass. At heaven's door, is what she likened the feel to.

Kiam broke the kiss and held her back at arm's length and soaked up her sexiness. She was rocking a pixie cut and her brows were perfectly arched. His eyes roamed down her body and he smiled in anticipation of watching her peel off those tight ass jeans.

At the same time that Kiam was checking her out Lissha's eyes were glued on his chest. "Somebody has been doing their pushups," she observed.

"Yeah, I've been gettin' it in," he said.

Lissha stepped in close and wrapped her arms around his waist "I got you now," she joked.

"You don't know what to do with all this man," he responded, looking down into her eyes as he reciprocated her hug.

"That's what you think."

"Well, I'm about to find out," he said, tasting her lips again. They had made some very specific promises to each other and today he was going to make her cash in on every one of them.

Lissha pulled back and took a deep breath. She was so overwhelmed all she could do was giggle like a teenager. "I can't believe I'm in your arms." She gushed.

"Let's get the fuck away from this shit hole so I can get into some other places," Kiam said, caressing her butt.

"I second that emotion." Lissha chuckled then turned to open his door.

Kiam got in and watched the jiggle of Lissha's butt as she walked in front of the car.

When she jumped in the passenger seat she reached in the glove compartment and passed Kiam a gun and a heavily padded envelope of hundred dollar bills. "Just a little something, something." She threw him that sexy smile and pulled out of the lot.

Kiam nodded his head as he fumbled through the neatly stacked bills. "Thanks, ma," he said then put his seat all the way back. "So what's going on with the team?"

"JuJu is handling the streets. You know we took some big hits but he was able to make sure our strongest arms are still in place and running well."

"What else?"

"Treebie and I have been stacking the money and making sure everybody stays on point. I have to walk light with this bail shit so Bay has been the only one making runs with JuJu and Dirty to meet with the new connect."

Kiam nodded. JuJu had told him the same thing.

"You know they all wanted to be in the parking lot to welcome you home as soon as your feet touched the ground. But I told them I was going to act a fool if they didn't allow us to spend the first day alone," she said as she turned corners.

"Where you going?" Kiam asked as she pulled onto the interstate.

"I copped a little townhouse out in Mentor. I wanted you to be comfortable and with all the police attention I thought you would feel better there instead of at either of our houses."

"That's what's up," Kiam said, relaxing in his seat.

"What you thought I was kidnapping you?" Lissha looked over at him with a wrinkled brow.

"Nah, nothing like that. I know you ain't trying to get fucked up," Kiam joked.

"Whatever. You spent a few days in the pen now you tough."

"You know I'm the muthafuckin' man," he boasted, turning up the radio.

Lissha didn't even respond. She twisted her lips to the side and shook her head as she picked up speed.

Kiam couldn't keep his hands off of her, he kept reaching over and rubbing up and down her thigh causing her foot to press heavy on the gas.

Lissha glanced over at him. "You're gonna cause an accident."

"Stop blocking and pay attention to the road," Kiam said smoothly as he slid his hand between her legs and rubbed his hand against her fat print. "Damn, this pussy fat," he said as she came off of the interstate stopping at a red light. "Give me kiss."

Lissha leaned over and did just as she was instructed. She pulled back licking her lips. "You taste so good," she cooed as Kiam looked at her with a low gaze.

"I got something else that taste better."

"The last time I tried to taste that, you pulled a gun on me," she reminded him.

Kiam chuckled at the memory. "I promise when I pull it out this time it will be all pleasure."

Lissha twisted her lips to the side and continued on with Kiam's hand causing a stir between her thighs.

When she pulled into the driveway she popped the trunk and pulled out some bags she had picked up for Kiam. He stepped out of the car and looked around the area then followed her up to the door. Lissha fumbled with her key in the new lock until Kiam stepped behind her. He pressed his body against her and placed his hands on hers and turned the key until the door came open.

Lissha pressed her butt back into him enjoying his strength all up on her. "Thanks, Boss," she jested.

"I do my best work in tight spaces." Kiam's warm breath caressed her neck, sending chills up her spine.

"You're so bad Kiam," Lissha said, moving into the living room and placing the bags down.

Kiam inhaled deeply as he looked around at the warm patterns of green, brown and rust. Lissha had the place fully furnished with a huge flat screen mounted to the wall along with a Bose stereo system. She moved to the radio and threw in a Sade CD.

Kiam sat on the couch and watched the sway of her hips as she moved around with purpose.

"Baby, just kick back and relax while I get things ready for my king," she said.

"I'm with that." Kiam put both arms up on the back of the sofa and chilled.

Lissha collected the bags and headed to the bedroom to get things straight. After she put away his clothes, she took a quick shower then ran Kiam a hot tub of bubbly water. Lissha threw on a pair of booty shorts and a tank top and headed to the kitchen to hook him up a blazing dinner.

"Let me start your food then I'll be right with you," she said as she passed him still seated on the couch.

"A'ight," Kiam said as he pulled off his boots and propped his feet up on the coffee table. He folded his hands on his chest and closed his eyes sinking into the soft suede of the sofa.

Lissha moved around the kitchen gathering her pots and ingredients. She rinsed and sliced two steaks into thin pieces, put them in a bowl of A-1 sauce and seasonings then diced her onions and peppers. After everything was cut just right she put the meat and vegetables in a Wok with a little olive oil. She cut up small white potatoes and put them on boil then sliced up the carrots. Turning everything on low, she rejoined Kiam in the living room.

"You ready?" she asked, putting her hand out.

Kiam's eyes came open and he took her hand rising to his feet. "I'm always ready." He looked into her eyes sending heat throughout her body. Lissha turned away and grabbed the remote and switched to the mixed R&B CD she had put together. Maxwell's *Pretty Wings* came on as they headed to the bathroom.

Kiam entered the bathroom to see it dimly lit with scented candles. The flames danced casting a shadow against the walls putting his whole body in relax mode.

Lissha moved silently around the bathroom putting everything in place. When she had everything set up she walked over to Kiam and began to help him out of his clothes. Her mouth watered with anticipation as her eyes roamed over his chest and abs. She rested her hands on his zipper, pulled it down slowly, and then allowed his jeans to drop to the floor.

"Why you acting like you scared of me?" Kiam asked, looking down at her.

"I'm not afraid of you." Lissha kept her gaze down because she didn't trust her heart to contain her feelings.

"We will see," he said, stepping out of his boxers.

Lissha led him into the tub then grabbed a body sponge and filled it with milk and honey body wash and began to rub over Kiam's skin taking away all that stress and strain of the last months.

Kiam put his head back and enjoyed her touch.

Lissha was in bliss. Finally she had him all to herself.

"Why you so quiet?" he asked.

Lissha thought for a minute then responded. "I wish I would have met you at a different time."

"Well, you got me right now. Don't worry about a different time." He reached up and grabbed the back of her head and kissed her deeply.

Lissha surrendered herself to his touch as her body heated up with every movement of his tongue. Her breathing increased as he took her breath and twisted her thoughts.

When he cradled her breast in his other hand Lissha pulled back. "Kiam, I have to check on the food."

"Yeah, you do that, with your scary ass," he chuckled.

"Whatever." Lissha got up and headed to the kitchen.

Kiam took the sponge and squeezed the hot water on his neck and chest. It felt so good to sit in that hot water. He embraced the moment of silence and unconsciously thanked God for seeing him through the toughest year of his life.

When Lissha came back in the bathroom he had the shower going rinsing himself off.

"Babe, I was going to hook you up." Lissha pouted.

"Oh, don't worry you're still going to." He turned off the shower and pulled open the curtain.

Lissha's eyes went to Kiam's steel as he held it firmly in his hand and stroked slow. She reached over, grabbed a towel and dried his chest and back then down his legs.

Kiam stepped out onto the thick bathroom carpet and Lissha went to her knees.

Lissha stared at all that thickness and just admired its beauty. Taking him into her hand, she kissed the head gently then ran her tongue around the rim. She put the tip in her mouth and sucked lightly then tightened her jaws and rolled her tongue back and forth sending intense sensations through Kiam's body. Lissha played with the head until she heard his breathing pick up then she slipped him to the back of her throat.

"Get that shit, ma," Kiam said on heavy breath.

Lissha put all of her skills to work rotating her head and giving him that heat. She caressed his balls playing gently with the line that separated them then she slipped him out her mouth and showed each one special attention with her lips and tongue.

Kiam fought hard not to come but she was doing everything he liked and he was getting ready to reward her.

Lissha put his dick back in her mouth and moved her head back and forth with precision. When he gripped her head and guided her movement she knew it was over.

"Ssss," Kiam hissed as he began to release in her mouth.

Lissha caught it all then spit it out all over his shaft then lapped it all up not spilling a drop.

"Make that shit nasty," Kiam moaned as he watched her drink his essence.

"Real bitches can spit and swallow," Lissha proclaimed, licking her lips.

"Talk that shit," Kiam said as he tried to recover.

Lissha rose up. "You deserve it all Kiam," she whispered.

"You know I'ma have to return the favor," he pulled her to him.

"Let me feed you and take care of you first then you can do whatever you want to me." She kissed his lips.

"You know that pussy gonna be in trouble right?"

"Yup and I want every inch with no restrictions." She washed him up, oiled him down, and then turned to head back to the kitchen.

Kiam smacked her ass on her way out causing her to giggle. He put on his boxers and looked at himself long and hard in the mirror. Tonight he was planning on burying the past and stepping into his future. There were things he would never let go of and Eyez was one of them. He replayed her mother's words. *My daughter would want you to live.* He internalized that and decided that was exactly what he was going to do.

Kiam walked into the living room to see Lissha coming in, carrying a plate.

"That's what I'm talking about." He took a seat on the couch.

Lissha handed him his plate and a tall glass filled with ice and grape juice then grabbed her oils and sat at his feet.

Kiam dug into the pepper steak, mashed potatoes and honey glazed carrots as she took his feet into her hands and massaged his calves.

"Am I distracting you from enjoying your meal?" she asked.

"Nah, you good, ma." It was the first time that he had ever gotten a foot massage while eating but the shit actually felt damn good.

They continued to share comfortable conversation and jokes as he enjoyed the tender meat that melted in his mouth and her delicate hands on his feet.

When he was done she stood up and took his plate, passed him his drink and left to straighten the kitchen. Kiam knew he was the king but she was making him feel his royalty.

Lissha came back into the living room to see that he had left out. She walked over to the stereo and changed the track then headed to where she guessed he would be.

Kiam was laid in the middle of the bed butt naked looking like a chocolate dream. "C'mere," he motioned her to him with his finger.

Lissha moved slowly to the bed unable to believe that she was about to actually give Kiam what she had been dying to give him from the first day they'd met. She climbed up on top of him and pulled her shirt over her head allowing her breast to sit up perfect to his view.

Kiam wasted no time putting his mouth over her erect nipples and sucking them just right.

Lissha rested her hands on his chest as she tried to control the heat that rose up from her core. "Kiam." She sucked in air.

"What's up, ma?' he asked, pulling at her shorts.

"I'm so scared." Her voice trembled as water rose in her eyes.

"I told you I got you. Don't worry I'ma give you everything you been wanting," he said as he slid down and positioned her pussy right over his face.

Lissha put her hand over her face and rested the other one on the head board as Kiam began to tickle her clit with the tip of his tongue.

Soft moans escaped her mouth as his lips and tongue slithered over her pussy causing it to gush with every movement.

Lissha put her head down and closed her eyes tightly when his warm lips covered her clit. She moved to the rhythm of his suckle as she heard Gerald and Eddie Levert singing *Baby hold onto me.*

Baby hold on to me, See I'm a special kind/ A man that is hard to find/ Told you a thousand times, Baby hold on to me.

When her body jerked uncontrollably he released his grip, flipped her over and climbed between her thighs.

"You ready to give me my pussy?" he asked, kissing her deeply.

"Yes," she moaned as tears eased out the side of her eyes.

Tonight nothing was going to stop what was destined to happen. Kiam pushed into her tightness and breathed deep before he began to penetrate further.

Lissha held him tightly as the tears flowed faster. All of her love and regrets flooded her emotions as he hit all the right spots. Kiam looked down into her beautiful wet face and for the first time saw all of her vulnerability. It turned him on to see her afraid of something.

"Let me have it, Lissha. Be all mine tonight," he rasped, throwing one of her legs over his shoulder.

Lissha was unable to speak as he stroked long, deep and slow. All she could do was cry.

"I'm sorry," she mumbled.

Kiam responded with his dick because his words would not properly explain. He gave her quick power strokes making her pussy real juicy. He placed tender kisses on her face and nibbled on her chin as her muscles hugged around his thickness.

Lissha held him tightly and put her head against his chest and let him have whatever he wanted.

For the first time Lissha knew what it felt like to be made love to. It was like he could read her mind with every stroke; he didn't miss one spot coming or going.

Kiam's feelings matched his push, he knew that Lissha had earned her position in his bed and he made sure she got that pussy handled thoroughly. He hit it and flipped it in every position possible until she could take no more.

"Baby, you gon' mess around and murk me," she muttered.

Kiam chuckled and looked down at the proof of his wicked dick game. Lissha was laid out on her stomach with her arms stretched straight out. When she drifted off to sleep he slipped out of bed to get a bottle of water.

A few minutes later as Lissha slept peacefully Kiam stood in the doorway looking at her. He wondered what it was that she had held back from saying before he loved her down.

Whatever it was had to be serious because she had begun to apologize and cry. Kiam ran a myriad of possibilities through his mind but couldn't settle on any one thing. He decided to allow time to settle the tiny suspicions that rose up in his gut. For now, Lissha had more than proven her love and loyalty.

Ca$h & NeNe Capri

Chapter 33
Back To Business

The next day Kiam and Lissha met with the crew at JuJu's house. Lissha was beaming like a bulb but Kiam's expression was as smooth as always. It was back to business.

The girls wanted to throw him a welcome home party at a nightclub to let the streets know that the king was back, but Kiam promptly deaded that suggestion.

"Just let them check their pockets in a few days and they'll realize I'm back," he said. "We're about to turn up on niggas. If anybody's head has gotten too big while I was away we'll quietly knock it off. Muthafuckaz better get back in line."

"That's what I'm talking about, Boss," said JuJu, whipping out his strap and posturing around the room before sitting back down.

Dirty said nothing he wasn't much of a talker, he preferred to let his gun speak.

"What do you need us to do?" Treebie asked, speaking for herself, Lissha, and Bayonna.

"I'ma keep Lissha glued to my side, I like the way her whistle twerk," said Kiam.

The compliment brought a smile to Lissha's face. She was ready to jump up and murk anyone that he pointed out.

Kiam looked over at Bay, who was sitting on JuJu's lap rubbing his arm affectionately. "Once I holla at Riz, Bayonna, you will roll out of town with JuJu to handle that. The shipment will be our largest yet so y'all gotta go pick it up and bring it back with no problems."

"You already know how we do," she replied.

"Indeed."

Kiam turned back to Treebie and held her stare. "What I need you to do is most important and it's very dangerous," he said as he validated risking her in his mind.

"That's how I like it," she confirmed. She pulled out her lighter, sparked a blunt, and put some weed smoke in the air as she waited for Kiam to define her mission.

"Wolfman," he said.

The name alone brought a whole different mood into the room. Every one of them despised Wolfman and lived for the day they could shove a gun in his mouth and send his thoughts up to the sky.

"Nigga, you're about to make me cum," said Treebie, wiggling around in her seat. "Just tell me how dirty you want me to do him."

Kiam shook his head *no*. That was not the game plan. "I know you're a beast, ma, but I don't want you to try to touch him yourself. That bitch ass nigga is mine. I just want you to put your ear to the streets and find out where he's at."

"Aww. I don't get to play?" she frowned and passed the blunt to Lissha.

"You'll get to bust your gun because when you find that mutha-fucka we're killing everything around him," Kiam said with venom dripping off of his statement.

When the meeting adjourned everyone was feeling Kiam's agenda. The streets was surely about to find out that he was back.

The pickup from Riz went down without a hitch and when the drugs arrived in Cleveland, it was back to business. The traps were soon booming again and any nigga that had set up shop in Kiam's territories while the drought was on was given two choices: get the fuck off the block or get put on their ass. Most knew not to test his gangsta but the few that tried would have to tell their stories in the afterlife.

"You're a beast, baby," Lissha said one night when she was lay-ing in his arms after a torrid round of sex during which he had sat her on the edge of the bathroom sink and fogged up the mirror.

"I tried to tell you to be careful of what you ask for," he boasted afterwards.

"Nigga, you ain't do shit," she teased.

"Yeah, right. Get your butt up and go hook me up something to eat. You have to pay for that good dick I just gave you," he joked back.

"Okay, Daddy."

Kiam's mouth tightened. "I'm not your daddy," he said.

"Sorry," Lissha apologized. But his reaction cemented her decision not to confess her betrayal.

Chapter 34
When It Rains It Pours

As one month ended and a new one rolled in Kiam had reestablished his stronghold on the city's dope game. Wolfman hadn't resurfaced so there was no team powerful enough to compete with his. Money was rolling in hand over fist and nigga's on his squad were eating and riding good.

But it would be short-lived because the feds were lurking, patiently building ironclad cases against the entire organization. The information that they were being fed was so accurate they almost knew when Kiam took a shit and wiped his ass. The only reason they hadn't moved in and snatched up him and his entire team was because they hadn't attained enough evidence on some of his associates yet.

The first chink in Kiam's armor came when two of his drug houses were raided on the same day. A week later, Dirty got pulled over with ten bricks in his truck. Before Kiam could bail him out of jail the spot on Miles Road got hit. And the next day the house on Hayden Road out in East Cleveland was raided.

The losses were huge and the bonds were high. Kiam always tried to get his souljahs out on bail as quickly as possible because he knew that the longer you let a nigga sit in jail the more likely they would flip.

It came out that Dirty had gotten popped on a gun charge before any of the raids began so his comrades began questioning whether or not he was working with po po to get the gun charge dismissed.

Kiam didn't think so but he wondered why Dirty hadn't told them about it. As soon as he made bond they were going to have to talk about that. In the meantime, Kiam had to make a move to offset his losses.

He went to his stash and spent all day counting up. By the time he left he was weary from seeing money but he was prepared to invest half of his bank, $2,500,000.00 on a re-up.

At home, while Lissha prepared dinner, Kiam hit Riz up and they set up the shipment.

Bones and his right hand Dro drove to the designated location with their faces tight and their guns cocked and locked on their waist. Bones couldn't understand why Riz would keep fucking with Kiam and his crew when he clearly didn't trust them. He concluded that it was the two and a half million dollars Kiam was spending that made Riz go against his instinct. Bones could understand that but it wasn't Riz's head on the chopping block if anything went foul—it was his.

"I want to switch cars with these muthafuckaz and be right back on the road. I don't even want the tires to cool off," Bones remarked as he pushed on towards their exit.

"You ain't gotta tell me twice. I hate this trip. This that bullshit I don't like." Dro was past grouchy and because it was a drop and pickup he couldn't smoke until they got back. His mood was anybody could get it.

Bones nodded and exited on the right.

Bayonna put her head back on the seat and took short breaths as she tried to convince her stomach that this was not the time to be sending her meal in reverse.

JuJu looked over at how uncomfortable she was and he too became uneasy. "Baby, you straight?" he asked as he pushed the rental down the highway.

"I'll be fine," she stated dryly, rubbing his arm as she kept her gaze out the window.

JuJu didn't push the issue. He had been watching her for the last couple of days and her random headaches and the sudden change in her sleeping pattern had him worried. He had charged it to her mother's health issue and tucked it away but on the real he was worried about his baby girl.

As JuJu turned onto the exit he began to look for the Exxon gas station where they were making the exchange with Bones. He spotted it up on the right and headed toward it, anxious to make the transaction and get Bay back home. *I'm making her go get a checkup as soon as we get back.*

Bones was already parked and waiting in the U-haul truck.

"You ready, ma?" JuJu asked, pulling right in front of the store and deading the engine.

"Always." Bayonna turned toward him and braved a smile.

"You know I love you, right?"

"Yes, and I love you more," she replied.

"Let me taste those lips so I know it's real." JuJu leaned over and she met him halfway.

After they shared a quick passionate kiss they climbed out of the car ready to take care of business. Bones and Dro hopped down from the truck.

Bayonna stood by JuJu's side as the men swapped instructions. Her forehead was wet with perspiration and she felt like she was about to pass out. She put her hand on JuJu's arm.

JuJu looked over at her and his face filled with concern.

"I'll be right back." She put her hand on her stomach.

"You alright?"

"Yeah let me go get some ginger ale real quick." She reached inside her jacket and passed him her banger then she hurried inside and went straight for the bathroom. As soon as she entered the stall she threw up all over the place. When she could finally stand she rinsed her face and put her head against the door and tried to regain her composure.

JuJu slid Bay's ratchet on his waistband next to his own. He and Bones exchanged keys then pulled the vehicles to the gas pump to prepare for the long rides back.

"Your girl look fucked up. You might want to check on her," Bones said as he lifted the nozzle from the pump.

"Nah, she straight. You know Bay is a rider." JuJu said as he began to pump gas into the U-haul.

"Look like all that late night loving might have caught up with her," Bones stated with a chuckle. He had been down that road a few times and the signs were obvious to him.

JuJu didn't respond he didn't like Bones well enough to chum it up with that nigga and he didn't believe in fake kickin' it. But he damn sure ran all of Bay's symptoms back in his mind and wondered if there was any accuracy to the man's words.

JuJu looked up at the store and watched as she moved from the cooler to the counter carrying her array of snacks. He smiled as he replaced the nozzle to its resting place. His shorty might not have felt well but she was a trooper.

After both vehicles were gassed up Bones asked JuJu to pop the trunk and let him see the dough.

"Nigga, ain't nobody tryna be out here on Front Street. If you don't trust me you can give me my keys back and be out."

Bones grilled him but had to let it ride because Riz trusted that those muthafucka's money would be right. "If it's a dollar short I'ma come looking for you personally," he said.

"And if you're a half of gram short you ain't gon' have to look for me, I'ma kick in your door."

Anticipating drama Dro put his hand in his jacket and moved in.

JuJu lifted the bottom of his shirt just a bit allowing him a peek at the butts of his fo-fo and the Glock .50. "What's up, Bleed, you wanna draw?"

"Don't be so quick to beef Junior. Life is short enough without rushing death." Dro was about that life too.

242

A camper pulled in the gas station followed by a bread truck and a van. JuJu let his shirt fall and smiled at Bones and his boy. "Next time," he promised.

As they turned to climb in their vehicles all hell broke loose. The back door of the bread truck flew open and DEA agents poured out barking commands, wielding guns and rifles that could penetrate steel.

"Police! Get on the ground!" they shouted.

Enforcements jumped out of the van and the camper.

From inside the store Bay looked out of the window and the gas station was flooded with cops.

Bones threw his hands above his head then went down to his knees in meek surrender. But JuJu and Dro's hearts didn't pump estrogen, they pumped an overload of testosterone and their balls hung to the ground.

JuJu whipped out both of his whistles and quickly ducked down behind the truck as the cops tried to take his head off. Dro dived inside the rental and threw the gear in drive but he had to remain low as bullets shattered glass and peppered the body of the car. As he tried to speed away, firing shots out of the window, a police cruiser came flying from across the street and slammed into the side of the rental. It spun around twice then flipped over on its side.

Dro crawled out of the shattered window letting his tool bark back at the cops, but he didn't get to fight back long. They chopped him down with more than forty shots.

Ten yards away JuJu was in a gun battle just as fierce. He already knew how it would end but he didn't give a fuck, he wasn't surrendering. He peeked around the fender and saw Bones punk ass scrambling out of harm's way. *Nigga quick to kill another nigga but bitch up when those boys draw down on him!*

He aimed one of his guns at Bones and knocked meat and skull out of that pussy muthafucka's head.

From his position JuJu could still see Bay in the store. She had a hand over her mouth looking out of the window in horror. There was no doubt in his mind that had she not left her banger with him, his girl would've ran out the door squeezing off every bullet in the clip at those bitch ass Jakes.

"I love you, shorty," he mouthed, though he knew that she couldn't see it. Still it felt good to tell her goodbye.

Now he was ready to go where he had sent dozens of others. He rose to his feet with both guns blazing. "This what the fuck y'all want?" he yelled.

He saw a cop drop from a head shot and he smiled just before they blew his ass to smithereens.

Bayonna's knees buckled as she looked on in fear. Without hesitation she bolted for the doors but felt a pair of strong arms snatch her back. She spun and looked into the face of a middle-aged black man.

"No, don't go out there you might get shot," said the stranger.

"Let me go!" She screamed and kicked but he wouldn't release her.

Bayonna wrestled in his arms as she screamed JuJu's name repeatedly. The world was moving in slow motion as she looked out of the door at her boo's tattered body slumped over the hood of the U-haul truck.

"Noooooooo," she cried as she slipped out of the man's arms and collapsed to the floor. "God why?" She let out a blood curdling scream and her body shook uncontrollably.

Tears ran from her eyes as she kept them on the movement outside. A half dozen police kept their guns trained on JuJu's body as they approached it with caution; like they were expecting him to rise up and start bustin' at them again. As they got closer, JuJu's body slid down the hood of the truck. The policemen's guns cackled like a barrel of firecrackers.

"Nooooooo," Bay cried out as she saw his head explode in a spray of red.

In the moments that followed there was mad confusion out in the lot. Bay stood up and stared out of the window as tears ran down her face in rivers. She wanted to run to where JuJu laid dead in a puddle of blood and hold him just one more time; kiss his lips just once more. Whisper *I love you* in his ear a final time before they covered his body with a white sheet.

"I love you," she mouthed.

The whir of a news station helicopter hovering over the gas station snapped Bayonna's mind back to survival mode. JuJu was dead and there was nothing she could do for him now. She had to move quickly in order to slip away while the pandemonium outside was still going on.

Bayonna tore her eyes off of JuJu's body and made her feet move although her heart remained right there were JuJu's blood covered the ground.

Hours later...

Bay sat on a Greyhound bus staring out of the window seeing nothing but a blur. Tears ran down her face and visions of JuJu's body stretched out on the pavement played in her mind non-stop.

A painful sob escaped her lips, breaking the silence on the bus. JuJu was gone. Living past this would be almost impossible. Bayonna closed her eyes and prayed for the hand of death to come for her too.

Chapter 35
The Hunt

Kiam knew that his dream was dead. There was no way to come out on top now. His best man was gone and he had closed down all of his drug spots. The only thing left to do now was to settle his debts then get ready to go out just like JuJu had.

Big Zo had been blowing up his phone but Kiam didn't have shit to say to that nigga. He looked around the hotel room at the remnants of his empire. Bayonna sat on the edge of a chair with both hands on her stomach rocking back and forth. Her eyes were vacant and she hadn't eaten in days. Listening to her cry herself to sleep night after night for the past week tore at all of their hearts. No matter what happened from here on, there was no doubt in any of their minds that she would never be whole again.

Treebie was posted up at the window with a choppa in her hand and her Kevlar vest on. She parted the curtains an inch or two and checked the parking lot. The devil was a lie if she didn't wet up the first thing that moved suspiciously.

Lissha sat on the bed next to Kiam with her head on his shoulder and her face wet with tears. Everything had come crashing down around them at once and she felt responsible. She closed her eyes and prayed to God that when she opened them it would all be a dream. The only thing she didn't want to wish away was her love for Kiam.

Lissha could feel the hotness of the blood surging through his veins on her skin. His face twitched with anger and his chest heaved in and out. She wanted to pull him away from the others and con-fess— anything to comfort his soul—but she was not that brave. And she still held out hope that somehow, some way they could walk away from this hand in hand.

All of a sudden Kiam stood up and began pacing the small room. His chest was bare and the waistband of his Polo boxers showed over the top of his jeans. A fo-fo was tucked on the right and a Nine on the left. He stopped in the middle of the floor and looked from one girl to the next, settling his lowered gaze directly on Lissha.

"There's a snake in my muthafuckin' garden and it ain't Dirty," Kiam spat.

Lissha almost peed on herself. Her heart started pounding and her mouth felt like cotton.

"Dirty wouldn't have known about the pickup. And he damn sure couldn't have told them where to find Riz," Kiam said.

Bayonna nodded in agreement. Yesterday the feds had raided Riz's spot up in New York and arrested him and some others.

"One of Riz's workers probably told that," Treebie interjected without taking her eyes off of the lot below.

Kiam conceded the possibility, but that didn't explain why the feds seemed to be locked in on his every move. Before he closed down the rest of his traps they had hit one after the other and they were still snatching his people up. "Somebody is talking," he spat, snatching the fo-fo off of his waist.

Lissha's eyes grew large with fear.

Kiam turned and walked to the window. "What's going on out there?" He peered over her shoulder.

"Everything is quiet but if anything moves slippery, I'm going to make sure that it never moves again," reported Treebie.

Kiam put a hand on her shoulder, silently communicating to her his appreciation for her gangsta. Behind them Lissha was trembling. She stood up and went to the bathroom to compose herself.

Treebie said, "Kiam, don't you think it's strange that all of our people are getting snatched up and none of Wolfman's crew? And now that this shit is happening to us, all of a sudden he has resurfaced."

The disdain she had for the man had her top lip curled.

"I want you to put a hundred stacks on that bitch ass nigga's head," said Kiam.

"Nah, Boss, you don't have to do that. I'ma bring you his head." Treebie walked away from the window and grabbed her jacket, a hoodie, and an extra clip.

Lissha came out of the bathroom. "Tree, where are you going?" she asked concerned.

Treebie looked her in the eye and replied. "I'm going to prove to the Big Bad Wolfman that he's more of a bitch than I am, and I got the pussy."

Lissha grabbed her jacket off the back of the chair and her strap off of the dresser. She looked at Kiam. "Babe, can I go with her to watch her back?"

Kiam nodded.

Lissha stood on her tippy toes and kissed him on the cheek. "I love you, Kiam. I honestly do," she said, tearing up. "If we don't come back please remember that."

Treebie walked over to Bayonna and gave her girl a hug. Lissha followed suit. "I love you," she said.

Together she and Treebie hit the streets determined to return with Wolfman's head in a bag.

When the crack of dawn came and Lissha and Treebie hadn't returned and they weren't answering their cells, Kiam grabbed his bangers and went to look for them.

He rode through the hoods calling on favors from those that he had extended a helping hand to in the past. Niggas said that they hadn't seen Lissha or Treebie, and Kiam could see that they were uncomfortable talking to him too long. Everyone knew that the feds were after him and they weren't trying to end up included in the indictment.

One man whom Kiam had given his first brick said, "Bleed, you're on fire. I can't be seen talking to you."

Kiam whipped out and hit him in the face with three shots. "Cool," he gritted. "Now you have nothin' to worry about cause you can't talk at all."

The man's body slid down the side of Kiam's car. Kiam stepped over him and hopped behind the wheel. As he pulled off he drove the tires over the nigga's chest. "Ungrateful muthafucka," he uttered.

The next two stops Kiam made netted him some valuable information but he still hadn't found Lissha and Treebie. Hours later he was still combing the streets when Lissha finally called. They hadn't found Wolfman but they were okay.

Kiam let out a sigh of relief. "Okay, I was worried," he said. "I want y'all to switch motels. We can't stay at one place too long."

"Can I get us a separate room?" asked Lissha. She had decided that she was going to tell him everything but she wanted them to be alone when she did.

"That's cool. Matter-of-fact, rent like six rooms. That way, if a muthafucka does find out where we're at they still won't know which room we're in. Get rooms on different sides of the building," he directed.

"Alright, baby. What are you about to do?"

"What y'all weren't able to accomplish," he said.

Without uttering another word Kiam ended the call and went to see if Wolfman was where he had been assured he would find him.

Chapter 36
Face to Face

The condos were in an affluent neighborhood so the grounds were quiet and few cars came in and out. Kiam had already spotted Wolfman's blue 2014 Bugatti. He had been told that Wolfman owned the entire complex but all he cared about was the one unit that muthafucka was in right now.

Sitting low behind the wheel, Kiam watched the door of unit 19A and patiently waited for Wolfman to come out. After hours of waiting Wolfman still had not appeared, but Kiam was not about to leave without that muthafucka's blood on his hands.

The hours crept by at a snail's pace. Kiam ignored the cramping in his legs and the ache in his back; there was a fire in his chest that overpowered time and the pain in his limbs.

As the sun began to fade from the sky the door of 19A opened. Kiam scooted further down in his seat and peered over the steering wheel. A blond white woman exited the condo. Kiam saw a large man standing in the doorway watching her walk to her car but he couldn't make out the man's face.

"Don't forget my cigars," the man called out to the woman.

Heat surged through Kiam's body. The voice was indeed Wolfman's and what he had just shouted had provided Kiam with his way inside.

Kiam grabbed a hunting knife out of a backpack on the back seat. He slid the sheathed blade down in his waistband between his two guns and got out of the truck. He looked around then casually strolled up the walk into the breezeway.

He stepped quietly pass Wolfman's door then reached up and unscrewed the light bulb in the hall. Dressed in all black, Kiam ducked around a corner, faded into the darkness, and waited like a trained assassin for the blond haired woman to return.

Twenty minutes later, he heard heels clicking on the ground. He squinted his eyes and made out the woman returning with a single grocery bag in her arms. Kiam waited until she stuck the key in the lock and turned the knob then he pounced.

One hand covered her mouth while the other pressed a gun to the back of her head. "Be real quiet bitch or I'ma spray your last thought all over the door."

He quietly forced her inside, scanning the layout with his eyes. Wolfman looked up from sofa to see Kiam holding his snow bunny at gunpoint but he did not panic.

"I figured we would come face to face again," he said, exhibiting no fear.

"Yeah and in a minute you'll do your next figuring face up in a muthafuckin' box." Kiam shoved the bitch to the floor and aimed his gun at Wolfman.

Wolfman smiled. "If you kill me you'll never find out who betrayed you."

"Fuck you." Kiam spat.

"No. Fuck *you*." The voice came from behind him, exclamated by a loud click-clack. Then Kiam felt cold steel press against the back of his head.

Wolfman laughed. "Don't kill him, Simon," he said. "It's time for me and Kiam to have a man to man conversation without any violence."

"Are you sure?"

"Yes," he replied coolly.

When Kiam felt the gun being removed from against his head he turned around and looked in the face of a man that he had seen on the local news countless times. Chief of Police, Simon Hubbard, lowered his gun but kept his finger on the trigger.

"I have friends in high places," stated Wolfman as he leaned forward and re-lit a half smoked cigar that was sitting in the ashtray.

The woman, who was a ten year veteran with the police department, got up off the floor scowling at Kiam. She gathered up the items that had spilled out of the bag and set them on the table then she took a seat in a chair to the left of where Kiam stood.

Kiam looked around him at all of the cool faces. He wanted to let loose on all three of them. Wolfman saw it in his eyes.

He took a puff of his cigar, leaned his head back, and watched the smoke leave his mouth and float to the ceiling. Staring at the ceiling fan, he spoke with a calmness that belied all of the pain that he and Kiam had caused each other.

"You know, Kiam, I respect you," said Wolfman. "You never back down no matter the odds against you. But in this game you have to bend or you'll break."

"Save the muthafuckin' sermon," Kiam spat. "It ain't necessary. I'ma kill you, your man gonna kill me, and who knows what the bitch gon' do. Point blank period."

Wolfman shook his head. "Nah, what's the point. Your beef is no longer with me. I lost two sons because you thought that I had Faydrah killed but I didn't and that's on my word."

"Nigga, your word don't mean shit to me," Kiam spat, ready to fill his chest with hollow points.

"Maybe it doesn't but it means something to me." Wolfman looked him in the eye. "Without his word a man ain't shit. My word and my reputation means more to me than my life."

"Right now your life ain't worth nothin' because I hold that bitch in *my* hands."

"And I hold yours in mine," Simon reminded him. His gun was pointed at Kiam's spine.

"Kiam," Wolfman continued unfettered. "I just want you to know that all of this talk in the streets that I sicced the feds on you is hater shit coming from the mouths of broke muthafuckaz that don't have nothin' better to do than hear themselves talk."

"It don't even matter. Everything is about to get settled right here, right muthafuckin' now," said Kiam. He didn't give a fuck.

"Oh, it matters," Wolfman disagreed. "You have muthafuckaz gunning at you right up under your nose. If you'll calm down and listen Simon will tell you about it. Have a seat."

"I never sit where I know I'm not really welcomed," spat Kiam. "If he has something to tell me I can listen just fine standing."

"Have it your way," said Simon. Then he told Kiam who the snake in his den was.

Kiam was floored. But it all added up. "That deceitful ass bitch," he grumbled as he turned and walked out of the door.

He was about to go floor her muthafuckin' ass.

Chapter 37
Confessions

Lissha opened the door with her gun down at her side. Kiam came in and she closed and locked the door behind him. She sat the Nine on the dresser and gave Kiam a hug.

He hugged her back with little affection. Lissha noticed it but chalked it up to the tremendous amount of stress that he was under. She stepped back and looked in his eyes. They were darker than the inside of a tomb.

"You look tired, baby. Let me give you a bath and then I want you to get some rest," she said tenderly.

"A'ight, but let's take the bath together," said Kiam.

"Umm." Lissha smiled in anticipation of some much needed stress relief.

As she darted off to the bathroom, Kiam quickly searched the room for police bugs. "Where's Treebie and Bay?" he called to her as he lifted the lamp and ran his hand across the bottom.

"They're in a room around the corner," she answered, testing the temperature of the water with her hand. She adjusted it with more warm water and began removing her clothes as the tub filled.

When Lissha turned around, Kiam was standing in the doorway staring at her. She jumped. "Ooh, you scared me." She giggled.

"Did I?" His face was stone.

Kiam pulled her to him and roughly ran his hands up and down her body, not missing a spot. When he felt under her arms Lissha looked at him with a raised brow. "Baby, why are you acting all weird?" she asked.

His hand shot up and he grabbed her by the throat and slammed her back against the sink. "Bitch, you're five-o!" he gritted and stared at her with pure hate in his eyes.

Lissha couldn't breathe, she tried to pry Kiam's hand from around her throat but his grip was like a vise. She kicked and squirmed as her lungs screamed for oxygen.

"Let me explain," she gagged.

"Bitch, ain't shit you can tell me." Kiam punched her in the eye, knocking her unconscious.

Lissha slipped out of his grasp and fell to the floor. Kiam bent down and slapped her awake. Lissha held her hands to her neck and started coughing and crying. "Kiam, just allow me to explain," she begged. "Please, baby."

Kiam chuckled and pulled out his knife. As he took it out of the sheath Lissha's eyes bucked out and she began scooting away. Kiam grabbed her by the hair and snatched her up to her feet. "Bitch, you working with your punk ass father to bring me down? You got my li'l nigga killed and your punk ass probably killed Eyez." He yanked her forward and ran her head into the mirror above the sink.

Blood poured down Lissha's head as she wobbled and fell to the floor on her face. Kiam rolled her onto her back and straddled her body.

"I swear, Kiam, it wasn't me."

"You're a muthafuckin' lie," he spat. "I got that from the horse's mouth.'*Big Zo's daughter is working with the feds*'. Y'all muthafuckaz tryna trade my freedom for his." He raised the knife over his head, ready to plunge it in her neck.

"Wait, Kiam!" Lissha screamed. "But I'm not Big Zo's daughter."

Kiam's arm froze in midair and Lissha blurted out the truth. "Big Zo isn't my father, he was my man."

Kiam looked down at her with shock.

Tears poured from her eyes and the truth spilled from her lips. By the time she told it all the tub had overran and water flooded the bathroom floor.

Kiam stood up and stared in the mirror. She and Big Zo had played him like a fiddle.

Lissha got up on wobbly legs. She came up behind him and wrapped her arms around his waist. Her head was light from the blood loss but her heart was heavy. "Baby, I love you. I know I fucked up but I tried my best to fix it. I swear to you I didn't kill Eyez and I never met with the feds. You have to believe me," she pleaded.

Big Zo's daughter is working with the feds. The chief of police had sworn on that.

Kiam didn't know if Lissha was lying about Big Zo not being her father or not but he knew that the bitch had violated. It didn't matter that she had tried to fix it, betrayal was irreversible. It was like ringing a bell—once you rung that muthafucka you couldn't *un-ring* it.

Kiam turned around and looked into Lissha's bloody, deceitful mug. She was crying and telling him how much she loved him. When she reached out to hug him Kiam plunged the knife in her stomach and warm blood ran down his wrist. A *whooshing* sound came from Lissha's mouth as she staggered back with her hands wrapped around the handle of the knife, trying to pull it out.

Kiam watched with no compassion as she sunk to her knees. He walked over and snatched her up. She looked at him with love in the one eye that wasn't swollen shut. Kiam drew his fist back and closed that eye too.

Lissha's back smacked the floor as her life began to flash before her in still pictures. So many sins— so many lies.

Kiam picked her limp body up and dragged her over to the tub. "This is the price you pay for disloyalty," he said as he threw her in the tub and held her head underwater until she stopped kicking.

Breathing heavily Kiam walked back into the sleeping area, grabbed his phone and dialed the number that Wolfman had given him.

"Yeah." Wolfman's gruff voice came on the line.

"Nigga, y'all assured me it was Big Zo's daughter that is working with the feds. I just killed Lissha—"

Before he finished Wolfman cut him off. "What you do that for? Lissha isn't his daughter, that's his bitch."

"Well, who the fuck is his daughter?" Kiam snapped.

"I don't know and Simon says his source wasn't able to get her name. But I know who would know and I can take you to her," said Wolfman.

"I'm on my muthafuckin' way." Kiam hung up the phone and cleaned himself up. Then he locked up the room and went to find the final piece to the puzzle.

Chapter 38
The Price of Deceit

Kiam sat in a rickety chair across from the woman who had just been introduced to him by Wolfman as Tracey. The small, dank efficiency was barren of furniture except the tattered sofa that she sat on, a coffee table, the chairs that Kiam and Wolfman occupied, and an old box-style television that sat in a corner on two milk crates that were stacked one on top of the other.

The lighting in the room was bad and Tracey looked like life was stomping a mud hole in her ass. But the more Kiam studied her face as she talked, the more he saw her resemblance to Lissha. They had the same mouth structure and they probably had the same brown eyes, once upon a time, before Tracey had seen how truly cold life could be.

Lissha and Big Zo's betrayal must have rocked her world, Kiam thought. When he asked about them Tracey's pain came out in a flood of tears and curse words. When she was done spewing Tracey grabbed the bottle of cheap liquor that Wolfman had brought her off of the table. She unscrewed the top, put the bottle to her mouth and turned it up. When she sat it back down on the table it was half empty.

Kiam looked at her and shook his head in disgust. But his distaste was not for Tracey it was for Lissha. He thought back to the time that he had seen them wrestling in the parking lot of a gas station. When he asked Lissha who the woman was, that bitch had lied.

"So Lissha is your daughter?" he reconfirmed.

"Yes, if that's what you want to call a tramp that stole her mother's man," spat Tracey.

"Does Big Zo have any children?" Wolfman cut in.

Tracey cut her eyes at him. "I'm not answering shit for *you*. You're not much better than that muthafucka." She leaned forward, grabbed the wine and finished it off.

Kiam went in his pocket and placed a stack of money in front of her. Tracey's eyes grew big. She looked up from the money on the table into his face, wondering what the fuck she would have to do to get her hands on that wad.

"I have some questions I need answered," he said, holding her stare. "Whether you can answer it or not the money is yours."

Tracey grabbed the loot off of the table and clutched it tightly. "What do you want to know?"

Kiam stood up. "Does Big Zo have a daughter?" he asked, looking down at her non-threateningly.

She didn't even have to ponder the question. "Yes," she said. "He has a wife and a daughter that lived somewhere out of state, the last I knew. That little girl should be about twenty-two or twenty-three years old now."

Kiam nodded his head but that didn't tell him much.

Beside him Wolfman sat up on the edge of his seat in anticipation of more.

"Do you know the daughter's name?" Kiam delved further.

Tracey shook her head *no*.

Kiam's shoulders slumped.

"Think hard," prodded Wolfman.

Tracey shot him an ice dagger. She turned back to Kiam and said, "It's been a long time and I never met that muthafucka's wife and daughter but I know that he loved *them*." Resentment of the favor he'd shown them was present in her eyes. "Let me think."

Kiam began pacing back and forth with his hands shoved down in his pockets. When he passed by Tracey for the third time, she reached out and grabbed his pants leg.

"Wait a minute," she suddenly said. "That girl's name was uh—uh—B-Bay something or another. Damn my mind is going bad."

Kiam's eyebrows creased and his hands got hot. "Bayonna?" Kiam assisted her.

Tracey's eyes lit up. "Yep, that's it," she said. "Bayonna. That's her name. She's his only child as far as I know."

Wolfman looked at Kiam. Kiam's eyes were as red as hot coals. "That dirty, cold-hearted little bitch!" he spat as he turned and headed for the door.

Kiam didn't wait for Wolfman, he hopped in his car and almost stomped the gas pedal straight through the floor. His chest heaved in and out as he bent a few corners and jumped on the interstate with the most vicious type of murder on his mind that he ever contemplated.

Bayonna was the last person that he would've expected to be the betrayer. But now it made sense why she had been able to get away from the gas station that day when JuJu was killed without being arrested. "Punk ass ho," he belted. "Crossed my li'l nigga out and he really loved her."

That shit brought hot tears to Kiam's eyes.

He replayed all the events in his mind and now the pieces to the puzzle fit. Big Zo had known Lissha better than anyone; he hadn't trusted her to go all the way with his plot so he had used his daughter as a backup.

Another cold realization hit Kiam in the chest and almost knocked the wind out of him. Isaac had said that before Faydrah had died in his arms she had muttered, "Bay."

All of this time Kiam had assumed that Faydrah had been trying to say "baby". But she had been trying to tell them who her killer was, he realized now.

Big Zo had me running around looking for Lissha that day so that I wouldn't be home with Eyez. And as soon I picked JuJu up Bayonna rushed out and murdered my world.

They had devised the most devious plot imaginable, knowing that he would turn the city into a killing field over Eyez' death. The more murders he committed, the more eager the feds would be to bargain with Big Zo.

Kiam was seething. As he got further down the interstate he had to decrease his speed almost to a crawl then to a stop. A seven car pileup up ahead had traffic at a standstill.

Kiam couldn't believe that shit.

"Fuck!" He pounded his hands on the steering wheel in frustration.

The last thing he wanted was for Bayonna's bitch ass to slip away. Fuck that, she was going to pay with her life for what she had done!

Bayonna stood over the sink watching the water run down the drain as she processed everything that had taken place in the last few weeks. JuJu was gone and that truly crushed her heart. She hadn't expected him to make the police kill him.

Before Bayonna agreed to set JuJu and Bones up, she had worked it out with the feds that after everyone was taken down JuJu would be offered a light sentence if he would turn on Kiam, Treebie, and Lissha. She had known that it wouldn't be easy to convince JuJu to flip, but she believed that the little life growing in her womb combined with their love would sway him in the end.

But everything had gone wrong when JuJu refused to surrender and chose to go out the same way he had lived. Bayonna could still see his bullet ridden body sprawled out on the ground in a pool of blood. The mere thought made her shiver.

She shook her head trying to dislodge that awful memory from her mind. But it was etched there forever. A constant reminder of the utter treachery that came from her hands.

Bayonna was so fucked up in the head, she hadn't been in contact with the federal agents since that day. *Why did I do that?* she asked herself with deep regret.

Bayonna knew the answer to her question. She had done it to free Daddy. She had loved JuJu but in her heart she was forever a daddy's girl. In addition, she had done it for her dying mother whose one wish was to have Big Zo hold her in his arms one last time.

Bay ran water over her face and looked at her reflection in the mirror. She hardly recognized the image that she saw. There was dark circles around her eyes and they were redder than her Blood Money contacts. Her face was gaunt and her mouth was turned down at the corners. Nothing was as it was before and not even a miracle could restore it back to normal.

Bayonna jumped when she heard the door to the room open and close. She reached for her gun but realized that she had left it in the outer room. Her heart raced with panic.

She relaxed when she heard Treebie calling her name. "I'm on my way out," Bay called back. She took a few more minutes to get herself together, then she came out of the bathroom in *fake ass bitch* mode, something that she was good at by now. "Damn that smells good," she said, forcing a smile.

"Hell, yeah. I'm about to fuck this up." Treebie said as she pulled back the lid from her Fettuccine Alfredo and Salmon. Then she handed Bay her order.

Bayonna widened the smile on her face as she uncovered her steak smothered with onions and mushrooms and two big baked potatoes with sour cream and chives. She sat down closed her eyes and prayed for the food to be blessed and that it stayed down.

Treebie had just smoked two blunts and her meal tasted like a slice of heaven. She was smacking and slurping.

Bayonna scrunched up her face. "Well, damn you wasn't lying, you're eating like that shrimp talked about yo mama."

"He did, this nigga gotta go," Treebie joked as she popped another one in her mouth.

Bayonna chuckled and shook her head as she cut into her tender meat.

"I can't wait for this to all be over," Bayonna said, taking a fork full of potatoes into her mouth.

"I know this shit is getting stressful. But hey, it's either be on the run or be stuck in a box." Treebie stated, continuing to dig in. She had already decided that she was gettin' in the wind in a few days.

Treebie put the last of her fish in her mouth then sat back fat and full and lit another blunt.

"Damn, do you have to chain smoke that shit," Bayonna asked, fanning her hand at the ganja clouds. Treebie had been smoking at least two ounces a day.

"My bad, ma, you know I need my medication. This keeps a bitch nerves calm. I almost fucked up the delivery man for not having enough napkins."

"You so crazy," Bayonna laughed as she ate the last of her meal.

Treebie was about to keep the laughter going when her phone rang. She paused and looked down and saw Kiam's number and picked up.

"What's up, playa?"

"What you doin'?"

"Just got finished eating and blowing this loud in the air," she said as she exhaled.

"Is Bayonna close by you?"

"Yup, why what's up?" Treebie went on alert.

"Smile while I talk and don't say shit."

"That's what's up." She put on a half-smile and pulled deep on the blunt.

"That bitch sitting across from you is the rat. That grimy ho is working with the feds." Kiam spat. Then he quickly told her what he had discovered.

"Well, stop and get me one," replied Treebie playing her role as she tried to remain calm and keep the anger she felt from showing on her face.

"That bitch set us all up and she killed Eyez, Tree. She took my son from me." Kiam growled into the receiver. "Whatever you do don't let that bitch leave. I'll be there as soon as I can, and when I get there I'ma make her pay for every bit of pain she caused me."

"A'ight, we'll see you when you get here." Treebie cracked a deadly smile and put her phone on the table as she tried to control her breathing. She put the blunt down and slowly rose to her feet. Muthafuck waiting for Kiam, she was about to handle that shit herself.

"Is Kiam good?" Bay asked.

"Yeah, he straight. You know he built for this shit." Treebie moved to the nightstand and picked up her gun.

When she turned around she had low eyes and a heart of stone. She looked down at Bay with her lips curled. "Let me ask you something. How long did you think you could hide your deception?"

Bayonna's eyes got wide as she looked at Treebie gripping her ratchet like she was about to make it spark. She opened her mouth to lie but Treebie made her rethink that shit real fast.

"Go ahead and lie, bitch," she gritted. "And I'm going to open up your whole muthafuckin forehead." She pointed her fo-fifth between Bayonna's eyes.

"Tree, it ain't like that." Bayonna produced the softest voice she could muster.

"Fuck you mean it ain't like that?" Treebie's voice boomed through the room causing Bayonna's heart to drop to her toes.

"Tree, please."

"Bitch, don't fucking beg me! You foul as hell. I broke bread with you, put my life in your hands and you turned us over to save a bitch muthafucka that couldn't do his bid like a man?"

"Treebie, he's my father. I love him," Bayonna shouted as tears ran from her eyes.

"I don't give a fuck. Your father is a bitch ass nigga. Somebody should've told his weak ass not to fuck with the game if he couldn't live with the consequences." Treebie clacked one in the chamber.

"I didn't just do it for Daddy," Bay cried. "I did it for my mother too. I just wanted to see her smile again before she left this world. You have to try to understand that."

"I don't have to understand shit. Bitch, you're wasting your breath!" She looked at Bay with disdain. "I don't even know who you are. Judas ass bitch."

Treebie placed the tip of the gun against Bayonna's forehead.

"Treebie, please I'm pregnant. Please don't kill my baby it's all I have left of JuJu. I'm begging you." Bay cried harder.

"Bitch, you watched them gun that boy down like a dog because of yo snitching ass. You didn't have any mercy for him, and you had none for Kiam's son. So you get the same verdict. Death."

"Treebie, please." She dropped to her knees and clasped her hands together in front of her. Tears flowed from her eyes and snot ran from her nose as she begged for a reprieve.

"Bitch, please." Treebie spat. "You was a fake all of this time. At least go out like a real bitch."

Bayonna covered her stomach and looked up at Treebie with pleading eyes. "Just give my baby a chance, please." She grabbed ahold of Treebie's leg and started weeping.

Treebie kicked her in the face. "Get the fuck off of me," she gritted. "Did you show Eyez and her baby pity? Hell no, you cut Kiam's heart out and you sold your sisters to the highest bidder. Bitch, your request is denied."

Boc! Boc! Treebie shot Bayonna right between the eyes.

Bayonna fell on her side with her hands wrapped around her belly. Her head hit the floor right next to Treebie's foot.

Treebie stood peering down at the woman that had sold her soul and theirs. "An eye for an eye," she spat.

She pointed the gun down at Bayonna's stomach and put one in her gut.

Chapter 39
All Debts Settled

Big Zo's eyes were misty as he walked back to the cell block. The chaplain had just delivered the news to him that his baby girl was dead. He knew that Bayonna's death was going to hasten her mother's and that worsened his grief.

He didn't know how all of this was going to affect his deal with the government. He did manage to get all of Kiam's workers in custody plus the feds had captured the big fish, Riz. But because Treebie and Kiam himself were still on the run, Big Zo hoped that his deal wouldn't be compromised. After everything that he had loss it would be beyond fucked up for them to not honor their agreement.

As he walked up to the second tier his heart was filled with the strongest hate imaginable toward Lissha. He promised himself that whenever he got out he was gonna dig that bitch up out of her grave and kill her all over again. What he didn't know was that his bitch ass was about to join her.

As Big Zo entered his cell Jason and four other convicts rushed in behind him and slammed the door. Big Zo spun around and came face to face with the long arms of the enemy that he had created in Kiam.

Jason lunged forward and stabbed him in the chest with a long piece of sharpened metal. Another man swung a steel pipe and cracked his head open. Big Zo stumbled back and fell onto his bunk. Blood poured down his face and the front of his shirt.

"Hold up," he cried, throwing his arms up in futility.

The four convicts attacked him with murderous conviction. "Kiam sends his love," said Jason as he plunged the metal shank straight through Big Zo's heart.

Ca$h & NeNe Capri

Kiam and Treebie drove in silence as he turned into the parking lot of the storage garage where he kept his stash. He pulled around to his unit and they got out and lifted the rolling door, prepared to divide the spoils of the war and get ghost. She was going to go her way and he would go his.

Neither of them were without scars. Their losses could not be quantified and their pain was eternal. It was with heavy hearts that they stood over multiple containers of money. *Blood money*. It was a bitter sweet moment. The result of their hustle was stacked high before them, but the empty spaces that weren't filled indicated that their casualties were just as astronomical. Those who had helped build up their riches were now dead.

The weight of those memories were more than Kiam wanted to think about right now. "Let's split this shit and get the fuck outta here," he said.

Kiam grabbed six empty large black duffel bags from on top of one of the money crates. He tossed three to Treebie. "Ain't nobody got time to count the dough. Just fill your bags up to the top and I'ma do the same with mine. It don't even matter if you end up with more."

Treebie sat her banger down on a table that was nearby and stepped to her business. She took the lid off of a crate and began stuffing her bag with stacks of Franklins. When it was full she sat it aside, grabbed a second duffel bag and moved over to another crate.

Looking up at Kiam, who was busy filling his own, Treebie remarked, "I never would have thought that we would be the last two standing," Treebie stated in disbelief.

"I guess what they say about real muthafuckaz is true. They can survive the war if they stay true to the code. We're standing here because we didn't let shit compromise our principles," Kiam confirmed as he moved to the second crate and began unloading it.

"I hear that slick shit. But on the real the only thing that I regret is leaving any witnesses." Treebie sat looking over at Kiam.

"Well, somebody gotta tell the tale, how else they gonna know about two real muthafuckaz?" Kiam looked at her with a firm gaze.

Treebie smile then bent over into the crate to collect a pile of loose bills that had scattered on the bottom when the rubber band had popped from around them.

Kiam leaned against the table and watched her almost fall into the large crate. He picked her gun up, fiddled with it and sat it back down. He smiled as she grunted, trying to hold onto the edges of the crate with both hands.

Treebie finally pulled herself up out of the crate. "Whew," she exhaled. "I almost fell over inside that muthafucka tryna get a handle of all this shit."

Kiam chuckled. "Did you get it all?"

Treebie turned to face him. "Every last dollar. You ain't know," she cracked.

"I feel you, ma," he said. "Don't leave a damn dime. It cost us way too much not to value every penny."

"Yep," she agreed. Then she walked up to Kiam and looked him in the eyes. "You know, I didn't like your arrogant ass at first. But you turned out to be official. You're my muthafuckin' nigga." She put out her hand and they shook to their success.

Treebie pulled out a blunt and fired it up as they continued bagging up the loot. When they were done they stood in front of the table with the six full duffel bags at their feet. Treebie pulled hard on her blunt and stared at Kiam. His eyes looked real sad.

"What's up?" she asked.

"Nothing. A nigga just got a lot of shit on his mind. I wish we would have found Isaac's body but Wolfman didn't know where Chino put it," Kiam said. "Plus some other shit I don't even want to talk about."

"Well, we got enough money to go lay back on an island and pay another muthafucka to carry our burdens." Treebie choked on the weed smoke.

When she stopped coughing Kiam said, "You need to cut back from that shit."

"I know but right now this is the only shit that keeps my hands steady." She picked her gun up off of the table and turned it back and forth in her hand.

"Well, get your unsteady hands together and let's take these bags out to the car."

Kiam threw a duffel bag over his shoulder and started towards the door.

Treebie looked down at the two bags he was leaving behind. "This nigga ain't learned his lesson yet," Treebie mumbled under her breath." Then she quickly grabbed her gun off the table and aimed it at his back.

"Stop right there bitch ass nigga or I'ma blow a hole through you," she barked.

Kiam stopped in his tracks.

"Drop that bag muthafucka or I'ma drop you instead. Play with this shit if you think it's a game." Treebie stood with her feet apart gripping her gun with two hands.

"You know what it is, ma," Kiam replied coolly. "You pulled that bitch now make it clap."

"Nigga, you ain't said nothin' hot to the coldest bitch to ever live," Treebie spat.

Then she squeezed the trigger. But nothing happened. She squeezed it again.

Click. Click. Click. The gun was empty.

Kiam turned around slowly with her clip in his hand. He looked at her and chuckled as he dropped the clip and snatched his Nine off of his waist and aimed it at Treebie's head. *"Trust No Bitch,"* he smirked.

"Fuck you nigga," she spat defiantly.

"Not in this life," he retorted as he stepped forward and fired two shots dead between her eyes.

Blood and skull blasted out of the back of Treebie's head and she landed on her back. Her empty gun fell out of her hand and skidded a few feet away.

Kiam walked over to where the bitch laid and stood over her.

Boc! Boc!

He shot her twice in her cold, merciless heart. Then he walked over and pulled a hand full of money out of a duffel bag that rested against the leg of the table. Stepping back to Treebie, Kiam bent over and rubbed the money in the blood that poured from her forehead. With a finality that settled all debts, he stuffed the money in Treebie's mouth and rose up.

"Blood Money, bitch," Kiam spat.

The End.

Ca$h & NeNe Capri

BOOKS BY LDP'S CEO, CA$H

TRUST NO MAN

TRUST NO MAN 2

TRUST NO MAN 3

BONDED BY BLOOD

SHORTY GOT A THUG

A DIRTY SOUTH LOVE

THUGS CRY

THUGS CRY 2

TRUST NO BITCH

TRUST NO BITCH 2

TRUST NO BITCH 3

TIL MY CASKET DROPS

Coming Soon

TRUST NO BITCH (KIAM EYEZ' STORY)

THUGS CRY 3

BONDED BY BLOOD 2

RESTRANING ORDER

BOOKS BY NENE CAPRI

PUSSY TRAP I, II, III & IV

DREAM WEAVER

TAINTED

Trust No Bitch 3

Coming Soon From Lock Down Publications

RESTRAINING ORDER

By **CA$H & COFFEE**

GANGSTA CITY **II**

By **Teddy Duke**

A DANGEROUS LOVE **VII**

By **J Peach**

BLOOD OF A BOSS **III**

By **Askari**

THE KING CARTEL **III**

By **Frank Gresham**

NEVER TRUST A RATCHET BITCH

SILVER PLATTER HOE **III**

By **Reds Johnson**

THESE NIGGAS AIN'T LOYAL **III**

By **Nikki Tee**

BROOKLYN ON LOCK **III**

By **Sonovia Alexander**

THE STREETS BLEED MURDER **II**

By **Jerry Jackson**

CONFESSIONS OF A DOPEMAN'S DAUGHTER **II**

By **Rasstrina**

WHAT ABOUT US **II**

NEVER LOVE AGAIN

By **Kim Kaye**

A GANGSTER'S REVENGE

Ca$h & NeNe Capri

By **Aryanna**

Available Now

LOVE KNOWS NO BOUNDARIES **I II & III**
By **Coffee**
SILVER PLATTER HOE **I & II**
HONEY DIPP **I & II**
CLOSED LEGS DON'T GET FED **I & II**
A BITCH NAMED KARMA
By **Reds Johnson**
A DANGEROUS LOVE **I, II, III, IV, V, VI**
By **J Peach**
CUM FOR ME
An **LDP Erotica Collaboration**
THE KING CARTEL **I & II**
By **Frank Gresham**
BLOOD OF A BOSS **I & II**
By **Askari**
THE DEVIL WEARS TIMBS
BURY ME A G **I II & III**
By **Tranay Adams**
THESE NIGGAS AIN'T LOYAL **I & II**
By **Nikki Tee**
THE STREETS BLEED MURDER
By **Jerry Jackson**
DIRTY LICKS

By **Peter Mack**

THE ULTIMATE BETRAYAL

By **Phoenix**

BROOKLYN ON LOCK

By **Sonovia Alexander**

SLEEPING IN HEAVEN, WAKING IN HELL **I, II & III**

By **Forever Redd**

THE DEVIL WEARS TIMBS **I, II & III**

By **Tranay Adams**

DON'T FU#K WITH MY HEART **I & II**

By **Linnea**

BOSS'N UP **I & II**

By **Royal Nicole**

LOYALTY IS BLIND

By **Kenneth Chisholm**

CPSIA information can be obtained
af www.ICGtesting.com
Printed in the USA
LVHW042048090522
718309LV00002B/338

9 781497 315464